NAT

MW01134468

RALPH COTTON'S
WESTERN CLASSIC

VENGEANCE

FORMERLY: VENGEANCE IS A BULLET

AUTHOR'S WORK SELECT EDITION

RALPH COTTON'S
WESTERN CLASSIC

VENGEANCE
FORMERLY: VENGEANCE IS A BULLET

AUTHOR'S WORK SELECT EDITION

Front cover photograph of an 1860 Army Colt .44
provided by Ralph Cotton Photo Archives.

Cover design & book layout by Laura Ashton
laura@gitflorida.com

Author's picture from a painting by
Malissa Beatty; her website can be viewed at
www.wavyspace.com/malissa

ISBN: 978-1479118663

Printed in the United States of America

For Mary Lynn ... of course

Other Books by Ralph Cotton

Series: The Life and Times of Jeston Nash

1. While Angels Dance*	1994	4. Cost of a Killing	1996
2. Powder River	1995	5. Killers of Man	1997
3. Price of a Horse	1996	6. Trick of the Trade	1997

* "While Angels Dance" became a candidate for the Pulitzer Prize in fiction in 1994. The entire series is being released as Western Classics and will be available from Amazon.com and other retailers, as well as on Kindle and other ebook formats beginning in 2011.

Ranger Sam Burrack (Big Iron Series)

1. Montana Red	1998	14. Black Mesa	2005
2. The Badlands	1998	15. Trouble Creek	2006
3. Justice	1999	16. Gunfight at Cold Devil	2006
4. Border Dogs	1999	17. Guns on the Border	2007
5. Misery Express	2000	18. Killing Texas Bob	2007
6. Blood Rock	2001	19. Nightfall at Little Aces	2008
7. Jurisdiction	2002	20. Ambush at Shadow Valley	2008
8. Vengence is a Bullet	2003	21. Showdown at Hole-In-The-Wall	2009
9. Sabre's Edge	2003	22. Riders from Long Pines	2009
10. Hell's Riders	2004	23. A Hanging in Wild Wind	2010
11. Showdown at Rio Sagrado	2004	24. Black Valley Riders	2010
12. Dead Man's Canyon	2004	25. Lawman from Nogales	2011
13. Killing Plain	2005		

Other Books by Ralph Cotton

PROLOGUE

From where the boy, Carlos, stood behind the low sandstone wall, he counted as many as four horsemen coming in from the west in the white harsh glare of desert sun. There might have been more, he wasn't certain. As soon as the thin wavering lines became recognizable to him, he'd dropped the water gourd to the ground and run the twenty yards from the well to the crumbling remnants of the old Spanish mission. His mother, seeing him run barefoot across the hot sand, lifted her eyes to the distant riders. In her own quick count, she noted there were now six—two more having risen upward as if out of the swirl of burning sand. She crossed herself and whispered the name of the blessed Virgin Mother. Then she reached out and caught her son around the waist as he bolted through the doorway.

Carlos struggled with her. *"Mama!* Let me go! The Wolf and his men, they are here! I must warn Papa!"

"No, Carlos, Papa knows," she said in a trembling voice. "He has already seen them! We must get you out of here."

"But he is asleep!" Carlos insisted, still struggling to free himself from his mother's grasp. "I must go wake him!"

"I'm awake, son," said a gruff voice. "You done good keeping watch for them."

Both Carlos and his mother turned toward the tall figure standing on the stone stairway above them. Tom Bannion swayed, but caught himself with his free hand against the sandstone wall. Flies buzzed in grisly harmony near the blood-caked bandage wrapped around his sweaty chest. Bannion tried shooing the flies with his gun hand, his pistol barrel only stirring them into a frenzy. "Go, do like your ma tells you," Bannion said in a weak voice. "This is no place for you—" His words were cut short, swallowed by a rasping cough from deep inside his shattered chest. He staggered down the last two steps and sank limply to his knees, both hands clutching his chest, his pistol falling to the dirt floor.

"Papa!" Carlos cried out, leaping forward, down into the dirt, steadying the wounded man against his small shoulder as he reached down and snatched up the pistol, shaking the dust from it. *"Por favor*, Papa!" he pleaded. "Take the gun! We must fight them. I will help you! I am not afraid!"

"I know, Carlos ... you're a brave lad," Bannion said in a shallow voice. He managed to take the pistol, but still he swayed back and forth on his knees. Lifting his hollow eyes to the woman, Bannion rasped, "Hurry, Murriala, take him and get out of here ... I'm done for." He nodded at an extra holster belt lying on the ground. The butts of two pistols glinted in the sunlight. "Take them with you," he said. "Look after yourself and the boy."

"No, Papa!" Carlos cried out, even as his mother reached forward and lifted him to his feet. "You are not done for! We must fight them. Please! Soon you will be well."

There were tears in Murriala's eyes as she hoisted the gun belt up over her shoulder and dragged Carlos backward toward the rear doorway. "Listen to me, Carlos! We must go! It is how he wants it to be."

"Come and get it," Tom Bannion called out, near delirium. "I've got all day."

Carlos shot a worried glance at his father, hearing his weak, rambling words. "No, *Mama!* I stay with Papa, you go!" Carlos sobbed.

Murriala glanced out across the sand flats and gasped as she saw even more riders spread out abreast. There were no less than a dozen, drawing closer, and no doubt seeing her now.

At the center of the riders and three feet forward of them, Major Avrial raised a gloved hand and slowed the men almost to a standstill. Their horses' hooves stirred a low rise of drifting dust, making the lower half of both horse and rider practically invisible from the distance of two hundred yards.

"What's the major stopping us for now, Pecos?" Calvin Galt asked the man beside him. "Seems like we'd hurry in and finish things ... as long as it's took us to run this fool down."

Pecos Bob Denton spit and ran a studded-leather gauntlet across his parched lips. "Why hurry now?" He shrugged, a sawed-off shotgun lying loosely across his lap. "Bannion ain't going anywhere."

"I say Bannion's already dead." Galt chuckled grimly. "If he ain't, he's damn sure top heavy ... that much lead stuck in his chest." Galt looked back and forth at the others with a faint smile, hoping they appreciated his sense of humor. If they did, they never let on. All eyes stared toward the old Spanish mission.

"It you knew Bannion as well as Major Avrial knows him, you would realize he is not a man to take lightly. He always keeps something up his sleeve," said Pecos.

"Yeah?" Galt sneered. "Well, you're sure starting to scare me, Pecos Bob. If he's still alive in there, I hope I can manage to hold my water, meeting him face-to-face and all."

Major Avrial shot a dark glance along the line of men toward the sound of Pecos Bob and Calvin Galt's voices, saying, "Anything needs saying, boys, come up here and tell all of us."

Avrial's eyes leveled and locked onto Pecos's for a second until Pecos shrank back beneath his lowered hat brim and nudged his horse forward a step, away from Calvin Galt. "You and your mouth," Pecos Bob hissed sidelong at Galt.

Calvin Galt only grinned to himself. He didn't give a damn

3

what the major thought of him. He'd ridden with tougher gangs than this. He couldn't believe it had taken this many guns to run down one man. He drew a deep breath, relaxed in his saddle, and gazed forward with the others. To hell with this bunch, Galt thought. He could do just as well on his own, and he would, too, just as soon as this war was over. He was a straight-up gunman. He didn't need anybody.

Major Jamison 'Wolf' Avrial lifted his dusty cavalry hat from his head, ran his fingers back through his damp, dust-tangled hair, then lowered the hat back into place. "Deacon," he said over his shoulder to the man nearest him, "come up here ... ride with me."

"Yes, sir." Deacon Stokes shot a glance at the others, then pushed his horse forward. "What do you think, Major, is he dead?" Stokes asked, lowering his voice so his words were just between the two of them.

"No, I think not, Deacon," said Avrial. "At least I hope not. I wouldn't want to think that all of this has been for nothing."

"I hate to say it, Major," said Stokes, "but if he is alive, I don't look for him to tell us what we want to know."

"You underestimate my power of persuasion then," said Major Wolf Avrial, staring straight ahead.

"Naw-sir, not at all," said Stokes. "I've seen your power of persuasion too many times to doubt it. But I also know how stubborn Bannion is. I'm afraid he's just apt to die before he'll give it up."

"We'll see, Deacon," said Wolf Avrial, nudging his horse forward, "we'll see."

Inside the old Spanish mission, Murriala Bannion worked frantically, saddling the little desert roan and shoving her son atop the horse against his will. When he tried to slide down from the saddle, his mother slapped him sharply across his face. But then she sobbed as she held his head to her shoulder for a moment and said, "Forgive me, Carlos! But you must do as I tell you! You must flee from this place and do not look back. Go across the border and into the north country."

As she spoke, she took one of the Colt pistols from the holster belt she had slung over her shoulder. "Here, keep this with you! Do not be afraid to use it if any of these men come after you! Now go!" She turned the horse roughly by its bridle and drew back her hand to slap its rump.

"But Mama! What about you?" said Carlos, realizing that his mother had no intention of leaving her husband to face these men alone. "Papa said that we must both go!"

"Do not argue with me, Carlos! You must live! No matter what, you must live!" There was a strange look in his mother's eyes as her hand fell to the horse's rump. Before the boy could say another word, he was snapped back in the saddle, then righted himself and held on as the game little roan shot forward and out across the desert sand, toward the mountain line ten miles away. Carlos managed to catch the pistol before it bounced out of his lap. He drew the heavy pistol up tight against his chest and, as his mother had instructed him, he did not look back.

As Major Wolf Avrial and his men drew closer in a widening circle around the old Spanish mission, he nodded at the line of dust leading out across the desert floor. "Cochio, Breeden, Shaney," he barked at the line of men to his left, "you three go after that horse ... it's his half-breed nit and his Mexican whore no doubt. Bring them back here, pronto!"

The three men spurred their horses forward and sped away from the others. Cochio Santavia took the lead. He was a big Mexican with a deep scar that ran jaggedly across his milky-white left eye and the bridge of his flattened nose. He looked over his shoulder at the other two with an expression of dark warning—they had better keep up with him if they knew what was good for them.

"Damn it," Bert Breedan growled under his breath. His tired

horse struggled forward as he reached back and laid a quirt to its rump. "Who the hell put him in charge?" he grumbled to Randall Shaney beside him.

But Shaney gazed straight ahead, concentrating on keeping up close behind Cochio. "Keep your mouth shut, Breedan. You don't want to make that big sucker mad." The three raced forward in Carlos Bannion's wake of dust, the boy having already gotten a long head start on them.

In the front yard of the old Spanish mission, Major Wolf Avrial stepped down slowly from his saddle, his men doing the same on either side of him. The rest of the men stood back beside their horses as the major and Deacon Stokes took a few cautious steps forward, then stopped, and stood staring into Tom Bannion's eyes from fifteen feet away. Bannion stood weakly, leaning in the open front doorway of the mission, his left hand raised and supporting him against the crumbling stonework. "That's close enough, Wolf," Bannion rasped, a big Colt army model hanging cocked in his right hand.

A silence passed as Wolf Avrial took his time looking around the old ruins. Then he cut his gaze back to Tom Bannion and said, "I'm not going to waste any more time on you, Bannion .... Where's that damned Yankee gold? This war'll be over soon. I aim to get something out of all this."

Tom Bannion shook his head slowly. "Nothing doing, Wolf." His eyes gestured toward the bloody bandage on his wounded chest where flies swirled and droned. "I'm the only one left who knows where it's stashed ... and you and your men have killed me. You think I'd tell you anything? Not a chance in hell. Let's just get this over with."

"Now, Bannion," said Wolf Avrial, feigning a sympathetic tone of voice, "I wouldn't have had all this happen to you for the world. All you had to do was put us onto that Yankee gold in the first place .... We'd never would have shot you." He looked off in the direction of the three riders on the trail of the little desert roan. "See, I can't believe a man like you, all shot up and dying, wouldn't tell his woman and boy where they could lay their hands on a fortune in gold. That would be plumb un-Christian, now wouldn't it?"

"They don't know anything, Wolf," said Bannion. "Besides, they're long gone into the mountains. Your men will never catch up to that little roan ... even with it carrying two riders."

Wolf Avrial chuckled under his breath. "You always did over rate everything about yourself, Bannion. Cochio will drag the boy back here kicking and screaming. The woman, too. We might have to carve a piece or two off them. But before we finish cutting, I expect you'll be telling more than we even ask for. Don't you think so, Deacon?"

Beside him, Deacon Stokes reached a hand down slowly, lifted a long skinning knife from his boot well, and laid the handle into Wolf Avrial's outstretched palm. "Hell, I'd bet on it, Major," said Stokes.

Tom Bannion had been forcing himself to sound strong, but now the vision Wolf Avrial had just created in his mind was too much for him. Dark rage boiled inside him, yet it sapped his strength. "You rotten ... bastard!" Bannion tried to raise his cocked pistol, the effort causing him to gasp for breath as fresh blood bubbled through his bandage. Flies rose away from the wound and hovered in a tight glistening swirl.

"Boys"—Wolf Avrial laughed, his hand raising his own pistol with ease and cocking it soundly, while beside him, Deacon Stokes did the same—"here's what you have to call a pitiful sight ... a man can't even get his gun up for one last shot." As Avrial spoke, Deacon Stokes rushed forward, grabbed Tom Bannion's gun hand and wrenched the Colt away with little effort. Then he took Bannion roughly by the shoulder and threw him into the hot dirt at Wolf Avrial's feet.

"There you are, Major," said Deacon Stokes. "Do some cutting just for practice till Cochio gets back with the woman and the boy."

"Good idea," said Avrial. "Collins, get up here. Give us a

7

hand," he called out over his shoulder. A tall lean man wearing a ragged sombrero and an even more ragged Confederate army tunic hurried forward and grabbed Bannion by one arm as Deacon Stokes grabbed his other.

"I suppose it wouldn't hurt to maybe cleave off his trigger finger," said Wolf Avrial. "It is the thing that's caused him the most trouble in his life. He grinned down at Tom Bannion. "If it makes you feel any better, Bannion, I'll dry it out and wear it around my neck—call it a keepsake from better times, when you and me were best of friends."

"Go to hell, Wolf," Bannion growled in a weak voice. "I still ain't telling you nothing. You'll never lay hands on all that gold."

"Oh, really?" Wolf Avrial's voice turned chillingly cold. "Now you've gone and hurt my feelings." He reached down and grabbed Bannion's gun hand, Collins holding Bannion's wrist securely against his knee.

"Hack off whatever you want to, Major," said Collins. "I've got his hand held."

Behind the remnant of the crumbling sandstone wall, Murriala Bannion held her breath and kept her eyes tightly shut, whispering a silent prayer, holding the Colt to her bosom in her steepled hands. But when Tom Bannion's tortured scream rose above the mission yard, she could wait no longer. She hurriedly crossed herself and stood up, wiping her eyes as she raised and cocked the Colt toward the men huddled over her husband in the dirt.

"Major, look out!" shouted one of the men. He had looked away just long enough to catch a glimpse of the woman standing there with the raised pistol, a hot breeze licking at her dusty hair.

Both Wolf Avrial and Deacon Stokes managed to jerk back a step, their pistols swinging toward Murriala Bannion and firing. But before their bullets pounded into her chest, her shot rang out. Kneeling beside Tom Bannion, Collins slumped and swayed in place with a blank look coming to his face. His eyes crossed upward, as if trying to inspect the large gaping hole in his forehead. Then he melted to the ground, stone dead.

"Murriala, no!" Tom Bannion screamed. But his words went unheard by her. A second shot from Murriala's pistol hammered her husband in his already wounded chest and flung him backward atop Collins on the sandy ground. Then Murriala spun around in a circle, as more bullets from the rest of the gunmen spiked into her. The force of the shots held her up in a broken death waltz until she pitched over the short wall, facedown in the dirt.

"Well, I'll be double-dog damned!" said Wolf Avrial, stunned, looking at the dead woman, then at her dead husband. Then he looked at Deacon Stokes, who raised up slowly from the dirt, his pistol smoking. "Where the hell did she come from, Deacon?"

Stokes stood up, dusting his trousers with his hat. "It's his woman, Wolf."

"Hell, I know it's his woman!" said Avrial. "How come nobody spotted her?"

"Beats me," said Stokes, passing a harsh glare at the rest of the men. "I reckon some of us wasn't paying attention like we ought to have been. She killed Bannion deader than hell," said Stokes. "Suppose she meant to?"

"Who knows?" said Wolf Avrial, disgusted with everything and everybody. "One thing for sure, Bannion won't be telling us a damn thing now." He looked at the dead woman. "Neither will she."

"Then we better hope to hell Cochio brings back that little half-breed, provided the kid even knows anything to begin with," said Stokes.

"Damn it," said Wolf Avrial, shoving his pistol down into his holster and turning back toward his horse. "Let's get out there and help Cochio round up that kid! He's our only hope. If he doesn't know where the gold is, we're never going to find it!"

9

"You smug sonuvabitch!" Stokes cursed down at Tom Bannion's body in the dirt. "I bet you're in hell right now, laughing your damn head off! Don't worry though, Cochio will find that boy .... Then the last laugh will be on you, won't it? You damn dead peckerwood you!" He drew back a boot and kicked Bannion's slack jaw. The dead man's head rocked back and forth in the dirt as if saying, *No.* The blank eyes stared upward into the blazing sun ....

When Major Wolf Avrial and the others caught up to Cochio Santavia, Bert Breedan, and Randall Shaney, the three men stood atop the first rising slope reaching up into the Mexican foothills. "Any sign of him?" Wolf Avrial asked, leaping down from his saddle and hurrying over to where Cochio stood with his sawed-off rifle cradled in his arms.

Big Cochio saw the worried look on Avrial's face. "No," Cochio replied, looking Avrial up and down. "Is there something wrong?"

"They died before we found out about the gold," said Wolf Avrial, his eyes squinting against the sun's glare, searching the hills for any sign of the boy. "Their kid is the only hope we've got now."

Cochio did not respond right away. Instead, he spit in disgust and ran the cuff of his dusty sleeve across his parched lips. "We cannot track him through these hills, across hard stone. We must circle left, away from these switchbacks and onto the shorter steeper trails. We must beat him to the water, higher up. He has no choice but to go there!"

"Are you sure, Cochio?" Avrial asked. "We damned sure can't take a chance on losing him. How do you figure he even knows where the water is up there?"

"He is Bannion's son. He knows. Bannion told him where to go and how to get there ... you can count on it."

"Then what are we waiting for?" Wolf Avrial said, raising his voice into the mode of authority, looking around at the

using this as a way of getting back at me, Sheriff, and you know it."

"Whether he is or not," said Tackett, "it makes no difference now. Nobody saw a pistol, Jarvis."

"Hell, I reckon not. The whole place went crazy soon as I shot him. You'd of thought it was the first time they ever saw somebody killed at a poker table."

The ranger listened to the two men as he raised his big Colt from his tied-down holster, checked it, then let it hang down his side, the long barrel at about knee level. His shoulder seemed to slump a bit from the weight of the pistol. Ranger Sam Burrack was no bigger than average. He was lean, and desert seasoned, and carried himself in an unimposing manner. Yet, there was something about the ranger that demanded respect, and got it.

"This is why I don't like working in town," the ranger said, glancing at Sheriff Tackett, then stepping over to the bolted front door. "There's always some underlying reason for stuff like this happening."

"Maybe you best let me handle it, Sam," Tackett said, seeing the ranger slip the bolt back and take the door by the knob. "I know these men .... What Jarvis said about Loman Gunderson is about half true. Maybe I can make him listen to reason. They're all whiskey drunk right now. They just need talking down."

No sooner than Sheriff Tackett had finished his words, a shot exploded through the small front window, hit the iron bars of an empty cell, and whistled through the air like an angry hornet. All three men flinched, then turned their eyes to the spot where the bullet thumped into the wall behind a potbellied wood stove.

Outside, a thick voice called out, "Sheriff, we're here to hang him! Save yourself some trouble—throw him out here! Jarvis Hicks has had this coming for a long time. Justice has finally caught up to him!"

"Yeah?" shouted Jarvis Hicks through the bars of his cell. "That ain't what your daughter said!"

At the sight of the fresh bullet hole in the front window, Sheriff Tackett's face swelled red with rage. "Of all the low, sneaking—"

His words were cut short as he stomped toward the front door. But the ranger blocked him, saying, "Hold it, Tackett. Let me handle this. They're not going to be talked down. They're already in a shooting mood. You've got to face these men come next election." He swung a glance at Jarvis Hicks and said in a warning tone, "No more remarks about anybody's daughter, or I *will* throw you out there in their arms."

"Sorry," said Jarvis. "The truth is I have nothing but respect for that young woman. I just don't want to hang for something I didn't—"

"You're right, Sam," Tackett said, cutting Jarvis Hicks off. "I better let you settle them down. I was all right till I saw that bullet hole. Now I'm apt to lose my temper and hurt somebody!" He let out a tense breath to calm himself. "I'll be right behind you with this scattergun, Ranger. Whatever play you make, I'll back it."

The ranger nodded. "This Gunderson, is he a poor man? Does he work a spread all by himself?"

"Naw, he's got more money than anybody around here. Has over a dozen men working for him. Why?"

"Just curious," said the ranger, turning the knob, and opening the door just enough to slip through it out onto the boardwalk.

In the street, raised torches flickered against the darkness. The angry mob had stopped short of the boardwalk, as if they knew their boundaries in spite of having already shot a hole through the front window. At the front of the mob stood a big man with a bald head and a thick, long, curving mustache. In one hand, he held a Smith & Wesson pistol; in his other hand, he held a coiled rope with a noose tied in it.

"You must be Gunderson," said the ranger in the short slice

16

of silence before anyone else got a chance to speak.

The big man glanced around at his followers, then said with a growl, "I hope you didn't come out here to talk, Ranger, 'cause we're past the talking stage!" His big thumb tightened across the hammer of his pistol.

"I see," said Sam in a calm voice. "Then let's not talk!" His pistol raised just as calmly and exploded on the short upswing. The crowd gasped and jerked back a step—all except Loman Gunderson, who screamed loud and long. He jerked his right foot up from the ground and swung it back and forth as if shaking bees from his boot.

"Lord God," cried a person in the crowd, staring wide-eyed at Loman Gunderson. "The ranger shot him! Blew his damn foot off!"

Gunderson clasped his right foot between both hands, hopping in a wild circle, blood squirting up through the bullet hole in his boot. His pistol and rope lay in the dirt where he'd dropped them. The ranger moved forward to the edge of the boardwalk, judging the mob, keeping everything in check, the big Colt smoking in his hand. "Take a good look, boys," the ranger said, gazing from one face to the next long enough to give his words a personal ring. "The next bullet hole you see might be in your own belly."

The men stood stunned, their torches sagging, watching Loman Gunderson stagger and scream, until he finally fell and rolled, whimpering on the ground. "He can't do that," said the same outraged man in the crowd. "Can he, Sheriff? Can he do this?" The men's faces turned from Loman Gunderson on the ground to Sheriff Boyd Tackett, who stood in the open door of the office with a shotgun raised and pointed with his good hand. Tackett looked as stunned as the men in the street.

"You're dang right he can," Tackett growled, collecting his wits, knowing he must back the ranger's play. "You just seen him do it, didn't you?" He took a step forward, acting as if he had known all along what the ranger came out here to do.

17

"Nobody gets away with shooting out the sheriff's window."
He gestured his head toward the bullet hole in the window
behind him. "There's some things even a lynch mob don't do.
You boys have all crossed a serious line here .... Far as the
law's concerned, once that glass was broke, you're all bought
and paid for." He stepped beside the ranger and said to him,
"Do whatever you feel like, Sam. These men asked for it."

"Good," said Sam, narrowing his gaze on the man who'd
been doing the talking. "Who's this one? Is he the spokesman
now?"

"Sounds like it," said Tackett. "His name's Melvin Hurd."

"Whoa! Wait a minute!" said Melvin Hurd, jumping back
a step, his hands raising chest high. "I'm not in charge of
nothing! I even told Gunderson this was a bad idea! I deplore
violence of any kind! That's the truth, so help me God!"

"Is that a fact?" The ranger raised his pistol and cocked
it. Two men, who'd started lifting Gunderson up from the
ground, dropped him and scurried backward, putting some
distance between themselves and the big pistol. Gunderson
groaned, still clasping his bleeding foot.

"Then you better get off this street quick enough to let me
know you mean it," said the ranger. His eyes scanned the
faces of the crowd once again as Melvin Hurd bolted away,
his bowler hat falling to the ground behind him. "That goes
for the rest of you, too," the ranger added. "Anybody else who
deplores violence better get on out of here right now. Stick
them torches down in the water trough as you file past it."

Sheriff Tackett stood stone faced beside the ranger as the
hissing of torches rose from the water trough. The two men
had pulled Loman Gunderson to his feet and started helping
him limp away toward the   doctor's office, his pistol and
rope still lying in the dirt. In a rage, Gunderson called back
to Sheriff Tackett, "You'll pay for this come next election,
Sheriff. I promise you that! The citizens of Halston won't
forget this, Sheriff ... do you understand?"

"Yeah, yeah, you dang troublemaker," Tackett grumbled, waving him away. "Halston will be lucky to still be here come next election day," Tackett said to the ranger, stepping down from the boardwalk and picking up the abandoned Smith & Wesson. He looked back up at the ranger as the last of the men hurried away, leaving the street empty and quiet, save for the sound of a barking dog a block away. "Lord, Sam," he said, keeping his voice low, "what came over you, shooting him that way?"

"You heard what he said, that we was already past the talking stage," said the ranger. "I knew it was going to take something hard handed to get them under control. Besides, what you said was true. There's some things even a lynch mob can't get away with. It showed no respect for the law, shooting out the window. A man who does that is asking for a bullet in the foot, at least." As the ranger spoke, he stepped down beside Tackett on the street. Both of them looked as they heard the sound of running footsteps coming toward them from the undertaker's.

"He's alive, Sheriff!" the undertaker's helper shouted, sliding to halt, his breath heaving in his chest. "He scared the bejesus out of me! I had just started to drop some hot wax under his eyelids! All of a sudden, he sat straight up on the gurney! I sent my boy Herman to fetch the doctor!"

"Take it easy, Earl," said Sheriff Tackett. "Who are you talking about, the peddler Jarvis shot?"

Earl Blume nodded briskly. "Yep, that's who I mean all right. I hurried here fast as I could, afraid that lynch mob might've snatched Jarvis and gone to string him up! They haven't, have they?" He looked around. "I heard gunshots."

"No, Jarvis is all right, Earl," said Tackett. "The shots you heard was somebody shooting through the window .... Then the ranger here shot Loman Gunderson in the foot."

The undertaker's helper looked at the ranger, astonished, his mouth agape. "You shot Mister Gunderson?"

The ranger didn't answer.

"You didn't leave that peddler alone, did you, Earl," Tackett asked, "the shape he's in?"

"Yeah, I did," Earl replied, calming down some. "But he seemed all right, for a man we all thought was going into the ground. He's got a bullet through his chest, but apparently it never hit nothing vital. It must have just missed his heart. Anyway, he's laying there right now, staring up at the ceiling .... Asked me for a drink of water. I gave him one, but it went down wrong or something. Then I came running here."

"What do you mean it went down wrong?" asked Sheriff Tackett.

But Blume was too excited to stop talking. "Oh, and let me tell you something else," he said to Tackett "Before he raised up, I found a small pistol in his boot, just like Jarvis said!"

"So it really was self-defense." Tackett shook his head. "See? Those fools would have hung an innocent man if they'd had their way. How come nobody saw the pistol before?"

Earl Blume shrugged. "I suppose in all the commotion, it went unnoticed."

"Went unnoticed?" Sheriff Tackett shook his head again. "A man is about to get his neck stretched, and a little detail like a hidden gun goes unnoticed?" With his shotgun cradled across his bandaged forearm, he shoved Loman Gunderson's pistol down into his belt with his good hand. Then he said to Earl Blume, "Do me a favor when you get to the doctor's office—tell Gunderson and his men everything you just told us. Maybe that bunch of peckerwoods will think twice next time before they want to hang a man." He turned to the ranger and gestured toward the open office door. "Come on, Sam, let's cut Jarvis loose and go check on that peddler. If he comes carousing around out here in the dark after everybody thinking he's dead, somebody else is apt to shoot him."

When Sheriff Tackett unlocked the iron door, Jarvis Hicks sprang out of the dark cell like a rabbit. "Thank you, thank you, Jesus!" Hicks sobbed, raising his steepled hands, his bloodshot eyes lifting to the ceiling. He then brought his gaze to the ranger as he sniffled and ran a finger beneath his nose. "And you, Ranger! I swear, nobody in my life ever done anything like that for me."

He stepped forward with his arms spread, but the ranger stopped him with a raised hand.

"Easy, mister," said Sam. "I was just doing the job, helping the sheriff out."

"Well ... thank God you was here," said Jarvis. "That's the first time in my life I was ever innocent of anything .... Imagine how I felt, thinking I was about to swing for something I didn't do. It's been an eye-opening experience for me, I'll say that. From now on, I intend on doing something good with my life— don't know what it is yet, but it'll come to me. Hicks's eyes shone with redemption. "A man's lucky to come to a place in life where he sees his errors and has a chance to—"

"That's fine, Jarvis," said Sheriff Tackett, cutting him off, "and we both wish you the best. But now we've got to get over and check on that peddler you shot."

"I want to go with you," Jarvis said eagerly. "I want to tell that man how sorry I am this whole thing happened. Not that I was in the wrong, but just that had I not been gambling and drinking in the first place, none of this would've happened."

"I don't think it's a good idea, you trying to talk to him right now," said Tackett. "Get yourself a drink or two and calm yourself down. Stay away from the Roi-Tan though. Don't want you having trouble with the men from the lynch party. For dang sure, stay away from Loman Gunderson."

"Unh-uh, no more drinking for me," Jarvis said firmly. Then his tone relented a bit. "Well ... maybe a quick shot now and then to be sociable on holidays and special occasions. But don't worry, Sheriff, there'll be no more trouble out of me. No more gambling, no more whiskey, no more whoring—that is, other than what's necessary for a man to keep up his morale and his image. But that's all, I swear it. I'll just drop in at the undertaker's with you, tell that peddler how I feel, then get on my way."

"I said you're not going with us, and that's that," said Sheriff Tackett. "We'll offer him your condolences, if that's all you want to do. Now get out of here."

Jarvis Hicks backed away with his hands held chest high. "All right, Sheriff. It's just that I've got all this good feeling welling up and I want to share it some way. But I'll do like you say ... I'll leave." He halted at the open door, then looked at the ranger and said, "Can I tell you something, Ranger?"

The two lawmen just stared at him until he continued. "I wouldn't have mentioned this, but I feel like I owe you something. That list of names you carry around? Of men you're always hunting for? If the name Carl O'Bannion is on there, I want to warn you about him." He stopped and waited for a response from the ranger.

"I never mention who's on my list unless there's good reason for it," said Sam Burrack. "If you know something, I appreciate any information you can give me."

"Well, this is something I always swore I'd never do, give information to a lawman ...." Jarvis Hicks licked his dry lips and rubbed his sweaty hands up and down his trouser leg. "But a man makes a big change, I reckon he needs to go all the way with it, eh?"

The ranger didn't answer; he only stared, waiting.

"Okay," said Jarvis, "there's a young outlaw named Carl O'Bannion from up in Wind River country. If his name ain't on your list, it ought to be." He checked the ranger's expression for any sign of recognition. But Sam's face didn't change.

"Go on," said the ranger, his mind recalling the name. Indeed, Carl O'Bannion was on his list of names. He had written down the name right before leaving the ranger outpost. But he wasn't obliged to mention it to Jarvis Hicks. For all he knew, Hicks could be O'Bannion's best friend. Sam knew little about Carl

O'Bannion, although he'd hoped to learn more about him before catching up to him. It paid to know the nature of his prey, he reminded himself, his gaze fixed tight on Jarvis Hicks.

Hicks saw that the ranger wasn't going to reveal anything. He shrugged, then went on. "The thing is, this O'Bannion is on the trail of some border guerrillas who kilt his mama and daddy back when he was just a little boy—back before the end of the war. He's a vengeance killer, this O'Bannion, and from what I heard, he'll kill anybody who tries to stop him."

"A vengeance killer," said Tackett, his brow darkening in concern. "That's the most dangerous man in the world." He studied the ranger's expression. If Sam was concerned, he managed to keep it from showing.

"Where'd you learn all this?" the ranger asked Hicks.

"I learned it from a big fellow named Cochio Santavia. Keeps a spread a day's ride from here, halfway twix here and Circle Wells. We was drinking together—another time I shouldn't have been doing what I was doing." Jarvis Hicks looked down for a moment of remorse. "Anyway, he got real nervous, followed me out to the jake and stuck a gun in my ribs. Started talking crazy. Accused me of being Carlos the Snake! I never heard of Carlos the Snake—I told him so, too. He searched me down. Said if he found any gold coins on me, I was dead."

"Gold coins?" The ranger's expression still didn't change, but Tackett noted that something had struck a chord.

"Yep." A faraway look came to Hicks's face. "See, that was another time I was fortunate, only I didn't know it. Luckily I was broke, and to tell the truth would probably have got him drunk and knocked him in the head if things hadn't gone the way they did." Hicks looked back and forth between the two lawmen for any sign of understanding. But seeing none, he shrugged again. "Of course, all that's in the past for me ... now that I'm changed and seen the light."

"What about the gold coins?" the ranger asked. "What did he mean by that?"

"After he saw I wasn't this Carlos the Snake, we got back into drinking and it turned out this Snake fellow had killed three men Cochio Santavia knew, and each time he stuck a gold coin in their mouths—old Federal coins from the war days."

"I see," said the ranger. "Now what has this Carlos the Snake got to do with Carl O'Bannion?"

"They're the same person," said Hicks. "That's what Cochio Santavia told me. Said the three men who'd been killed had all been in the same Union guerrilla band in the war. Cochio said he'd happened to have ridden with the same band out of Kansas, led by none other than Major Wolf Avrial himself. Cochio Santavia was worried about this Carlos the Snake, you could tell."

Hicks stopped and stared at the ranger in anticipation, awaiting whatever question he might ask. But Sam Burrack only nodded, as if dismissing it. "That's quite a story. Thanks for telling me."

"So," said Hicks, spreading a slight grin, "you do have the name O'Bannion on your list?"

Without answering Hicks, Sam turned his eyes to Sheriff Tackett.

"Get going, Jarvis," said Tackett. "Try to stay sober for at least an hour or so, after making such a big change and all." There was a sarcastic snap to the sheriff's words.

"I'm being genuine, Sheriff .... You'll see," said Jarvis Hicks, backing toward the open door. "I wish I had a Bible to read, or a guitar to play, or something. This is no small passing thing that's happened to me. I feel like I've been saved and given a new lease on life."

"That's great, Jarvis, now go!" said Tackett, with little enthusiasm. He and the ranger stood watching until Jarvis Hicks backed out of the office and disappeared into the night. Then Tackett said to Sam as they both stepped through the door and headed for the undertaker's, "Something about the gold coins got to you, Sam. I saw it."

"Yep, it did," said the ranger. "I've got Carl O'Bannion's name on my list. But it's for shooting a faro dealer in a gambling dispute up in the badlands. But the thing is, there's an unsolved murder happened there around the same time—a fellow named Tom Renner. Guess who he rode with in the war, and guess what he had in his mouth when they found him?"

"No kidding," said Tackett. "So, what Hicks is telling you could be true, about them both being the same person?"

"Could be," said Sam, as they headed along the empty dirt street. "At least, I believe this Cochio fellow might be worth talking to."

"You be careful getting caught up in some of that war vengeance," said Tackett. "That stuff can get awfully dangerous, especially when an old guerrilla outfit is involved. I ought to know. Don't forget, I once rode guerrilla myself."

The ranger managed a thin smile, staring ahead as they walked along. "You're not carrying any gold coins, are you?"

"Ha! If I was, I'd quit this job," said Boyd Tackett.

At the undertaker's, Tackett stepped inside warily, knocking on the open door as he entered, the ranger right behind him. Sam stepped quietly to one side as Sheriff Tackett called out in a low voice toward the next room, where a dim lamp glowed through the doorway, "Hey in there, Peddler ... are you all right?" Tackett's good hand held the sawed-off shotgun with his thumb over the hammer.

"Yeah," said a strained voice, "I'm okay .... Hell of a lot better than anybody thought, I reckon."

"That's for sure," said Tackett, lowering the shotgun and giving the ranger a look. They both walked into the room. The peddler sat on the side of a gurney, buttoning his shirt cuffs. Seeing the two badges on the lawmen, he lowered his gaze to the front of his flared open shirt and said, "Look at this: Somebody ripped my shirt down the front and cut off my britches legs." He dangled his legs showing where his

25

pinstripe trousers had been cut off just below the knees. "What the hell was the meaning of that?"

"I don't know." Sheriff Tackett shrugged. "Undertakers do curious things before they plant a man ... but this beats all I've ever seen."

"You're telling me?" The peddler's hand went carefully to a red mark above his right eye. "I woke up with some peckerwood fixing to pour hot wax in my eyes! Look where he burnt me."

"Oh, well, that's to hold your eyelids shut," Tackett offered. "Keeps them from flying open during a funeral, scaring the hell out'n the kids."

"My eyelids are working just fine ... but there'll be a funeral sure enough, if I can get my hands on the man what shot me."

"Easy, mister," said Tackett. "We heard the truth about what happened. Who are you, anyway?"

"Maurice Benfield is who I am," said the peddler. "And what do you mean you 'heard the truth'? The truth is I was shot for no reason."

"We heard about the hidden pistol in your shoe top, Mister Benfield," said Tackett. "Both the man who shot you and the undertaker's helper told us about it."

"My shoe top? Then they're both black-hearted liars!" Benfield swung his feet up one at a time, revealing the tops of his black, high-topped dress shoes. "There. Do you see any hidden pistol? Hell no! I was unarmed and assaulted with the intent to be killed. I hope you've got that man in jail, 'cause I'm not responsible for what I'll do to him." Benfield started to stand up, but Sheriff Tackett put a hand on his shoulder, holding him down.

"You best settle down, Benfield," said Tackett, noting the bloodstain on his ripped shirt. "You've still got a chest wound to worry about."

"Bull, I don't," said Benfield. He jerked one side of his shirt back and showed the bloody streak of the bullet that had run two inches across his chest, then tore itself free and sped away. "I just happened to have had a wallet full of money in. my breast pocket, sir," said Benfield. "You might say money saved my life. It deflected the bullet and left me un-conscious—yet unharmed." Benfield's hand went to the back of his head and carefully touched a large bump there. "I believe hitting that floor was the worst thing that happened to me, leastwise till I got here." Irritated by all the undertaker's helper had put him through, he looked around.

"Where's the little turd that done this to me? Why didn't somebody check first to see if I was alive? How do I get my britches legs back, so's I can get out of here? I asked that man for a glass of water. He gave me pure rubbing alcohol—liked to choked me to death. Then he ran off, shouting like a lunatic! I ain't seen him since."

"He's just an undertaker's helper, mister. Our undertaker, Max Tennison, had to go pick up his new bride in Montana."

"I don't care if he picks her up in Montana and drops her in Kalamazoo! I hate this damned place, Sheriff, I don't mind telling you. Being treated like a dead man makes my skin crawl!"

"I understand," said Tackett. "Don't know if this helps you any, but the man who shot you wanted to come by here and apologize."

"Apologize," Benfield said flatly.

"Yep, he talks like he's real repentant about everything," said Tackett.

"I'll repent him," Benfield fumed. "Let me get my hands around his neck."

Beside Sheriff Tackett, the ranger said under his breath, "See why I never like working in town?"

CHAPTER 2

At daybreak, the ranger swung his saddlebags up behind his saddle and ran a gloved hand along the big Appaloosa stallion's neck. As he reached down and checked the cinch, he said to Sheriff Tackett, who stood on the edge of the boardwalk, "Think you're going to be all right? I can stay another day or two if you need me. I've got plenty of names on my list, but nothing that won't keep a couple of days longer."

Tackett took his forearm out of the sling and studied his stiff fingers, opening and shutting them. "Looks like my arm is healing right along. I ought to be able to manage things here. Much obliged for your help, Sam."

"Don't mention it," said the ranger. He glanced up and down the dirt street through the sheen of silver morning light. "What about Gunderson, that peddler, and Jarvis Hicks? You expect any trouble out of them?"

"Gunderson's had enough. He'll get on back to his spread and lick his wounds. As for the other two, I told Benfield to be on today's stage to Humbly—said if he ain't I'll throw him in jail for disturbing the peace. I expect this morning his chest is too bruised for him to be wanting to fight. And I don't look for any trouble out of Hicks .... To tell the truth, I about halfway believe he means it about seeing the error of his ways. I hope so anyway."

"I reckon you have to take a man at his word till you see something otherwise," said Sam. He dropped the stirrup and stepped up into his saddle.

"You keep an eye out for that Carlos the Snake, or Carl

O'Bannion, or whoever he is," said Tackett. "I wish you knew more about him."

"So do I," said Sam. "I'll go see this Cochio Santavia as soon as I can get over that way, hear what he's got to say about it. I've got plenty to do between here and there. I've got the Glover boys over in Shuller. They killed three men up in the badlands a few weeks back."

"You mean Stevie Boy and Mudcat Glover?" Tackett asked. "Those boys are as cold-blooded and crazy as any I've ever seen."

"Yep, that's them all right," Sam replied. "Carlos the Snake will have to wait until I get to him."

"Adios, Ranger," said Tackett. "You be careful fooling with Stevie Boy and Mudcat"

"I intend to." The ranger touched his fingers to the brim of his gray sombrero and turned the Appaloosa to the street. On a wooden bench out in front of the stage station, Sam saw Benfield the peddler sitting with his head bowed and his hand raised to his chest as if to soothe it. Benfield only glanced up with a pained expression, then dropped his head and stared at the boardwalk. A block farther along the street, Sam saw three men helping Loman Gunderson up onto a buckboard.

"Watch my foot, damn it!" Gunderson growled at the men without so much as glancing in Sam's direction.

In the alley beside the Roi-Tan Saloon, Jarvis Hicks stood talking to two drunken miners as they passed a bottle of rye back and forth. When one miner offered the bottle to Jarvis Hicks, Sam saw Hicks refuse it, shoving it away as it were full of spiders.

Seeing Sam ride along the street, Jarvis Hicks waved at him with both hands, a broad smile covering his face. Hicks started to step forward, but Sam nudged the Appaloosa into a trot. "Let's get out of here and back to work, Black-Pot," Sam whispered to the stallion. "Let's go find out what this Carl O'Bannion is up to." The, stallion rode in the direction of

29

the north trail, with its string of small towns and stage stops between there and the badlands.

Randall Shaney's heart pounded in his chest. His breath had given out on him as he topped the steep rise of sand. Now his burning lungs could only make a desperate gasping effort to keep him alive. He collapsed to his knees, the scalding sun feeling like a cruel heavy hand pressing him down. The weight of the Colt pistol was far too heavy for his sweaty exhausted hand. He let the gun slip free and drop to the sand with a soft plop. Then he forced his scorched head around enough to look out across the sand flats below him. "Jesus ...." he whispered, breathlessly, barely able to murmur the word through his parched lips.

Through the wavering heat below, Randall Shaney watched the big desert roan pound forward relentlessly across the burning sand. The rider sat straight and tall, the sun seeming to have no effect on him. Shaney pitched forward onto the ground, sand clinging instantly to the corner of his gaping mouth. What was the use? He couldn't fight this man, he couldn't stop this man. The man was not even human, he thought. And how did this man pick him? There had been four other men with him—riders for the Broken Bar Ranch headed back from Humbly.

Shaney hadn't noticed the rider following them until he'd split away from the Broken Bar men. That had been yesterday evening. The rider had dogged him ever since. First a rifle shot had knocked his hat off his head. Shaney had looked around and saw the rider plain as day. He was just sitting in the middle of the trail, staring at Shaney from fifty yards away, a big Remington rolling-block rifle propped up from his lap. Maybe then Shaney should have made a stand ... should have drawn his own rifle and shot the man down on the spot. But it was too late now to think of what he should have done. Death was coming for him, reaching right up from the sand flats, and would be here any minute.

Vengeance

As soon as the first shot had sliced his hat away, Randall Shaney did what any man might do, given the same circumstances. He'd made a run for it. He hadn't been expecting trouble. When it came upon him so sudden and for no apparent reason, Shaney did what was instinctive to a man's nature. But running was a mistake. Now that mistake would cost him dearly. Before he'd gotten ten yards farther along the trail, a second shot ripped into his horse's hip and took it down, sending Shaney headlong into the sand.

When Shaney had tried crawling back to his saddle boot for his rifle, another shot shattered the rifle stock right before his eyes. Then a steady pounding of shots into the sand had forced him backward until he could struggle to his feet and run. "Lord God, please ... help me," Shane pleaded, sand inside his mouth now, gritty and sharp beneath his tongue.

Randall Shaney's fingers crawled to the pistol butt in the sand, but he didn't have the strength to lift the big gun. There had been a time last evening when he thought the man dogging him might be a thief, but he'd long since given up that notion. The first thing the man did was destroy anything Shaney had of any value: the horse, the rifle.

During the night, running wildly across the sand flats, the rider close behind him as if to torment him, Shaney had pulled his money from his pocket and pitched it to the ground. Seventeen dollars, all he had to his name. Surely if this man was out to rob him, that would satisfy him. But when the rider was still on his trail come morning, Shaney had to accept the cold hard truth. This man wanted his life, nothing else. "God ... help me," Randall Shaney sobbed again, feeling the world grow dark and small around him.

Carlos the Snake took his time, letting the roan climb the sandy slope at its own pace. At the top of the steep slope, he walked the roan in circle around the sweaty trembling body. He took note of the hand lying atop the pistol, but was not concerned about it. The face turned slightly up toward him, the lips moving, but no words came out. Carlos tried to imagine what he must look like from that angle, the blazing sunlight forming a broad halo above his shoulders and hat brim. He knew the man could not see his face with any clarity. Carlos formed a thin smile. What did he look like from up here? He looked like Death, of course. That was exactly how he wanted to look.

"Randall Shaney," he said, staring down at the face streaked with sand and sweat, and convulsing in terror. "I believe this is yours." Carlos tossed the seventeen dollars he'd found the night before down near Shaney's pistol in the sand.

"Who ... who are you?" Shaney rasped between short, stabbing breaths. "What ... do you ... want?" Even as he spoke, Randall Shaney concentrated on the pistol beneath his hand, weighing his chances, wondering if he could raise it and fire in one last surge of energy. What did he have to lose? he asked himself.

Carlos the Snake took his time, swinging down slowly from his saddle and lifting his canteen by its strap from the saddle horn before answering. "I am Carlos," he said, knowing his name would mean nothing to this man. He uncapped the canteen, took a sip of warm water, swished it around, and squirted it out.

"You're going ... to kill me?" said Shaney, already knowing the answer. Then, without waiting for a reply, he asked, "Why? I don't know you ... what have I—"

"Ah, but you do know me," Carlos said, cutting him off. "You know me from many years ago."

Randall Shaney squinted in the sun's glare, trying for a better look at the face as he tried to recall having ever seen this man before. "You ... you're Mexican?"

"*Sí,* I am *Mejicano,* on *mi madre* side." Carlos reached out with the canteen at arm's length, and poured a trickle of water down on Shaney's upturned face. His voice was heavily accented in Spanish as he spoke, yet, the accent vanished as he continued. "But my pa was black Irish through and through." He paused and stared at Randall Shaney, as if waiting for recognition to come to him. After a moment, when it didn't happen, Carlos said, "You killed them both, you and the border militia you rode with."

"Mister ... I swear to God"—Shaney shook his head slowly—"I never kilt ... nobody, not even—"

"Unh-uh now," said Carlos, wagging a finger, with the canteen in the same hand. "Don't deny it. It won't help you any." He tipped the canteen slightly, letting another trickle run down Shaney's cheek into his parched, gaping mouth. "There is nothing that's going to save you. Here, sip this." He bent down closer and pressed the canteen to Shaney's lips, cradling the exhausted man's head in one gloved hand. As Shaney sipped, Carlos kept an eye on the hand lying on the pistol. Water would revive the man's strength and with it perhaps his will to live. So much the better, Carlos thought.

"The only thing you might get now is a quick ending, but that's up to you," said Carlos.

"Please, mister...." Shaney's words trailed away.

"Who are the men you rode with back in the war, Shaney?" Carlos asked, as if not even hearing the man's plea for mercy.

"I ... I can't remember them" Shaney replied. "Not most of them anyway. That ... was a long ... time ago." His voice came broken and weak from his chest. His breath still panted.

"Yeah, I suppose so," said Carlos with bitterness, "yet it seems like only yesterday to me." He drew the canteen back and held it loosely in his hand. Looking up into the blazing sky, as if in contemplation, Carlos said, "I'll have to shoot you in both knees and stake you out here. By nightfall, if you're not dead, you'll wish you were .... You'll be a warm meal for whatever crawls out of the shadows."

"Mister ... I swear to God," said Shaney, sobbing, "I don't recall them days. I've tried to ... forget them." But then he forced himself to settle down enough to press his memory. "Wait! Now I know. That was ... Major Wolf Avrial I rode with."

Carlos grinned thinly. "There, you see, it's all starting to come back to you. But I already know about Avrial. Who are some others?"

"Deacon Stokes?" said Shaney, as if questioning his own memory.

Carlos handed him the canteen again, saying, "I already dealt with him, too. Go on."

Shaney held the canteen in his trembling left hand, his right hand still resting on the pistol. But that was fine with Carlos. The pistol being there gave the man hope—helped him try to remember. "What about Duke Davenport?"

"He's dead, too," said Carlos, flatly, with a knowing expression on his face. "Yep, they found him over in Bismarck last fall. Had a knife shoved down in his eye. Looked like he'd died hard, they say."

Randall Shaney swallowed a dry knot in his throat. "Bert Breedan?"

"He died in jail," said Carlos.

"Moose Hendricks?"

"Also dead." Carlos stared down into Shaney's eyes. "So is Andrew Butler. You don't want to hear the details." Carlos's pistol moved slightly, the tip pointing at Shaney's kneecap. "Better come up with something quick, Shaney. I'm losing interest."

"There was a fellow ... they called Pecos Bob," said Shaney. He took a short sip from the canteen, feeling the pistol beneath his right hand. "There was a Calvin Galt ... but he goes under the name Dan Bristoe. He's a drifter and a gunslinger. I saw him in Halston today, but he never saw me—he's the reason I left there. You'll find him at the bar."

"Go on," said Carlos.

Shaney concentrated. "There was a Vernon something-or-other, rode with us back then, too. And there was Cochio Santavia—"

"A big Mexican, had a long scar, one eye missing?" Carlos asked, running a finger down the side of his nose, depicting Cochio's scar.

Shaney nodded. "That's him, all right ... that's Cochio. He was one tough hombre. I could take you to him," Shane offered in desperation. "He's over near Circle Wells."

"Not a chance, Shaney," said Carlos. "I already knew about these men, except for the Mexican's name, and this fellow Vernon. Can't recall his last name, huh?"

"Believe me, if I could—"

Carlos cut him short. "I know, you would tell me." As he spoke, Carlos the Snake took out a single gold coin from his vest pocket and held it down close to Shaney's face. "Remember these?"

Shaney nodded. "Yeah ... they was minted during the war. Few of them still around." He closed his fingers around the pistol butt in the sand, keeping his eyes upward on Carlos's.

"I have saddlebags filled with these big gold babies," said Carlos. "This is the gold you and Wolf Avrial and the others killed my father and mother over. But they never told you where it was hidden, did they?"

"Mister, you've got to believe me, I never ...." Shaney's voice trailed to a halt as shadows of the past took form and grew clearer in his mind. "Bannion," he whispered in astonishment. "My God, he had a boy ... who got away." Shaney laid his thumb across the pistol hammer, still staring up into Carlos's eyes.

"Yep," said Carlos the Snake. "I was that little boy. And to think that you could not even remember taking part in something so terrible." Carlos's eyes glistened. "Shame on you, Shaney." A shot exploded from his pistol without his taking his gaze from Randall Shaney's. Shaney screamed, his hand jerking away from the pistol, both hands going to the gaping hole where his right kneecap had been only a second before. The canteen had flown from his hand and lay spilling water into the sand. As Shaney

35

lay writhing in agony, Carlos stepped over and picked up the canteen and capped it.

"Damn you!" Shaney bellowed. "I told you all I knew! I never killed them people! I was just there! You can't blame me for their deaths! I was just a soldier! All I did was follow my orders!"

"I see," said Carlos. Another shot exploded, this one shattering Shaney's left kneecap. Carlos walked away to his horse, where he holstered his Colt and draped the canteen strap over his saddle horn while Randall Shaney screamed and rolled back and forth in the sand, his legs useless to him now.

"Why? Why? You rotten, dirty—!" As Shaney ranted in agony, he managed to grab the pistol from the ground. Carlos was standing with his back to him. The pistol was covered with blood, bits of gristle, and small splinters of bone "You gave your word!"

"My word?" Hearing the sound of the pistol cocking, Carlos turned around slowly. He stared into Shaney's eyes, as if not seeing the gun pointed at him. "What good is the word of a man whose family you killed?"

"I got you! You sonuvabitch!" Shaney screamed. "I'll die out here, but I won't die alone! You're going with me!"

"You fool," Carlos said in a calm, almost soothing voice. Shaney saw only a blur as Carlos's hand streaked upward from his holster. The very disbelief of something happening so fast was enough to stun him, keeping him from reacting. Three shots exploded. The first shot ripped the cocked pistol from Shaney's hand. The second shot sliced through the joint of Shaney's right shoulder. The third shot did the same to Shaney's left shoulder. Shaney slammed backward on the ground, his eyes dazed and staring into the merciless white sunlight.

Carlos the Snake stood over Randall Shaney, staring down at him and speaking in a low, even voice. "My father and mother made me leave that day. Although I wanted to stay and fight beside them, to die with them if I must ... they forced me to leave. Do you know what that does to a little boy? To know that death has come to take those most precious to him ... and to be powerless to do anything about it? I used to lay awake at night praying I could go back and change things, to make it all different. But such are the foolish dreams of a small boy, eh?"

"Damn you!" Randall Shaney lay helpless, his shoulders and legs torn apart, no feeling in them, other than crushing pain where the bullets had ripped into him. "Finish it, mister," Shaney growled through his pain. "Only an animal would leave a man laying to die like this ... finish it."

"Sí, you are right," said Carlos the Snake, "only an animal would do this." He holstered his pistol. Stooping down, he hefted Shaney up enough to give him a hard shove over the edge of the rise. Shaney tumbled, his useless arms and legs flapping like a bloody scarecrow's.

Carlos stood up and watched Shaney come to rest at the bottom of the rise in a cloud of sand. Shaney sobbed and begged for mercy to the wide empty sky. Carlos looked upward, as if to see if the sky had heard, or if such mercy was forthcoming.

Then, satisfied it was not, he smiled to himself. He dusted his hands off, walked back to his horse, mounted, and rode away.

CHAPTER 3

The team of horses pulling the big black hearse stopped at the edge of the flatlands, the driver barely having to pull back on the reins. "Whoa, Bob, whoa, Oscar." As soon as the two big whites settled, the driver stood up and visored his hand across his brow, beneath the skimpy brim of his cloth cap. "I can't see a blasted thing in this sun," the man said, squinting, feeling his eyes starting to water with the strain.

"Perhaps you should have worn a brimmed hat after all, Maximus," said his new wife seated beside him. She rose and visored her brow in the same manner as she spoke.

"I told you, Darcy, no more call than I ever have for traveling clothes, buying a wide-brimmed hat would only be a waste of money." He jerked a white handkerchief from his hip pocket and blotted his eyes. "Besides, newlyweds need to be saving ... if we ever expect to someday raise a family and get ahead in this world." Maximus Tennison smiled, still squinting from the afterimage of sunlight. "I promised your pa before he died that I'd take good care of you. I intend to keep my word."

"Of course," Darcy replied, having only lent half an ear to her new husband's words. Her attention was still drawn toward the distant wavering rises of sand, cactus plants, and dried sage. "Must we continue on this same trail, Maximus?" she asked, sounding apprehensive.

"It's the way I came, Darcy. I hate to start changing directions on the way back. This is powerful-large desert country. You never know where you might end up."

"But those gunshots we heard, Maximus," said Darcy. "I

don't like the idea of riding right toward them."

"Neither do I," said Maximus Tennison, "but I'm afraid we have little choice." To console her, he took his watch from his vest, opened it, checked the time, then added, "It's been nearly a half hour since we heard the shots. I'm certain there's no cause for concern." Together they both sat down on the seat. Maximus nodded back toward the empty hearse and said, "It would be much cooler for you back there. Maybe you could sleep a while." He smiled, saying in a childlike voice, "When you wake up, we'll be past the spot, and it will all be gone."

Darcy returned his smile, although she saw no humor in his acting that way. She was no child. And hearing the gunshots was no laughing matter to her. She looked back at the dark empty hearse, then said to her new husband, "No, thank you, I'll ride right up here. Whatever is out there, we'll face it together." She sat erect and stared straight ahead.

"I hope you're not still upset with me over traveling in the funeral rig," Maximus said, smoothing his palm across his sweaty forehead. "Had there been a train line running this direction, I would have gladly brought you by rail. I just couldn't see renting a rig when we own these two strong horses and this fine stout wagon."

"No, I'm not upset," said Darcy. "I understand we need to be frugal." Maximus's bringing up the subject caused her to once again look around at the ornate black hearse. Dark red curtains covered the glass viewing windows on either side. When they had started their trip, she'd agreed that if they ran into bad weather, a sandstorm or a heavy rain, they would take shelter in the hearse for the night. Fortunately, that hadn't happened. They had slept each night on the ground, close to a campfire, something she had done in the past, growing up as a rancher's daughter.

Seeing the look on her face as she took in the whole scene of the big black hearse and the two dusty white horses, each of them wearing a tall red plume atop their foreheads, Maximus offered in an apologetic tone, "Darcy, it's the profession I'm in. I try to make do."

"I know," she said, offering a slight smile, reaching a hand up and brushing a strand of hair from his wet forehead, tucking it beneath his cloth cap. "We talked about all this before, Maximus. It will just take some getting used to."

Maximus settled in the seat and gave a short slap of the reins. The big horses were so well trained they needed no more than a quick reminder of what the driver wanted from them. Maximus said as the two horses started forward across the sand flats, "I sure hope you get used to it. Nothing would suit me more than you taking a hand in my business and working right alongside me. It would save me keeping a helper on the payroll."

"We'll see," said Darcy, staring straight ahead into the wavering heat and the sun's glare.

On the other side of the sand flats, near the bottom of the slope, Randall Shaney lay more dead than alive. In the short time he'd been lying there, the sun had fried his exposed skin to no less a degree than a slab of bacon thrown into a hot skillet. With each shallow intake of breath, Shaney prayed death would quit taking its time torturing him. Whatever was keeping him alive, he couldn't begin to guess. It certainly wasn't his will. His will had played out not long after Carlos the Snake had ridden out of sight and left him here to bake in the sand. "God, please kill me ...." Shaney murmured skyward. His tongue was thick and dry; a coppery taste of blood lingered in the back of his parched throat from where his lips had cracked open under the intense sunlight.

Carlos was right about the night and what it would bring. Shaney didn't want to even consider what would come crawling, sniffing, then sinking its teeth into him, should he still be alive after dark. There would be no mercy here, not on this barren hot griddle where the fallen became the feast.

Shaney trembled deep inside and managed to roll his face sideways, still pleading in a broken whisper, "God, please ...."

In his near delirium, Shaney thought for a moment that he might have heard God respond to him. But as he listened closer, he realized it was not the voice of God, but rather the low, blowing sound of a horse drawing near. He tried staring through the swirl of blazing heat, but saw nothing, only blinding silver light. He heard the sound again, and squeezed his eyes shut for a second.

As he opened his eyes again he heard the creaking sound of a harness and wagon. Then, as if parting the wavering shroud of heat, two big white horses, red funeral plumes fluttering atop their heads, came forward toward him, pulling a glistening black hearse.

"Thank you, Jesus," Shaney moaned, realizing that his plea had been heard, that he was finally dead. This was how it happened, he realized, taking relief in understanding at last the mystery of death. He looked up as the hearse drew nearer, then let himself sink into a dark cool place as the horses stopped and an angel wreathed in soft golden light swooped down and cast shade upon him.

"Careful there, Darcy," Maximus warned his young bride. Darcy had already left the wagon seat. She dropped down onto her knees, a canteen in her hand, and looked around at Maximus, who hurriedly secured the reins around the brake handle.

"Hurry, Maximus, he's still alive!" Darcy called out. She turned back to the burnt and tortured face as she uncapped the canteen and poured a trickle of tepid water onto a gathered handful of her hemline She touched the wet dress cloth to the cracked lips, seeing only a quiver of life run across the chin. "Oh, my God, Max! Who would do something like this?" Her eyes went from arm to arm, knee to knee, seeing the gaping holes, the black stiff blood there.

Maximus swallowed hard, took a quick wary glance around the barren land, then said, "Lord, I don't know, Darcy ...

Indians? Apaches maybe? We better get out of here." He reached down to take her by her shoulder, but she drew herself away. She went back to the task of wetting the blistered face and gently squeezing a drop of water between the slightly parted lips.

"I don't think it's Indians," Darcy said, "but get your rifle anyway, Maximus. If there were Indians this close, they would have attacked us already, if they had a mind to." She heard Maximus run through the sand, then return as she continued squeezing drop after drop of tepid water into the dry mouth. The water brought what sounded like a faint death rattle up from the parched throat. At length, she could feel a faint trace of breath against the back of her wet hand. "That's it, mister," she coaxed, "breathe for me .... You can do it. Breathe, breathe!"

Behind her she heard her new husband wrestle with the lever on the rifle. "Oh, no, Darcy, it's stuck. I can't get it to lever a round into the chamber! Get up, come on! We've got to get out of here!"

"What about him?" Darcy asked in disbelief, looking back over her shoulder. "We can't leave him here to die."

Maximus's voice turned shaky and harsh. "We've got no choice but to leave him! For God sakes, think about us!"

"Shame on you, Maximus." Darcy stood up slowly, her gathered, wet hemline still in her hand. "I'll pretend I didn't hear you say such a thing as that." She turned loose of her dress and jerked the jammed rifle from his hands. "Pick him up and carry him to the hearse. Then we'll leave. When we don't have time to help a man in this shape, we're no better than the ones who did this to him."

"But, Darcy ... I'm only trying to think of both our welfare," Maximus said, his voice going shallow.

"So am I, Maximus," Darcy replied. "Do you think we could face one another the rest of our lives after leaving a man to die out here?"

She palmed the stuck rifle lever a solid forward blow, then jerked it back quickly, not giving it time to catch on the rim of a cartridge. Maximus stared as if dumbstruck, seeing his gentle new wife handle the big Winchester like a cavalry trooper. "There, all done." She threw her small thumb across the cocked hammer and laid it down expertly, cradling the rifle across her forearm as her eyes began to scan the desert like a hawk's. "Hurry, pick him up. Let's get moving. I don't like being here ...."

Throughout the afternoon, the big whites labored across the rise and fall of the rolling desert floor, slowly, but steadily, keeping their natural funeral pace. Inside the hearse, Darcy had opened the glass viewing windows to allow a cross-draft of air. Randall Shaney lay stretched out on a blanket, his wounds washed and compressed by wet blood-soaked rags Darcy had torn from her spare petticoat. Shaney had drifted in and out of consciousness until, by dusk, when the hearse stopped on a stretch of flatlands, he stared upward wordlessly at the low ceiling of the hearse. He listened to Maximus ask Darcy through the open window, "How's he doing?"

"I think he's going to make it," Darcy whispered in reply. "I'll be along in a moment to help you make a camp."

Hearing their words, Shaney asked Darcy, as Maximus stepped away from the window and toward the horses, "You— You said I'm going to make it—? You mean I ain't dead?" He saw Darcy in his peripheral vision, yet was afraid to face her eye to eye. "I can't move my arms ... or legs."

"I know," said Darcy in a tired voice. "You've been shot bad. But, of course, you're not dead." She raised his head enough to tip a few drops of water from the canteen into his mouth. "Luckily, we found you when we did. Who are you, mister, and who did this to you?"

"I thought ... I was dead ... that you were an angel," Shaney murmured.

"Listen to me," Darcy insisted, leaning down close to his face, making him look at her as she spoke. "It's important that we know who did this. Who's out there? Was it renegade Indians? Bandits?"

Randall Shaney forced himself to loll his head back and forth in reply. "No ... it's a man who's held ... a grudge since the war."

Darcy listened as Shaney struggled with his words and told her the story. Outside, as twilight turned to darkness, Maximus struck a small campfire, unhitched the tired horses, wiped them down, watered and grained them, and walked them to a sparse stand of wild grass. Then he hobbled them. When he returned to the campsite, he found Darcy beating the campfire out with a blanket. "What are you doing?" he shouted, running forward, seeing her slapping wildly at the fire. He grabbed her arm as she stepped into the blackened smoky spot of earth and kicked the remaining coals out across the ground.

Darcy pulled herself loose from Maximus's grasp and continued stamping out the glowing sparks in the dirt. "Quick, Maximus, help me! He'll see this for miles! He'll be back!"

"Oh, Lord!" Maximus said, catching on right away, his gaze darting out across the desert night. "What have I done?" Together, the two of them finished off the campfire and stepped back, panting, watching the remaining drift of smoke move away on the night air. Maximus wiped a trembling hand across his clammy forehead. "I'm sorry, Darcy, I didn't realize—"

"Hush, Max," Darcy said. "It's done. All we can do is hope he didn't see it." Her voice had taken on the authoritative tone that had been Maximus's up until they found Randall Shaney lying wounded in the sand. She looked warily out across the darkness. "If he saw the fire back here on his trail, he'll know Mister Shaney might still be alive .... He'll come back to finish him."

"Mister Shaney? That's his name?" Maximus asked. He

glanced toward the hearse. "You mean, he told you what happened? The man who did that to him might come back here?" Maximus's face paled at the thought.

"Oh, yes," said Darcy, moving over to where Maximus had propped the Winchester against the hearse before tending the horses. "This man's name is Mister Shaney, and he told me everything." She started to mention that it was foolish of him to leave the rifle there, knowing there could be trouble. But by now Darcy had seen enough to know that her new husband did not possess the kind of cool head this sort of situation called for. Without saying so, she picked up the rifle, checked it, and cradled it over her left arm, keeping her right hand around the stock, her finger close to the trigger.

"We're going to have to be awfully careful from here on, Max. There's a very dangerous killer out there. This was a personal vendetta that goes back to the war."

Maximus looked sick with fright. "Then ... then it has nothing to do with us, Darcy. It's between them. Surely to God, all we have to do is get out of the way! We're not a part of this!" As he spoke, his voice quivered with fear. Darcy took note of it and forced herself to remain calm.

"If he's seen the fire, we're a part of it, whether we like it or not, Max. Not only will he want to finish killing Mister Shaney, he'll want to do away with anybody who can tell what happened out here. The best thing we can do is be ready, just in case."

"No, no, wait!" said Maximus, getting more and more nervous and edgy. "I'll get the horses! We'll clear out of here! He comes back, we're gone! I think that's the end of it!"

Darcy shook her head slowly. "Stop it, Max," she said with resolve. "We're in this up to our necks. We might as well accept it and be ready to fight, if we want to live. We're not abandoning Mister Shaney to that killer. And what's the use if we left here right now? He'll pick up our tracks and be on us until he catches us."

"But we could reason with him, let him know this is none of our business!" Maximus offered.

"There's no reasoning with this kind of man," Darcy said. "The only smart thing to do is wait here for him. If he comes back, we'll face him here tonight, while we're expecting him."

Maximus paced back and forth, his fear overcoming him. He gripped his forehead as he spoke. "But, Darcy, how on earth do you know that's the best thing to do?"

"I don't know that it is the best thing to do," said Darcy, "but unless you've got something better, this is where we make our stand." She stared at him, her eyes clear and calm, unwavering in the dim moonlight.

Looking back on his trail from a cliff in the circling hills, Carlos the Snake had seen the distant glow of fire in the early darkness. He sat watching the firelight twinkle like a fallen star on the desert floor. Then he watched it go out. Too late, he thought knowing that back on his trail someone had found Randall Shaney, either dead or alive. He nodded to himself, knowing that whoever had struck the fire had, at that very mo-ment, realized their mistake and were trying to cover it up. But they knew they had given away their position. So now they would be expecting him to come back. They would be ready and waiting for him.

He stepped down from the roan, uncinched the saddle, and lifted it from the horse's back. Let them wait. When he'd attended his horse, he gathered dried brush and built himself a campfire behind a stand of rocks. Even in rock cover, he kept the flames low and thin, and banked sandy soil and loose rock up around it.

He made coffee, and warmed jerked beef, and ate, staring with dark contemplation into the dancing flames. Leaving Randall Shaney alive had been a mistake. He'd have to be more careful from now on. But each time he caught up with another of his father and mother's killers, he'd felt a need to inflict a crueler form of punishment than the time before. He thought of the men he'd killed, and how their deaths, rather than bringing him the satisfaction he'd expected, had only left a restless gnawing feeling inside him.

The first man he'd found was Duke Davenport. He'd simply goaded the big man into a gunfight and shot him dead and left his body in a urine-soaked ditch behind an adobe cantina near Taos.

The second killer he'd found was a thin sickly man named Moose Hendricks. Apparently, Moose had been given his robust nickname during healthier times, before consumption had ravaged him. It would have been easy to put a bullet into Moose Hendricks, but instead Carlos had taken a knife to him. He'd taken his time, killing Hendricks slowly, until at last he'd forced the tip of the blade into the man's eye, to the hilt, and watched his life glaze over and come to a stop.

Yet, killing Hendricks had done nothing for the fire of revenge burning in Carlos's belly. Hendricks seemed to have almost welcomed death, or to at least not have been at all surprised by it. Carlos finished the last bite of the jerked beef and stood up with his tin coffee cup in his hand. He stepped away from the tall rock sheltering his campfire and gazed out across the shadowy black desert.

After Moose Hendricks, Carlos had tracked Tom Renner living up in the badlands in a mining camp. He'd found Renner asleep on a canvas cot inside a ragged tent. He'd choked him to death slowly with his bare hands, whispering to him as he did so, repeating the story of what Renner and the others had done to his family. He had taken some satisfaction in watching Renner's face swell red, then blue, then go slack in death as he released his fingers from around his throat.

But choking Tom Renner to death had brought Carlos the Snake no more satisfaction than knifing Moose Hendricks or shooting Duke Davenport. He'd left Tom Renner's tent with a cold killing rage beating inside his chest. That rage had spilled over less than an hour later, in a faro game that ended with his killing the dealer, and backing out of the gambling tent with his smoking Colt flashing back and forth, covering the crowd.

Carlos stared out into the dark desert and sipped his coffee. That had been a mistake, shooting the faro dealer the same day he'd killed Tom Renner. There were people in that mining camp who could identify him, if anyone ever connected the two killings. He'd promised himself to be more careful after that. Yet today, leaving Randall Shaney alive was one more foolish thing he'd done in an attempt to quench his thirst for vengeance. Letting the man lie there and bake to death slowly in the sun had been fit punishment, he'd thought at the time. But now he had no idea if the man was dead or alive. Either way, Carlos had left the body in his own trail, when all he'd had to do was kill the man quickly, drag him out of sight, and toss him into some brush.

Carlos finished the last sip of coffee and slung the grounds from his cup. Tomorrow, he would have to clean up his mistake and be careful not to make another one. He still had too much killing left to do. He couldn't take a chance on getting caught before he finished. His next stop would be Halston, the man Galt, now going under the name Dan Bristoe. Whoever was down there on his trail could sleep tonight. He'd take care of them in the morning when they were least expecting it.

CHAPTER 4

At the end of a sleepless night, Maximus Tennison leaned against the hearse, with a blanket wrapped around him to stave off the cold desert air. At first, he and his new wife had agreed to take turns standing watch. But after a few hours, it became obvious that neither of them were capable of any fitful rest. Knowing what might be lurking in the darkness just outside the circling moonlight, Maximus remained tense. He was operating on nothing more than raw nerves and fearful anticipation by the time sunlight rose in a thin wreath on the eastern horizon.

The unexpected sound of Darcy's voice startled Maximus as she stepped down from the hearse and said with regret, "Poor Mister Shaney is gone, Max,"

"Huh, gone?" In his nervous state, Maximus looked around quickly in the grainy dawn light.

"Max, he died, only moments ago," said Darcy. "I was holding his head in my lap and he let out a breath and just seemed to go to sleep." She moved in close to her husband for comfort.

"So now all of this has been for nothing," Maximus said. "We risked our lives helping him, and now he's dead anyway." There was bitter irony in his voice.

Darcy stopped abruptly and Maximus saw the hurt in her eyes. He lowered the rifle from his arms and held her to his chest, reaching out with the blanket and wrapping it around the two of them. "I'm sorry, Darcy ... I didn't mean that. We did the right thing, helping Mister Shaney. You did everything you could for him," he consoled her.

A silence passed as she collected herself and touched her sleeve to her eyes. "All right, enough of this," she said aloud to herself. "Since we have the facility to take him to the next town, perhaps that would be best, instead of burying him out here. You're the undertaker, Max—what do you think?"

"Yes, of course," Max replied. "We'll be in Shuller by this afternoon. It's no more than a wide spot in the trail, but the mining company has a private constable on their payroll there. We can tell him what happened." As Max spoke, his eyes went back to searching the gray farther out from their campsite.

"If we have any trouble out of Shaney's killer today, maybe the constable will accompany us a ways," said Darcy.

"Do you think we will have trouble today?" Max asked in a hushed tone. "If he saw our fire, it seems like he would have come back in the night. Since he didn't, maybe we were worried for no reason. Maybe he missed seeing the fire altogether, and rode on."

"Maybe," said Darcy. "Let's hope so anyway." She stepped back from her husband and looked out into the dawn with him. "We'll have to be very watchful the rest of the way."

When the big whites were hitched and the body of Randall Shaney lay securely wrapped in a woolen blanket, the hearse began its trek across a rolling stretch of flatlands toward a circling hill line. Both Darcy and Maximus Tennison searched the land ahead and surrounding them, Darcy with the rifle across her lap. Her hands were wet with sweat by the time the sun rose to mid-morning height above them.

Across the stretch of flatland, Carlos the Snake held the telescope to his eye, watching the hearse roll slowly toward him. At first, he'd been surprised to see the big funeral rig out here in the middle of the desert, the big white horses wearing red plumes atop their heads, but then he afforded himself a trace of a smile. *Why not ...?* He collapsed the telescope between his palms and put it away. He relaxed in the shade of a large boulder for over a half hour, the big Remington rolling-block rifle propped against a smaller rock beside him. Next to the rifle stood a pair of hickory cross sticks, for long aim.

Carlos sipped tepid water from his canteen and only looked directly at the hearse now and then, saving his eyesight, keeping his vision sharp and fresh in the white glare of sunlight. Only when he judged that the big dusty black hearse had moved within the distance of a thousand yards from him, did he show any interest in it or its passengers. Then he rose up onto his knees, took out the telescope once again, and looked through it into the grim faces.

First, the man, the driver. Carlos studied the worried expression on the taut face through the magnifying lens. The young man's face looked as close to Carlos as his own face would look to him in a shaving mirror, he thought. The young man's most distinctive feature was fear, mixed with regret. Too bad, Carlos thought. He had nothing against this man, or the young woman seated beside him. They just happened to find themselves in the wrong place at the wrong time— traveling on the wrong person's trail. In the whole of this broad endless land, fate had put them here, in his gun sights.

Carlos moved the telescope from the man to the woman and saw the same pensive look on her face. Yet, there was something missing in the woman's expression, and it took Carlos a moment to realize what it was. He studied the face for a moment longer, then it came to him. He saw no regret in the woman's expression. She looked tired and afraid. But for whatever she knew of her situation, or what she feared might become her ... she showed no sign of regret for this cruel hand coincidence had dealt her. There was no doubt they had come upon Randall Shaney, Carlos told himself, studying the woman's face. But then he quickly lowered the telescope and put it away again. He could afford no mercy for this woman, or the man beside her.

Carlos took a second to clear his mind. Then he breathed

deep, picked up the hickory cross sticks from beside the big rolling-block rifle, and spread them open into a wide X.

On the seat of the big hearse, Darcy had fought against sleep as long as she could. She dozed off in the mid-morning heat, with the Winchester rifle across her lap, fully loaded, a cartridge belt with over thirty rounds looped around her shoulder.

Maximus drove the hearse, barely staying awake himself, a half-full canteen resting in his lap. His eyes were red and raw from lack of rest, his head nodding despite the nagging fear down low in his belly.

In his exhausted state, he caught a glimpse of sunlight glinting on gun metal in the distance. But before the alarm could go off in his mind, the silent lead bullet hit his chest with the impact of a hammer. A second passed before the sound of the shot reached down from the hills. By then, Maximus had already slammed back in the seat and fell forward. He lay stone dead, slumped over the ornate iron railing.

"What was that?" Darcy gasped, coming suddenly awake. She felt something warm and wet running down her face as she turned to Maximus and saw the gaping hole in his exposed back. Her hand went to her face and she realized she'd been drenched with Maximus's blood. "Oh, God, Max!" she screamed.

Feeling the slack on the reins fall upon their backs, the big whites quickened their pace. The big hearse swerved slightly. A second bullet struck the back of the seat between Darcy and her dead husband. She screamed again. Yet, even as she did so, she scrambled with both hands, snatching the reins and taking control, lest the big horses bolt on her.

Feeling the impact of the bullet, followed by the sound of the big rifle, Darcy instinctively laid back heavily on the left rein, forcing the horses to turn in a narrow circle. She had to get out of the line of fire, put the big hearse between herself and the shooter. There was no time to even think about Maximus lying dead beside her. Darcy's moves were pure reaction, her survival instinct taking over.

A third shot resounded from the hills as the big hearse slid sideways and made its turn in a rise of sand. Oscar, the big white on the left, let out a long pitiful nicker, a red spray of blood gushing out of the wound in his neck.

Feeling his teammate go down thrashing beside him, the other big white panicked and struggled to complete the turn. Neighing loudly and dragging the dying horse beside him, the horse barely managed to turn the hearse quarterwise before bogging down beneath the weight.

Darcy sprang down from the hearse with the Winchester in her hand. The turn had caused Maximus's body to sway. Now he toppled from the driver's seat and hit the ground like a bundle of rags. Darcy gasped at the sight, then ran to Maximus's body, rolled him over onto his back, and rummaged frantically through his trouser pockets until she found the folding knife he always carried.

A shot hit the ground at the remaining white's hooves, causing the big horse to jump sideways against the fallen horse on the ground. "Whoa, Bob!" Darcy shouted, jumping in with the pocket knife open, cutting the horse free of the tangled reins surrounding it. Before another shot resounded, she had scrambled back through the dirt to the coupling pen and freed the animal. Holding one long rein, she slapped the horse's rump with all her might and circled it back behind the cover of the hearse. Then, gasping for breath, she fell to the ground coughing and clawing sand from her eyes.

Beside his rock cover eight-hundred yards away, Carlos the Snake raised the big Remington from the cross sticks and laid it across his knee. He closed the cross sticks and dropped them to the dirt. Then he took out his telescope and focused it on the grisly scene down on the flatlands. "Quick thinking, lady," he murmured, seeing the hearse turned quarterwise to him. "You almost made it." He watched the final throes of the dying horse, its big white body streaked with dark red blood.

Carlos knew that had she managed to turn the big hearse before he shot the horse, she could have made a run for it—not that he wouldn't have caught up with her eventually. But it would have prolonged her life, making his bloody work more difficult.

Now, as it stood, she was trapped down there. She could make a desperate run on horseback. But without the bulk of the hearse protecting her, she wouldn't make it twenty yards before he put a bullet through her. Carlos was certain she realized that. He wondered if she would even bother trying, or if she would lie huddled down there awaiting death, and perhaps hoping that she could beg her way out of it.

Taking his time, he scanned with the lens. Through the dusty viewing window, he saw the body wrapped in a blanket. Of course he would have to check and make sure once he got down there, but Carlos felt sure it was Randall Shaney inside the hearse. That made him feel a little better about killing these people. It would help to know he'd been right about their finding Shaney. He moved the telescope's range out across the ground to the body of the hearse driver lying sprawled on its back, its dead eyes staring up into the blazing sun.

A few feet from the body, Carlos scanned across a canteen lying in the dirt. He passed the canteen, then jerked the telescope back to it. If there was water in the canteen, it could bring an end to things a little quicker, he thought. Lowering the telescope, Carlos hurried, picking up the cross sticks and propping them up on the ground. He took the big Remington rifle and had started to lay the barrel down in the X of the cross-sticks when he saw the woman dart out from behind the hearse, snatch up the canteen, and race back behind her cover.

"Lady, you are no slow thinker," Carlos said, letting the cross sticks slump in his hand. He stood up with the rifle in his hand and dusted his knees with his free hand. He hadn't seen the Winchester lying anywhere on the ground down there, so he was certain she had it. Could she hit anything with it? Would she even *use it* when the time came? Oh, yes, he said to himself, answering the *use* it part of the question. He might not have known it until just the past few minutes, but seeing the way she handled herself down there, this woman wanted to stay alive.

Twenty miles away in Shuller, Stevie Boy and Mudcat Glover had tossed back shot after shot of tequila ever since the owner of the saloon tent had opened for business at daylight. Now, at midmorning, the two young thugs were wild drunk and looking for trouble. There had been a few other day drinkers—miners who worked the second shift—when the Glovers entered the tent and pulled the cork on the first bottle of tequila. But those drinkers had vanished by the time the first empty bottle sailed up against the tent ceiling and exploded.

Mudcat Glover had stood grinning at the miners with a strange dark glow in his eyes, his big Russian .45-caliber pistol still smoking in his hand. The miners' eyes flashed up to the big hole in the tent canvas. Then their empty glasses dropped quietly to the bar and stayed there. That had been over two hours ago. Since then, the Glovers had drunk another whole bottle of tequila and shot four more bottles off the shelf.

Broken glass littered the bar, liquor spots covered the canvas wall. Flies droned and swarmed.

Stevie Boy Glover stood with his right arm draped across the bartender's shoulders, having dragged the helpless old man from behind the bar and forcing him to drink with them. "Felix, it's like this," Stevie Boy said, hugging the old man roughly, "either you hold out those shot glasses on the backs of your hands and let us clip them off, or we'll forget the shot glasses and just shoot you straight out."

"Boys, please," Felix Devore pleaded, "I've got a bad heart. I can't stand that sort of thing .... Doctor says too much excitement'll kill me."

Mudcat grinned. "Your doctor's probably right, but you've got to look at this from all the angles. Me or Stevie Boy, neither one mind shooting you dead right here, heart or no heart. At least, this way we're offering you a sporting chance."

Outside, Sam Burrack stepped down from his saddle and looked back and forth along the deeply rutted street. He spun the Appaloosa's reins around a hitch post out front of the saloon tent. On his way into the small-plank shack and tent community, a nervous miner had seen the badge on his chest and come running alongside the Appaloosa, saying up to the ranger, "I hope to God you've come for the Glovers ... they're getting wilder by the minute!" He gestured toward the large, ragged saloon tent. "If you don't hurry, you'll find Felix Devore dead!"

Sam had only nodded and rode on toward the saloon. A hand-painted picture of a frothing beer mug hung above the open fly of the tent. Next to the beer mug, a big hand pointed downward to the tent fly as if without it no patron would likely find the place, in spite of the empty whiskey bottles strewn about on the ground, or the large pair of lady's pantaloons hanging from a short flagpole. The pantaloons flapped in the beat of a hot desert wind.

Sam only flinched slightly at the sound of two pistol shots from inside the tent. He saw a whole side of the tent quiver as the bullets ripped through the canvas. From inside the tent, he heard a loud peal of drunken laughter rise above the bartender's pleading voice.

"Sounds like our boys all right," Sam said softly to the big Appaloosa. He drew his rifle from his saddle bolt, checked it, cocked it, and let it hang down his side. Then he stepped backward a few steps into the middle of the narrow, deep-rutted dirt street.

"Serves you right, old hoss," Stevie Boy Glover said to the sobbing bartender. "If you kept a couple of whores working this time of morning, none of this might have happened."

Felix Devore stood clutching his right wrist to slow the flow of blood from where one of the bullets had grazed the back of his hand. "I've got to go get this hand looked at," said Felix, his voice pleading. "It's deep and bleeding something awful!"

"Naw, you ain't going nowhere," said Stevie Boy. "We enjoy your company." He jerked his head sideways. "Now get back there and get us both a cigar. See if you've got any jarred pickles back there somewhere, too. A man ought not drink on an empty stomach, I always heard."

Felix Devore had started around the corner of the bar when the ranger's voice called out from the street, "Steve Glover, Mudcat Glover! This is Ranger Sam Burrack. Both of you come out with your hands up."

Mudcat looked at his brother, Stevie Boy, with an expression of stunned surprise. "How the hell did he know what we was doing in here?"

"He didn't, you idiot," Stevie Boy snapped. "Think he rode all this way just knowing we'd show up this morning wanting a drink? He's come after us for killing them three miners up in the badlands."

"Aw, hell," said Mudcat, "that's been over a month ago. Surely that's all forgotten by now. Don't you think?"

Stevie Boy just looked at him for a second. Then without attempting an answer, he turned and looked across the bar at Felix Devore. "Reach down and hand me up that shotgun you've been thinking about making a grab for."

"Me?" Felix's hand jerked back away from beneath the back edge of the bar. "No, sir, Stevie Boy! I wasn't thinking about making a grab for nothing!"

"You going to hand it to me?" Stevie Boy squinted at him with a harsh glare. His hand rested on the pistol at his hip. "Make that butt first," Stevie added.

"Sure thing!" Felix Devore lifted the shotgun by its short barrel and handed it over with a trembling hand. "Honest to God though, I wasn't thinking about making a grab for it! Alls I want to do is get along with everybody, not have any trouble—on account of my heart and all." As he spoke, Felix hurriedly wrapped a clean bar towel around his wounded hand.

"Yeah, well I'm all torn up over your bad heart, Felix," said Stevie Boy Glover, opening the shotgun, checking the two loads of buckshot in it, then snapping it shut. He let the tip of the double-barrel hover beneath the bartender's chin. "Now you holler out there and tell that ranger what you think we'll do to you if he comes poking his nose inside this tent." He tweaked Felix's chin with the shotgun barrel. "Better make it sound convincing, for your own sake."

Without wasting another second, Felix Devore called out to the dirt street, "Ranger! I'm Felix Devore. This is my saloon here. I want you to know these boys have a shotgun against my chin! Don't do nothing stupid, or they'll kill me!" He gave Stevie Boy a glance, looking for approval.

Stevie Boy Glover flashed a grin at Mudcat, then lowered the shotgun from the bartender's chin.

"He ain't answering," said Mudcat, nodding toward the street.

"Maybe he can't figure what to say," said Stevie Boy. He and Mudcat both stared toward the front of the tent through the open fly. Stevie Boy said over his shoulder to the bartender, "Go on, Felix, you're doing good. Tell him he best get on down the road. Tell him me and Mudcat ain't the kind of boys he wants to fool with, if he knows what's good for him."

"Why ain't he answered?" asked Mudcat.

"Maybe he's shy," said Stevie Boy.

"Can I leave if I tell him that?" Felix asked, his voice shaky.

Without turning his gaze from the front of the tent, Stevie Boy said over his shoulder, "Let's put it this way, you damned sure ain't going nowhere if you *don't.*" He chuckled. Mudcat joined in, standing at the end of the short bar, his pistol out and cocked toward the tent fly.

"Uh, Mister Ranger!" Felix called out, his voice tighter, more frightened. "These boys ain't joking around! They said tell you if you come poking your nose in here they'll—"

"I heard him." The ranger's voice spoke from close behind them cutting Felix Devore off. Stevie Boy Glover swung around toward the sound, just in time to see the butt of the ranger's rifle swipe a vicious blow across Mudcat's unsuspecting jaw as Mudcat turned.

"You dirty, sneaking—!" Stevie Boy raised his cocked pistol as he shouted, but his words stopped short. The butt of the ranger's rifle came out in a short powerful stab, the butt plate making a solid thud on the bridge of Stevie Boy's nose. The bartender winced at the sight of Stevie Boy's head snapping back at such a dangerous angle.

"Lord have mercy! You broke his damned neck!" said Felix Devore, staring down at Stevie Boy Glower sprawled out on the dirt floor.

"No, but I probably should have," said Sam, reaching behind his back and pulling out handcuffs and a three-foot length of posting chains. "I've got a feeling these boys will be trouble all the way back to the station."

Felix looked down at the two unconscious gunmen, then put his towel-wrapped hand on the ranger's arm as Sam started to reach down with the handcuffs. "I tell you what, Ranger," Felix said in a guarded whisper, "if you want to save yourself the trouble, put a bullet or two in them .... I'll bear witness they made the first move on you." He gave Sam a sly wink.

Sam pulled his arm free of Felix Devore's hand, nodding at the thick, bloody bar towel. "Go tend to yourself, bartender," Sam said. "Don't make me sorry I didn't come in through the front, and let them splatter you all over this tent!"

"Lord, Ranger ... I was only trying to help!" Felix Devore jumped back with his hands raised chest high.

"You want to help?" said Sam, leaning down, snapping the cuffs on Stevie Boy Glover's wrists. "Tell me where to find the constable, to get these boys behind bars."

"Uh, well, Ranger," Felix said, scratching his head, "the thing is we never got us a place to keep jailbirds. The company

59

was suppose to bring up a barred wagon, but they haven't yet. Far as the constable ... he gets drunk sometimes and wanders off for days. There's no telling where you'll find him."

"That's just dandy," Sam said, a bit put out. He stared at Felix Devore for a moment, then said, "Tell me what you know about a Scots-Irish gunman named Carl O'Bannion ... or else a *pistolero* called Carlos the Snake."

CHAPTER 5

Darcy couldn't wait any longer. Whatever move she made, she would have to make right now, while the sun stood high overhead. At this point the sun showed no partiality to either her or the killer. But as time passed, the sun would be behind whoever rode down from the hills. She knew little of these matters other than what her father had passed on to her. He'd told her tales from his days of first settling their Montana ranch on the cusp of Indian country. But he'd only told her these things in passing, or so she'd thought at the time.

Before she'd turned twelve and gone off to live with her Aunt Greta and Uncle Herb in Cleveland, Ohio, her father had taught her many useful things. He'd taught her how to use a rifle, shoot a pistol; he'd taught her to ride a horse, to treat a snakebite. "These are the things you have to *know* how to do in life, then hope to God you *never* need to use them," she could recall his telling her. She looked out across the high wavering veil of heat, seeing the seriousness in her father's face when he'd said those words to her.

I was listening, Papa .... She felt a warm tear form in the corner of her eye and she wiped it away—no time for that sort of thing. Her father had passed away only last year, shortly after she'd come home to be with him those last terrible days of his illness. Her mother had died four years earlier while she was attending teacher's college in Cleveland. Now there was only her and her older brother Willis. Willis would run the ranch. She would see a share of any profit, Willis insisted. But that had mattered little to her. She had long since grown distant to this harsh land and its raw toughness. There had been a time when she loved this country, respected its fierceness, but those feelings had slowly faded away from her, living a gentle life in a large civilized city like Cleveland.

Darcy ran her dress sleeve across her wet forehead, considering the irony of it. Her parents had sent her east, for an education, a more gentle life ... and yet here she stood, a rifle in her hands, her brain feeling as if it were about to boil inside her skull, and what was she thinking about? She was searching her memory for anything she might recall about staying alive should such a thing as this ever happen. Beside her, the big white horse blew out a breath and raked a hoof back across the hot sand. Darcy had already seen enough about the killer to know that he would kill the horse no sooner than his sights fell upon it. And yet, the horse was all that could save her ... the only thing that could get her to safety.

She looked back across the stretch of flatlands behind her, trying to recall the terrain. Back there in the moonlight she'd seen a dry creek bed that cut across their path and snaked around southward. But for how far? Enough to get her around past the killer without his seeing what she was doing? She hoped so, because that was exactly what she planned on doing. It would be too hard pushing the big white all the way back to the shelter of the rocks. Both she and the horse would be exposed for too long, especially with the kind of rifle the killer was firing.

Darcy knew enough about rifles to realize that the shots which had killed her husband and one of the whites had come from a long way off ... possibly as far as a thousand yards. It was one of the big rifles preferred by the old buffalo hunters, the men who had come by their ranch when she was only a child. She could not recall the name or the model of those rifles, but she remembered they were all single shots. Maybe knowing that would help. After each shot, there would be a second or two she could use to her advantage. This was slim hope, but it was the only hope she had.

With the Winchester in her hand, and the single remaining canteen of water slung over her shoulder, she reached down, gathered her dress up around her waist, and climbed atop the big horse, using a foothold on the back of the hearse to get herself up there. "Bob, I hope I'm not going to get us both killed," she whispered, adjusting her dress down over her knees as best she could, "but we've got to try something, even if it's wrong."

She sat bareback on the horse, feeling the heat of it beneath her. Using one of the long traces she'd tied into a clumsy hackamore stay around the horse's muzzle, she reined back, getting the big white to understand this new form of signals. For a moment, the horse only raised its head and tried to toss its muzzle back and forth. But then, as if knowing their predicament, he stepped back with the reins guiding him, turned in a tight circle without stepping out from the cover of the hearse, and righted himself in the direction the reins asked him to go.

Darcy took a good deep breath in preparation. She looked over at the body of her young husband lying in the dirt, his arms and hands already bloating, something slim and black crawling across his sunbaked forearm. "I'm so sorry, Maximus," she said, her words sounding as soft as a prayer. Then, with a long length of the leather trace in her hand, she reached back and slapped the big white's rump, sending it forward.

"That's an awfully stupid move, lady," Carlos the Snake said, watching with his naked eye, seeing the horse bolt away from behind the cover of the big hearse. "Just when I figured you to be a real thinker, you turn around and do something like this." He rubbed his eyes, the strain catching up to him from staring through the wavering heat and glaring sunlight. "Guess it's time I put you out of your misery." He took the cross sticks, spread them, braced them with his hand, and laid the rifle barrel to rest between them.

Carlos slumped down behind the rifle stock, getting comfortable, settling in for the kill shot. Yet, when he sighted down onto the woman, ready to put an end to the situation, the rifle sights steadied on the center of her back, she swerved the horse sharply to the left. Carlos stopped short of pulling the trigger. "Easy, lady," he murmured, moving the rifle sight along with her, making his adjustment. But just as he started to shoot again, she swerved the big horse back in the other direction.

"All right," said Carlos, "I see what you're doing. Not bad. But it won't buy you more than a few extra seconds." He settled behind the rifle stock again, this time determined to anticipate the zigzagging motion of the horse and make it work for him. He took a deep breath, held it, watched the white horse make a left swerve and drew his rifle sights a bit ahead of it, giving the shot some leeway.

Darcy saw the bullet kick up a tail of sand a few feet in front of her. Luckily, she had cut the horse shorter this time as she swerved it left. Knowing it would take a second for the killer to reload, she now gave the big white a straight path toward where she knew the dry creek bed lay waiting to give her shelter. She pushed the horse hard, needing these few slim seconds of straight ride to gain some distance.

Timing herself like the second hand on a watch, she yanked hard on the right rein, then felt the big horse shift direction just in time to see another tail of sand, this one falling a bit shorter than the one before it. "Yes, God! Thank you!" she shouted aloud.

Carlos raised his face from the rifle butt long enough to see her straighten the big white out into a hard run. A bemused look of respect came to his face for only a second. Then, seeing how much ground she was gaining, how close she was coming to getting out of his rifle range, he leaned back down behind the butt, an even more determined look coming to his eyes. "You're dead this time, lady," he whispered.

Carlos centered his sights onto her back. The wavering heat and rising dust made her grow more obscure as he squinted in the sun's glare and concentrated on his shot. He watched for the move of her body instead of the horse's. When he saw her begin to sway to the right, he gave his barrel leeway as she topped a small rise. But then, instead of swinging the horse to the right, she cut hard to the left. She'd feigned the move to the right and sent his sights away from her. Carlos couldn't stop the shot, even though he knew she'd tricked him. The recoil of the big rifle hammered back against his shoulder with a useless thud.

"You're good, lady," he said, a somber impatience in his voice. He raised his head and watched the shot kick up sand at the rim of the low rise. He reloaded the big rifle, drew his pistol from his holster, and lay back down for his next shot. This one would do it. She was all out of tricks. He would fire the pistol. She wouldn't know the difference between its sound and that of the rifle's. Then, when she straightened the horse, thinking he needed to reload, he'd let her have it.

Carlos raised the cocked pistol and waited for her to come on the other side of the rise. He lay ready, his shoulder steady against the rifle, his pistol poised to fire into the air. But what was this? She didn't come up. He waited for a second longer. She still didn't come up. He looked back and forth along the edge of the rise. No dust, no nothing. Carlos stood up, with his rifle in his hand, his cross sticks falling to the ground.

On the other side of the low rise, Darcy walked along stooped at the waist, keeping the big white's head down as low as possible, the horse walking light, not letting it give up any telltale dust from its big hooves. She moved slowly but steadily along with the contour of the land, using the slight dip for cover, praying silently that the dry creek bed she'd crossed would run this far around to the left and head on southward. If it did, she would go around the killer, put the sun to her back for a change, and get too far ahead of him for the big rifle to do any good. Thinking about her plan for a second, she almost panicked. She grew nauseous, realizing how ridiculous it was, her trying to outsmart a hardened killer. Yet, what had been her choices? She crept along, telling herself the creek bed would be there. Please, God! It had to be there.

"All right, lady, I get it now," Carlos the Snake whispered aloud to himself. "You saw something back there on your way here last night. What was it, the creek bed?" He smiled, gazing out to the west where the creek bank would lie unseen, then upward to the scalding white sunlight. "Yep, that's what it was." With the rifle and cross sticks in his gloved hand, Carlos walked to the horse, stepped up, and headed down onto the flatlands. It seemed almost a shame after her struggling so hard to stay alive, but all he needed to do now was to cut over and find that creek bed himself. He'd ride down into it and follow it around until he met her face-to-face. *Too bad, lady, it has been interesting ....*

Darcy had found the meandering creek bed, led the big white down into it, and followed it nearly a hundred yards before stopping long enough to venture a look out across the flatlands. Crawling up the side of the sandy bank, rifle in hand, she stayed low and stared out at ground level. At first, she saw no sign of the killer, but she kept scanning closely until finally she caught sight of his dust standing on the hot desert air. Her heart sank as she realized he was riding west toward the creek bed. She hadn't fooled him at all.

The killer had seen what she was up to. Now the question was, could she outrun him, get past the point where he would drop down into the creek bed and come charging toward her? It looked doubtful, but she had to give it a try. She had to get the sun behind her, make it work to her advantage instead of his. He knew that was her plan as she did, Darcy thought, so he wasn't going to give an inch if he could help it. All right then ... she had to hurry!

Vengeance

Darcy slid down the bank beside the big white and quickly climbed atop. She wasn't giving up without a fight. She still had water, a rifle with fifteen shots in it, another thirty-seven rounds in the cartridge belt on her shoulder. She still had a heart beating in her chest. She was alive!

Darcy swung the barrel of the Winchester back like a riding quirt and slapped the white's rump. "Let's get going, Bob," she said in a harsh, determined voice. "We've still got a trick or two up our sleeve."

From a long way across the flatland, Carlos saw the thick dust began to bellow up in a long sheet, as if rising from out of the ground. He smiled grimly to himself, pushing his roan at a quick, steady pace. He was right, she'd seen him out here and was making a run for it, wanting to get past him, wanting to get the sun out of her eyes. True, that would've helped some, he thought. But he wasn't about to blow out his horse in this kind of heat just to keep her from getting past him. Didn't she realize that they could play that game from now on. She could get ahead for a while, then he'd circle around and do the same thing.

Without pushing his horse too hard, Carlos closed the gap between himself and the rising dust from the creek bed. At a distance of three hundred yards, he saw that the woman was going to get past him, so he slowed the roan and let it happen. "Okay, lady, you've made it, now what?" He turned his horse slightly parallel to the stretch of rising dust, watching it spread farther south along the creek bed. All he had to do now was wait for her to wear the big horse out. Wherever she stopped, he'd leave her lying. Sun to her back, to his, it made no difference to Carlos.

Surprisingly to Carlos, the big wagon horse made it another two thousand yards before its dust fell slowly to a halt. Watching it, Carlos had kept an easy pace, keeping the roan rested as much as possible, riding across the sandy flatlands while the woman had to push the big horse along the rough, rocky creek bottom. Foolish, he thought. And now it was time to ride in and make his move. She'd taken up too much of his time already.

At the edge of the creek bed, Carlos stopped the roan and stepped down from his saddle. He left the big Remington rifle in his saddle boot and drew his Colt instead. He led the roan cautiously down the sandy bank, not about to go charging in blindly. He'd seen enough to know that this woman deserved a little respect. He had no doubt that she would start shooting as soon as she caught a glimpse of him.

Dust still lingered heavily in the creek bottom. Carlos pulled his bandanna up across his nose and ventured forward, seeing a rocky turn fifty feet ahead.

He stepped just short of the bend in the creek when he heard the big horse nicker under its breath. Quickly, Carlos pulled the roan to the side and hitched it to a brittle stand of brush. He crept forward in a crouch, the Colt cocked and ready in his hand.

"All right, lady, this is the end of the line," Carlos called out, flattening back against an exposed boulder where the creek bed made its bend. "Come on out, and we'll keep it quick and painless."

No more than fifteen feet ahead of him, around the rocky bend, Carlos heard the big horse shuffle back and forth in the loose rock bottom. There was no sound of the woman, and while it could have been that she had taken position and was waiting silently to meet him head-on, Carlos let out a depleted breath, already knowing better.

"Son of a bitch," Carlos said, standing up in full view and pushing his hat up on his forehead. Uncocking his Colt and holstering it, he stepped out and around the boulder and looked at the big lone white standing a few feet away. The white was staring, its breath pounding in its chest. Carlos shook his head and stepped back, in no hurry now. He went to the roan, unhitched it, and led it to where the big white stood blowing out its tired breath. Carlos ran a gloved hand down the white's sweaty side. The big white shied away from him.

"Woman you beat all I ever seen," Carlos said to the dusty creek bed, looking back toward the north, realizing the woman could have jumped off the horse anywhere between here and where he'd first seen the dust rising. "You got me good," Carlos murmured, realizing that if he pushed the roan hard back in that direction, all he would do is wear the animal out and put himself afoot.

His guess was that the woman had made her leap as far back as possible, over a mile or more away, he thought. She was back there, putting more and more distance between them. By now, she could have disappeared into the rocks at the base of hills on the western edge of the basin. He looked back at the big white. She had emptied the cartridge belt and tied it to the end of the leather trace, leaving it short . . . letting it slap back and forth as the horse ran.

"The oldest trick in the book, lady," Carlos said. "So old, I wasn't expecting it." He shook his head again and allowed himself to chuckle under his breath. Then his eyes grew dark and more serious as he gazed off toward the hills. "Tomorrow, we'll see what all this was worth to you."

CHAPTER 6

Felix Devore couldn't tell him anything about Carl O'Bannion, or Carlos the Snake. He told the ranger he'd heard the names and was pretty sure he'd met Carl O'Bannion and served him a beer across the bar. But Sam doubted it. He knew that most bartenders like to make you think they knew everybody— especially outlaws, Sam Burrack thought, as he readied his Appaloosa for the trail. But it took only a few minutes for Sam to realize that if O'Bannion ever came through here, regardless of which name he was going under, he'd managed to keep his presence quiet. And that made sense, Sam told himself, if a man was on the move, hunting down men he intended to kill.

Sam gave it some more thought, checking his saddle cinch. It was hard to fault a man for hunting down the men who'd killed his family. Under the given circumstances, Sam couldn't say he wouldn't be doing the same thing. But the law was the law, and Sam knew better than to imagine what he would do if he put himself in the other man's boots. Of course he would go after the men who'd killed his ma and pa. What man wouldn't? Finishing with the saddle cinch, Sam dropped the stirrup on his Appa-loosa and stepped over to the pack mule standing on the end of a lead rope. What man, indeed …?

Sam cautioned himself against thinking that way. He'd seen enough to know that revenge was never a simple thing. Revenge had a way of rolling from one set of shoulders to the next and of spilling over into the lives of innocent people. Sam gave the supplies a once-over, then made sure everything was tied down securely. Yet, what did you say to a man whose family had been murdered? Let the law handle it? In a case like this, what could the law do about it? This went back to the last days of the Civil War. The mule looked up at Sam and twitched its ears.

There was nothing Sam could say or do that would bring any consolation or offer any settlement to a revenge situation. That didn't matter anyway, he reminded himself. Sam's job was to put a stop to the killing, nothing more, nothing less. He leveled his sombrero on his forehead and looked up at the Glovers atop their horses, their hands cuffed in front of them and resting on the saddle horns.

"Are you boys ready to travel?" Sam asked, the gray early light already heating up from the hot wreath of fire sizzling white in the east.

"Hell no," Mudcat Glover grumbled in a slurred voice. "I been saying all night, my damn jaw's broke. Nobody'll do anything for me. I can't travel like this." A short chain linked his wrist to his brother's.

"Neither can I," said Stevie Boy Glover in a thick nasal twang. "Just look here at my nose. It's broke sure as hell! I got no sleep at all last night ... just ached and tossed and turned. Had some of the worst nightmares I ever had in my life."

"You had no business doing us this way," Mudcat said, with much effort through his purple swollen jaw. "We need some serious medical attention here."

"Sorry, boys," said the ranger, a slightly bemused look on his face, "turns out the doctor is as about as dependable as your constable. Nobody's seen him in days. All I can give you is sympathy, if that's any help."

"Hummph," said Mudcat, looking away in disgust.

"I'll tell you one damn thing, Ranger," Stevie Boy Glover said, raising his voice as the ranger stepped away and climbed up into his saddle. "It'd be a whole different story if you'd faced us man-to-man ... not come slipping up behind us. Fair's

71

Ralph Cotton

fair, by God! One-on-one, me and Brother Mudcat would've killed you graveyard dead."

"You and Brother Mudcat?" Sam stared at him. "How do you call that one-on-one? If you look around, you'll see there's two of you."

"That's right," said Stevie Boy. "Everybody knows we come as a pair. The point is, you took unfair advantage, Ranger ... and we ain't forgetting it, not by a long shot!" Stevie Boy's face glowed red behind his swollen nose and black eyes.

"Hush up and settle down, Stevie Boy," said Mudcat, seeing his brother ready to go into a fit of rage. "We'll just bide our time." He gave the ranger a sinister threatening look. "Lots of things can happen between here and where we're going."

Stevie Boy collected his temper and gave his brother a quick nod. "You're right, Brother ... thank you for reminding me." He cut a glance to the ranger. "Don't worry about us, Lawdog. Time come, we'll fix your wagon."

Sam backed his Appaloosa from the hitch rail, taking up two lead ropes, one running to the mule's harness, the other keeping the Glovers' horses coupled together. "After you boys," the ranger said, pulling the Glovers' horses out from the rail and nudging them forward.

"We can make this trip as easy or as hard as you want it to be," Sam said to their backs as he led the pack mule along behind them. "But you best remember, you're making threats on your way into the desert ... only one of us with a gun. Get too tough, and you might never be seen or heard from again."

They rode in silence for a moment along the narrow dirt street, the Glovers side by side with four feet of slack in the rope connecting them. They seemed to consider the ranger's words, until finally Mudcat leaned slightly in his saddle and said to his brother, "Think he meant that, about us not being seen again?"

"I don't know," said Stevie Boy, staring straight ahead.

"What do you know about this lawdog?" asked Mudcat

72

"No more than you do," said Stevie Boy. "Just that he carries a list of men he's hunting. He killed most of the old Junior Lake Gang deader than hell last year."

"Killed Junior Lake?" said Mudcat, his eyes widening in surprise.

"His whole gang," said Stevie Boy.

"Damn…." Mudcat Glover whispered, glancing back over his shoulder. "How come you didn't mention that before?"

"Before what?" said Stevie Boy.

"Damn it! Before we started making threats! Mudcat hissed through clenched teeth, his swollen jaw starting to pound with each beat of his pulse.

"I don't know," said Stevie Boy, his voice going down to a whisper. "What's the difference? First chance I get, I'm breaking loose anyway. I ain't going to jail, even if it means he kills me. Are you?"

Mudcat Glover didn't answer, but then he didn't think he needed to. His brother Stevie Boy already knew what his answer would be.

They traveled slow and steadily throughout midmorning until the sun stood straight above them, baking the desert floor mercilessly. To their left lay the stretch of red rocky hills where shallow caverns reached back beneath cliff overhangs, affording scant, but precious shade against the fiery heaven. The ranger guided the Glovers into a long black sliver of shade. They rested there for over an hour when the sound of distant rifle fire drew the ranger's attention toward the peaks of the hill line above them.

"Somebody's sure got a mad-on at somebody," said Stevie Boy Glover, grinning at the ranger, who stood out from beneath the overhang and scanned the hills. "One thing for sure … there ain't nothing over in that basin for folks to shoot at except one another."

Two shots had echoed in across the hills before Sam had gotten up and stepped out into the burning sunlight. Now a third shot resounded as he listened closely and tried to pinpoint its location.

"It's not coming from the basin," said Mudcat. "That's coming from up there in the hills."

"Yeah?" said Stevie Boy Glover. "Well, wherever it's coming from, it ain't costing me nothing. Let them bang away at each other if they've got no better sense, this kind of weather." He sank down in the shade against the rock wall and, with his cuffed hands, pulled his hat down over his swollen nose. "Be sure and wake me if they go to getting too close."

Two more shots echoed in, separate and distinct sounds that the ranger recognized as coming from different types of rifles. "Get on your feet," Sam said, stepping back inside the black shade and reaching for the lead ropes and his horse's reins. Stevie Boy Glover had just settled. Now he moaned in protest, his brother doing the same.

"Hellfire, Ranger," said Mudcat, "can't you just mind your own business? So long as they ain't shooting at us, what's the—"

"Get on your feet now," the ranger said, grabbing the four-foot length that held the two prisoners together. He yanked hard, forcing them up.

"All right, all right!" said Stevie Boy, his voice sounding astonished at the ranger's unreasonable demand. "You don't have to get crazy on us! We're coming!" He shot his brother a guarded glance, the two on the lookout for anything they might use to their advantage. "You're going to take us into a shoot-out *handcuffed,* are you? Surely to God not!"

The ranger grabbed him by his shirt and yanked him in close, almost nose to nose. When Mudcat also tried to step in, Sam raised a boot and kicked him back, the four-foot length of chain drawing taut between the two men. "Listen good, Stevie Boy," the ranger hissed. "The only reason I'll take those cuffs off you right now is to put them on you behind your back. Next time I tell you to do something, if you don't do it right then ... you'll finish this ride facedown over a saddle. If you think that won't happen, you say so right now. We'll get it over with and save us both a lot of trouble." His Colt streaked up, cocked, and jammed beneath Stevie Boy's chin.

"Don't kill him, Ranger," Mudcat pleaded, seeing the cold killing look in Sam Burrack's eyes. "He'll do what you say! We both will, won't we, Stevie Boy? Tell him we will."

"We will," Stevie Boy said, staring back into the ranger's eyes, closely checking them, trying to decide if this ranger was real or bluffing. "I lost my head there for a minute ... it won't happen again."

But Sam knew better. He could tell by the tone in the man's voice that this was only the first in a long line of testing that Stevie Boy was going to be doing all the rest of the trip. "Get moving," Sam said, shoving him forward. Mudcat had to hop up and go with him, the chain making them move together.

Darcy Tennison was nearly blind from the sun's glare, and half out of her mind from the blazing heat. There were no more than a few drops of water left in the canteen. Somewhere the night before as she'd clawed her way up the steep hillsides, she'd spilled most of the cartridges from her dress pocket. Now, lying against the shaded side of a rock partially hid-den by a deadfall of scrub piñon, she wiped a strand of hair from her eyes and tried in catch her breath. The rifle barrel was still hot from firing it down the hillside at the killer as he made the mistake of getting too close.

"We showed him ... didn't we?" she rasped in a thick hoarse voice, having no idea who or what she was speaking to. She'd seen the killer back away when she cut loose on him with the Winchester. One shot had grazed a rock less then a foot from his head.

"Good shooting," she whispered to herself, recalling how he had scrambled backward looking for better cover.

"No ... frightened little girl here." She managed a weak

smile to herself, her parched lips stifling her words in pain.
"Come on, you son of a ...." Her words trailed off as she
swooned forward against the rock, feeling the world grow
dark and silent around her.

Two hundred and five yards down the side of a steep rocky
hillside, Carlos the Snake lay flattened to the hot ground
behind a brittle stand of broom sage. Looking up through the
telescope, he watched the three horsemen wind slowly down a
narrow switchback trail. He noted the cuffed wrists of the two
in front. Then he caught the glint of sunlight on the ranger's
badge. This was bad, he told himself. He couldn't allow a
lawman to find the woman, not alive anyway. He was starting
to reveal too much about himself across the desert.

Carlos pulled the big Remington up from his side and wiped
his hand along the barrel. This would be an easy shot for
him. Take down the lawman, the other two would scatter—
no trouble out of them. He eased the rifle barrel out through
the broom sage, then tossed a quick glance down the hillside
to where he'd tied his horse, making sure it was still there.
When he looked back up, he saw the ranger sitting still atop
the big Appaloosa on the edge of the trail, looking out across
the flatlands. Carlos took his time, eased his thumb forward
and cocked the big rifle.

At the edge of the hill trail, Sam Burrack felt a dark, knowing
chill run the length of his spine. With no more than a flick
of his wrist, he stepped the Appaloosa back quickly, putting
himself out of position from any gun sights lurking farther
down the hillside. A few feet away, the Glovers sat watching.

"What's wrong, Ranger ... did you see a rattlesnake?" asked
Stevie Boy Glover, a sly grin on his face.

"Never mind what I saw," said the ranger. "Get moving,
keep back from the edge."

"Aw, now look here, Brother Mudcat," Stevie Boy purred in
a mocking tone, "something's got the lawdog spooked. Pray

what might it be?"

Stevie Boy started to laugh, but his expression turned wide-eyed as a rifle exploded farther along the trail in front of them. A bullet whistled past the side of Stevie Boy's head, close enough to lift his hat in the air and spin it away.

"Lord have mercy!" Stevie shouted, his horse rearing beneath him. The lead rope connecting his horse to his brother's caused both animals to jerk back and forth against one another in panic. The ranger jumped his Appaloosa forward, helping the Glovers calm their horses down.

Another shot resounded, the bullet slicing across the side of a rock and spinning away with a loud whine.

"Damn it, Ranger! Do something!" shouted Mudcat, ducking low in his saddle.

As the ranger tried to settle the men and their horses, Stevie Boy saw his chance to reach out with his cuffed hands and make a grab for the ranger's pistol. But Sam saw his move, grabbed the pistol first, and swung it around sideways, cracking Stevie Boy across his forehead, sending him to the ground. A third shot exploded as Sam jumped down from his saddle and pulled the horses over against the rocky hillside, giving them some cover. He yanked Mudcat down and threw him against the rocks. "Stay there," Sam demanded.

"Don't worry, I will!" said Mudcat.

Sam jumped out from the wall long enough to grab Stevie Boy and drag him out of the line of fire. Stevie fell against the wall, his head lolling back and forth like a drunkard's.

"Can you see who's shooting, Ranger?" Mudcat asked, hugging back flat against the rocks. "How many are there?"

"I don't know. Stay put," said Sam. He leaned out a bit with his pistol up and cocked, venturing a look toward the rock and the scrub piñon where the shots were coming from. He caught a glimpse of the woman's hair as she peeped up over the rock, the rifle pressed to her shoulder, ready to shoot. "It's a woman," the ranger said.

"A woman?" Mudcat gave him a dubious look. "What the hell is a woman doing up here?"

The ranger didn't answer him. Instead, he called out, "Ma'am, hold your fire .... I'm Arizona Ranger Sam Burrack. I mean you no harm. Do you hear me?"

A silence passed, then an exhausted voice said with strained effort, "A— A ranger?"

"Yes, ma'am, I am a ranger," Sam called out, hearing an undertone of fear and desperation in the woman's voice. He stepped slightly out from the rock wall, giving up his cover.

"You're crazy, Ranger," said Mudcat Glover. "She'll shoot your eyes out!"

"Shut up, Mudcat," Sam hissed. He took a cautious step toward the scrub piñon. "Don't shoot me now, you hear? I'm trying to come forward, show you my badge." He paused for a second, then when she offered no protest, he moved in closer. "I heard the shooting, earlier, from down the other side of the hills. Who was shooting at you?" As he asked, his eyes made a quick scan and came back to her position. "What can I do to help?"

Darcy raised her face for only a split second, just long enough to catch a glimpse of the badge on the ranger's chest. When she dropped back down behind the rock, she hugged the Winchester rifle to her and sobbed softly, "I'm alive, Maximus ...."

She raised a dirty palm and rubbed her eyes. She stared at her hand, fascinated by the wet smear of tears on it, as if never having seen such a thing before. As she stared, transfixed, her sobbing turned into a low, painful-sounding chuckle that quickly grew out of control. With delirious laughter, she called aloud, "I am alive, Papa! Do you hear me? I am alive!"

Sam Burrack reached down gently, slipped the Winchester from her hands, and said, barely above a whisper, "Yes, ma'am, you are alive." he looked her up and down: the torn dress, with her dirty knees, raw and blood-smeared, showing through her tattered petticoat. Her face was parched, and blistered, her lips dry and cracked, and scabbed with black dried blood.

"I'm alive ...?" she murmured, her laughter waning a bit as she tried to focus on the ranger's face. Rising to her burnt and aching feet with the ranger's help, she swooned forward, Sam catching her against his chest.

"Easy, ma'am ... yes, indeed, you are."

A shot whined in from the sloping hillside beneath them, followed by a resounding explosion. Stevie Boy and Mudcat ducked down against the rock, raising their cuffed hands to shield their faces.

"Hey, Ranger" called Stevie Boy, "You can't leave us cuffed like this. What if that long shooter kills you? At least take these cuffs off us ... give us a fighting chance!"

"Only chance you got is to stick close to me, Stevie Boy," said the ranger. "He's shooting from a far ways down the hillside," Sam added, lowering the woman back down to cover behind her rock "You two tie the horses where they are, then keep low and crawl over here."

"Crawl?" said Stevie Boy Glover. "I don't like crawling for no man."

"Then walk standing just as tall as it pleases you, Stevie Boy," said Sam. "It won't cost me nothing."

Another shot clipped a chunk of rock off a few inches above Stevie and Mudcat's heads. "Damn it, Stevie Boy, get down, you fool!" Mudcat spun the horses' reins around a spur of rock as he dropped down and the two came crawling along the path toward Sam and the woman.

"Why do you suppose this peckerwood is shooting at her?" Stevie Boy asked, he and his brother scooting in beside the ranger. They both looked closely at the woman as she lay, barely conscious, against the rock.

"I don't know," said Sam, "but my guess is he won't last, now that we're here." Sam looked over at their tied horses, then down the slope in the direction of the rifle fire. "I'm going to have to show him that he's not the only one with a long-range rifle."

"What have you got, Ranger?" Mudcat asked.

"I've got a big Swiss in my blanket roll," said Sam. "That's why I wanted you two over here. Stay with the woman while I stick a shot or two down his shirt. That ought to shake him loose."

"How do you know, Ranger?" said Stevie Boy. "This could be some heated lovers' quarrel we're involved in here. For all you know, that fellow might not rest until he kills her and us, too!" Stevie shook his cuffed wrists at the ranger. "You've got to get these things off us!"

"Shut up, Stevie Boy," said the ranger. He looked at Mudcat Glover. "Can I trust you here, Mudcat?"

Mudcat gave him a skeptical look. "Ranger, I can't promise nothing. I hate thinking about going into that hot cell, maybe even hanging."

"I understand," said the ranger, "and I appreciate you being honest about it." He gave a strained glance down the hillside. "I'll be right back." Then he lowered into a crouch and hurried over to the horses. No shots exploded while Sam took down his bedroll, rolled it open, and picked up the two pieces of the Swiss rifle, hastily snapping them together. He picked up a long brass-trimmed scope, attached it, and loaded three big cartridges in the rifle chamber. Only when he hurried back in a low crouch did a shot come ripping up over the edge of the trail and strike the rock wall above him.

Back inside the cover of rock and scrub piñon, Mudcat said, as the ranger came rushing in and took position at the side of the rock, "Lucky we're above him. This hill is just steep enough to keep him from hitting anything."

"Yep," said the ranger, "and if this man's smart, he'll realize that and pull out." As he spoke, the ranger worked the bolt back and forth on the big Swiss rifle, putting a round up into the breech. He looked down at the woman, then said to Mudcat, "How about covering her ears for me?"

"Sure," said Mudcat.

"You'd be wise to get back a little and cover your ears, too," Sam said to Stevie Boy Glover, noticing how Stevie had managed to inch in closer. Sam knew he was hoping to get a chance to make a move on him.

"I ain't worried about a little rifle noise," said Stevie Boy, with a flat grin.

"Suit yourself," said Sam, making a final check on the big Swiss rifle. "But you've tried making one move on me .... The next one is apt to get you killed." Sam took two small cotton balls from the rifle's small butt compartment and stuffed them into his ears.

Stevie Boy didn't respond, but he cast a glance at his brother and winked. Mudcat gave him a sharp warning stare and shook his head.

"Everybody ready?" Sam asked, standing slowly, bringing the rifle butt up to his shoulder.

"Do you always use those ear plugs?" asked Stevie Boy.

"When I've got time," Sam replied. As he aimed down in the direction the last three shots had come from, Stevie Boy Glover also rose slowly a few feet behind him. But just as Stevie Boy took a step closer to the ranger's back, a hard deafening explosion ripped from the barrel of the big Swiss rifle and caused Stevie Boy to sway sideways, almost staggering from the impact of the blast. Brittle needles showered down from the scrub piñon.

"Lord God!" Mudcat shouted. "What does that big sucker shoot anyway, a cannon ball?"

The ranger didn't answer. His hand quickly bolted a fresh round and sent the old cartridge case flipping upward in the air. It hit the ground smoking at his feet. Behind him, Stevie Boy shrank back away, with his hands going over his ears in time for the next shot to explode.

* * *

Down the long slope near the base of the hillside, Carlos the Snake ducked down securely behind his cover as the second shot shattered a large portion of a rock a few feet to his left. The first shot had kicked up a long tail of sand after whistling over his head. "All right, Lawdog," Carlos said to himself, "I get your message. We've got ourselves a standoff here."

He ventured a quick glance around the edge of his cover, then dropped back out of sight. The only difference was that Carlos's rifle was a single shot, shooting uphill. This ranger had the advantage of shooting downhill, with a repeater of some sort. Carlos reached into his pocket and took out his remaining three cartridges. This was something else to consider, he thought, putting them away.

Carlos wondered if this lawman was going to let him just back away and clear out of here. Carlos had only caught a glimpse of the two prisoners with their hat brims low, blackening out their faces. What was the ranger going to do, come after him with two men in cuffs and a woman half dead from the heat? No, Carlos didn't think so. The ranger would let him back away now without a fight, so long as he didn't make himself into an easy target—something he wasn't about to do. As far as the woman went, she hadn't gotten a good look at his face. Maybe he'd bide his time, let her get settled in somewhere. Then he'd make his move. He wasn't going to ride away and forget about her. Instead, he would lag back and follow, unseen. Carlos the Snake still had a lot do in this part of the country. He wasn't about to leave any loose ends.

"Hell, Ranger," said Stevie Boy, rounding a finger in his right ear, "you can go on and get him…. Me and Mudcat's got things covered here for you."

"Not a chance, Stevie Boy," said Sam. "You heard your brother. That cell starts feeling awfully hot the more you think about it."

Stevie Boy looked at his brother and said, "I can't believe you said something like that, Mud. What the hell got into you anyway?"

Mudcat Glover took his hands from the woman's ears now that he saw the ranger was through firing. Instead of answering his brother, Mudcat looked out across the bare, hot land and said to Sam, "Do you think he's gone, Ranger?"

"Yeah, I figure he's leaving right about now. I'm going to give him time to clear out .... Then we'll head on to Halston and get her some help," Sam replied, reaching down and picking up the two spent cartridge cases.

"I call that shirking your duty, Lawman," said Stevie Boy. "You don't know what that man's done. He might be a killer, for all you know."

Before the ranger could answer, the woman opened her eyes and murmured in a weak, broken voice, "He is .... He killed ... my husband." As she spoke, she managed to raise a limp hand and point out toward the desert, where the remains of her husband lay baking in the sun.

"Hear that, Ranger?" said Stevie Boy. "You're letting a killer get away!"

"Maybe," said Sam, having already weighed his chances at catching up to the man, trying to stay alive in the sights of that big long-range rifle, with two prisoners in tow, and a woman suffering from heat and exhaustion. "But at least you're not going anywhere. Not if I've got any say in it."

"Damn it to hell," Stevie Boy cursed defiantly. "So what have I got to lose if you kill me out here? It beats hanging or sweating to death in a steel cage."

"I won't kill you then, if that's really how you feel about it, Stevie Boy," said the ranger. "I'll just shoot you through the foot. That's becoming a common practice it seems," he added in a resolved tone. "You just sit still and not make things any worse for yourself."

Stevie Boy moaned and lowered his eyes in defeat.

Moments later, the ranger ventured out of the cover and eased over a spot along the edge of the trail where he could look out across the flatlands below. What he saw was a settling sheet of dust that snaked upward across a long low rise, then sank down out of sight. Headed southwest, the border, the ranger noted.

"Don't know who you are, mister," Sam said under his breath, "but you just made it onto my list."

He considered it for a second, and added, "If you ain't on it already, that is." Then he turned, with the big Swiss rifle under his arm, and walked to the horses.

CHAPTER 7

At first the ranger had intended to move everybody to a different position on the upper slope, in case the rifleman returned. But, looking around, Sam could see no better place of defense than right here beneath the bent bough of the scrub piñon, and behind the shelter of the broad rock overlooking the hillside below. Looking at the woman, who lay with a wet rag Mudcat Glover had placed on her forehead, Sam wondered if she had chosen this place to make a stand, or had simply stumbled in here out of desperation. "How's she doing, Mudcat?" he asked, seeing the woman roll her head back and forth slowly.

"She's coming around again, Ranger," said Mudcat, scooting a bit to the side, out of the ranger's way.

Sam stooped down beside the woman and adjusted the wet rag back on her forehead. She opened her eyes slightly and tried focusing on him, a look of fear returning to her face. "Easy, ma'am, it's still me," Sam said softly. "The shooter is gone .... You're going to be all right."

"Ha!" said Stevie Boy, standing back against the rock wall beside the horses and the mule. "Why don't you tell her the truth? A person can die days later from the heat and—" Stevie Boy stopped short under a cold glare from the ranger.

"Pay him no mind, ma'am," the ranger said. "You're young and strong. You'll make it sure enough."

Stevie Boy's words seemed to have stirred an extra surge of determination in Darcy Tennison. She raised up onto her elbows, the ranger supporting her head in the crook of his

85

Ralph Cotton

arm. "Don't you worry ... mister," she managed to hiss toward Stevie Boy Glover. "I'll ... make it." Her eyes went to the cuffs on his hands. "I'm not ... being defeated by the likes ... of your kind."

"Defeated?" Stevie Boy smiled a sarcastic grin and shook his head. "What does she mean, *'my kind,'* Ranger?" He took a step closer, his cuffed wrists raised for her to see. "Lady, this don't make nobody any better than me. Everybody's guilty of something. I was just unlucky enough to get caught."

"See if you can shut him up, Mudcat," said the ranger. "If you can't, I'll have to. I won't have him upsetting this woman."

"Don't worry... Marshal," Darcy said, her voice growing a bit stronger. "I mean what I said... he doesn't bother me."

"Good," said Sam, swabbing her forehead with the wet rag. "It's *Ranger,* ma'am. I'm an Arizona ranger, not a marshal. But that's all right. Many people make that mistake."

"I won't make that mistake again, Ranger," Darcy said. "After all, you ... saved my life."

Sam helped her sit up against the rock behind her. One of her shoulders was exposed and showing red scrapes through her torn dress. "Judging from all the shooting I heard earlier, ma'am, it sounded like you saved your own life." Sam studied her face for a moment, realizing she'd forgotten what he'd told her when he'd first found her. "I'm Ranger Sam Burrack, ma'am," he said. "These men are my prisoners. I heard the firing and came to see what it was about. When you feel stronger, you can tell me."

"I'm Darcy Judd— I mean Darcy *Tennison,"* she said, correcting herself. "If it will help catch... that killer, I feel like talking now."

Sam listened closely as she told him the whole grisly story. When she finished, they sat in silence for a moment until Sam whispered, "Ma'am, I'm so sorry for you and your husband. I can promise you I'll do everything I can to bring that ambusher

86

to justice—you have my word."

"I had thought that ... perhaps I would go after him myself," she said calmly in her weak voice, "but I suppose things aren't done that way, are they?"

Sam gave her a curious look. Realizing the heat must still be clouding her thought, he said, "Well, no, ma'am. It's probably best you let the law take care of it. That's what people like me get paid to do."

"Yes ... I believe you're right," Darcy said wistfully. "I don't know why I thought such a thing."

"Yeah, lady," said Stevie Boy Glover in a sarcastic voice, butting in as he circled wide around the ranger and the woman, toward where the ranger had propped her rifle against a rock. "You best let this man handle things. In case you don't know it, this here is rootin'-tootin' Ranger Sam Burrack, the man what killed Junior Lake and his whole gang!"

"Shut up, Stevie Boy," said Sam, rising slowly. But before Sam made it to his feet, Stevie grabbed the rifle and cocked it.

"Put it down, Stevie," the ranger warned. "I'm only going to say it once."

But Stevie Boy only grinned, pointing the rifle. Seeing the position he had the ranger in, the woman sitting at his feet, Stevie Boy knew Sam wouldn't risk getting the woman shot. "And I'm only going to tell you once, Ranger, raise the keys from your pocket and pitch them over here. Don't let me see your hand near that pistol butt, or I'll just start shooting!" He gestured with the rifle barrel toward the woman. "You know where that puts her."

The ranger looked down at the woman, then back at Stevie Boy with a bemused expression. "Stevie Boy, you ain't shooting nobody with that rifle. You should have paid more attention."

"What do you mean?" Stevie Boy asked, a strange look coming on his face. "Don't fool with me, Ranger! I'll kill her! You better know I will! Won't I, Mudcat? You tell him!"

Ralph Cotton

"Stevie, you best put it down," said Mudcat, seeing the intent look in the ranger's eyes.

"Unh-uh," said Stevie Boy, his finger on the trigger. "Ranger, do like I'm telling you, or she'll die with you!"

Sam looked down at the woman. "I'm not afraid of dying. Are you?"

The woman's eyes grew cold and fearless. "Not in the least," she said, turning an unyielding gaze to Stevie Boy Glover.

"There, you see, Stevie Boy?" said the ranger. "You're not killing nobody with that rifle unless you use it like a club."

A sick look of doubt rose on Stevie Boy's face. He saw the ranger draw the big pistol from his hip slowly, with all the time in the world. "You unloaded it, didn't you?" Stevie asked, a tremble seeping into his voice.

"You'll just have to pull the trigger and find out for yourself, Stevie Boy," said the ranger. "Do you really think I'd leave a loaded rifle laying around, as bad as you hate going to jail?" Now the big pistol was raised and cocked, and pointed at Stevie Boy's chest from just fifteen feet away.

Stevie Boy's eyes flashed to his brother. "I don't know, Stevie," said Mudcat. "I wouldn't risk it! Not now, you idiot, you've let him get the drop on you!"

"Come on, Stevie Boy," the ranger goaded him. "Show some sporting blood. I'm tired of your mouth anyway. I'd rather leave you feeding the buzzards than take you all the way in."

Stevie Boy sweated; his hands trembled.

"Make your move!" the ranger demanded, taking a step forward, his fist tight around his pistol butt.

Stevie Boy's nerves couldn't stand it any longer. Letting out a long scream, Stevie slung the rifle away and threw his hands high above his head. "Don't shoot!" he bellowed.

The discarded rifle hit the rock wall and fell to the ground. A shot exploded from the barrel. Stevie Boy's face took on a strange twisted. expression. He screamed again, this time losing control and springing toward the ranger, bare-handed. "You son-of-a-!"

A shot exploded from the ranger's pistol. Darcy's eyes reflected the flash of gunfire as she watched, transfixed by the sight of it.

The ride to Halston took three days longer than it should have. Sam rode at the end of his ragged, dusty procession, the woman cradled in his arms. The big Swiss rifle lay across her lap just in case the long shooter had decided to circle back and resume the fight. In front of Sam, the Glovers rode low and sweat stained. Mudcat's horse led the supply mule, with the mule's lead rope tied to its tail. On the boardwalk outside the sheriff's office, Sheriff Boyd Tackett stood, having squinted at the black, watery figures for the past ten minutes. Now as they came onto the street at a slow walk and he saw who it was, he whispered under his breath, "Lord have mercy, Ranger."

At the sight of the haggard band, some men stepped out of the shade of the Roi-Tan Saloon's boardwalk and came forward to assist them to the hitch rail and down from their saddles.

But the voice of Loman Gunderson boomed out of the saloon doors. "Hold it, men, look who it is... it's that blasted ranger who shot me!"

The men slowed to a quick halt, then returned to the boardwalk as Sam kept the tired Appaloosa moving step after labored step toward the sheriff's office. "Looks like... you ain't ... real popular here, Lawdog," Mudcat Glover said over his shoulder in a parched, raspy voice.

"It comes with the badge," said Sam, more to himself than in reply.

Boyd Tackett ran forward and alongside the sweat-streaked Appaloosa. Slipping his bandaged forearm from its sling, he reached upward with both arms toward the woman. "Hand her down to me, Sam."

The ranger did so without even stopping the slow-moving

stallion, fearing that, once stopped, the big animal might not want to move forward again. Ahead of the ranger, the Glovers looked back, ready to stop themselves. "Keep moving," Sam called out to them. "Don't stop till you reach the sheriff's office."

Boyd Tackett walked along briskly beside Sam's stallion, carrying the exhausted woman in his arms. Looking at the Glovers, Tackett saw Stevie Boy's left foot was wrapped in a thick bandage of torn blanket strips. "Another one shot in the foot, Sam?" Tackett asked.

Sam nodded. "It ain't something I enjoy doing." He fell silent the next few yards to the hitch rail. Then he looked at Tackett as he slid down from his saddle with the big Swiss rifle in his gloved hand. "For some reason, Stevie Boy here must've thought I was bluffing."

Stevie Boy cursed under his breath.

At the hitch rail, the Glovers dropped from the saddles and let their reins fall to the ground. "I don't care if I go to your jail, Sheriff," Mudcat panted, "so long as you've got some cold water."

Sheriff Tackett looked over his shoulder at the ranger as he carried the woman up onto the boardwalk. "Are you going to be staying here a while, Sam, instead of going on to the outpost with these two?"

"Yep, it looks like it," said the ranger. "I want to get on the trail of the man who killed her husband. From what he done, it sounds like the work of this Carlos the Snake I've been hearing about."

"Really?" Tackett stopped in his tracks, holding the woman.

"Yep, but go on, take her to the doctor's. I'll put these two in a cell and join you there." The ranger nodded at the door to the sheriff's office. "Got anybody who can watch the prisoners for us?"

"I'll get little Stanley Baggs, one of the livery hostlers. He's itching to put on a badge," said Tackett.

In Tackett's arms, Darcy Tennison rose into consciousness for a moment and looked around through blurry eyes. "Where are we?" she asked.

"You're in Halston, ma'am," said Sheriff Tackett. "This is my town—you don't have to worry about a thing."

"Halston," she whispered. "This was to be my home."

"What?" Tackett looked stunned.

"Her husband was your undertaker, Sheriff," said the ranger.

"Oh, no," said Tackett, "poor Maximus. That young man wouldn't hurt a fly." Tackett shook his head. "Lock them two up and hurry on over, Sam. I want to hear what all happened out there."

"What about my wound?" Stevie Boy asked, limping as Sam nudged him and his brother forward. It was the first thing Stevie had said aloud since Sam had put a bullet through his foot.

"We'll get the doctor to look at it as soon as we can, Stevie Boy," said the ranger. "Meanwhile, you just go on being as quiet as you have been. It looks good on you."

Once both of the Glovers were locked inside a cell, leaving them cuffed for the time being until someone was there to keep an eye on them, Sam sat a bucket of drinking water and a tin dipper against the bars, within reach. "You boys behave yourself while I'm gone. We'll see if we can get you a good meal this evening."

"We'll be good, Ranger, *gracias,*" said Mudcat.

Stevie Boy only gave the ranger a defiant stare.

No sooner had Sam left the building, Stevie Boy turned to his brother saying in a mock tone, "'We'll be good, Ranger, *gracias*.' Why don't you just kiss his lawdog ass, and make the show complete!"

"So?" said Mudcat. "What's wrong with acting like I've got some sense, not causing trouble all the time? You took your best stand, look what it got you. I never seen a man do so many stupid things so close together in my life. If Pa's been watching, he's turned over in his grave by now."

"Well, to hell with Pa, the ranger, and you, *Brother* Mud!" said Stevie Boy. "While you and that ranger make friends and start holding hands, I'm going to be busy looking for a way out of here."

"That's exactly what you ought to do," said Mudcat. He stood staring at Stevie Boy with a smug grin. "Now you're starting to get the picture."

Stevie Boy had started to rave on, yet the crafty look in his brother's eyes made him stop. For a second, he seemed at a loss. But then, seeing what Mudcat was getting at, Stevie Boy let out a breath. "Well beat me with a hot skillet! You're just shining him on, ain't you, Mud?" Stevie grinned to himself now. "Hell, why didn't you say so?"

"Because you've done such a good job making him want to kill you, I didn't want to do anything to slow you down." Mudcat chucked cruelly. "Don't you think I'm as keen as you are to stay away from the hanging rope, or that sweat bath, Yuma prison? I'm just playing the same song to a different pitch—biding my time, is all. When I make my move, nobody's going to be expecting a thing."

As Mudcat spoke, he reached through the bars, picked up a dipperful of cool water, and raised it dripping to his lips. He took a long drink, then handed the dipper to his brother. "First thing we got to do is get rested and fed. Once we're in shape, we look for our best break and take it."

"I'm with you, Brother Mud," said Stevie Boy, tipping the water dipper in a toast before pouring back a long cool drink. "Just say the word when you're ready."

By the time the Glovers had rested and drunk their fill of cool water, a knock on the front door drew their attention. They looked at one another as the knock came again. Then, grinning, Stevie Boy called out across the empty sheriff's office, "Do come in, please."

The door opened a crack. A thin young man, wearing a broad, floppy hat, stuck his head inside and looked around before proceeding any farther. When he did step through the front door and over to the Glovers' cell, his face was pale with restrained fright. Stevie Boy and Mudcat remained slumped on their cots as the man looked them up and down with uncertainty.

"Can we help ya?" Stevie Boy asked, the flat grin still on his face.

"I'm— I'm Stanley Baggs," the young man said in a shaky voice. "I'm the new deputy. The sheriff hired me to look after you boys, make sure nothing happens to you."

"Nothing happens to us?" said Stevie Boy. The Glovers looked at each other again, this time with a sharp gleam of hope in their eyes. "Well, that's mighty big of you, son .... I feel better already." Stevie Boy chuckled.

Ralph Cotton

CHAPTER 8

Bone-weary, Sam led the tired horses and the mule down the dusty street. Out front of the doctor's office, he dropped the reins over the hitch rail and spun them one loose turn. Before he could walk up onto the boardwalk, Sheriff Tackett stepped out through the door to meet him, his forearm back in the sling. "Doc said for us to wait out here until he gets her cleaned up and looked at."

"All right," said Sam, half turning toward the horses. "I'll take these animals to the livery and get them attended."

Before he could go, Sheriff Tackett stepped down beside him. Tackett rubbed his chin with a concerned expression. "Sam, are you sure this is Carlos the Snake's work?"

"Yep," said Sam, "as soon as she told me everything that fellow told her out in the desert before he died, I knew it was Carlos the Snake. It fits with what Jarvis told us." Sam looked toward the door to the doctor's office, then back at Sheriff Tackett. "She's a brave woman, Sheriff. I've never seen anybody work any harder at staying alive then she has."

Sheriff Tackett eyed him up and down. "On the way over here, she said something about you going back out there and bringing back her husband's body, and that other fellow, for proper burial?"

"Yeah," Sam said, reluctantly, "I told her I would, so I reckon I've got to. I tried to tell her as gently as I could that there wouldn't be much left to bury by the time I got back to him. I don't think she wanted to hear it .... Leastwise, she didn't seem to."

Tackett shook his head. "Well, since these are my townspeople, I reckon I ought to go with you. Can't say I enjoy the prospect of hauling in the leftovers from a coyote feast, though."

Sam nodded in agreement. "Far as I'm concerned, I'll go get the bodies while you stay here and keep an eye on the Glovers."

"You've got yourself a deal there," Tackett said quickly.

"I told her I'd take along a team and bring the big hearse back here, too," said Sam. "She said it's a pretty expensive rig. I suspect she'll want to sell it to whoever takes over the funeral parlor."

"Yeah, I expect so," said Tackett. "Young Maximus ran a good respectable funeral business .... He'll be hard to replace." He stood in silent contemplation for a moment, then asked, "What about Carlos the Snake? I reckon you'll be going after him, once everything else is settled?"

"Yep, he's on my list," said Sam. "Looks like his vengeance has already spilled over onto innocent folks, the way we said it would."

Sheriff Tackett gave a concerned look out across the flatlands to the west, to where the hills loomed like apparitions in the wavering heat. "Think he might have trailed you here? Maybe he's waiting out there for you right now?"

"It's crossed my mind," said Sam. "But if that's how it is, I might as well get to it."

"I'll tell you again, Sam," Tackett said, "you be careful out there."

Sam nodded, taking note of the grave look on Sheriff Tackett's face. "I'll sure try, Sheriff," he said in a mock sober tone, as if he needed to be reminded. He took the reins to the horses and the mule from the hitch rail.

Leaving the sheriff, Sam led the worn-out animals to the livery barn, where he was met by a young boy whose eyes turned large at the sight of the ranger badge on Sam's chest.

Turning the other animals over to the boy, Sam attended the Appaloosa personally, looking the stallion over closely before putting him into a stall by himself. "What's your name, lad?" Sam asked.

"I'm Willie Burns," the boy said. "There's me and Stanley Baggs both working here 'tending horses. Stanley wants to be a lawman. I do, too, someday I reckon. It would beat going to school."

"I bet it would," Sam said wryly. "Listen to me, Willie, I'll need a good strong mount and a wagon team, pronto." As he spoke, Sam took out a coin from his vest and flipped it to the boy.

He snatched the coin out of the air and made it disappear into his loose fitting shirt "You mean, first thing in the morning?" Willie asked, seeing Sam's tired dusty condition.

"No," Sam replied, "I'll be back within the hour .... Have them ready to go."

As Sam turned to leave, he saw Jarvis Hicks walk in from the street. "There you are, Ranger. I've been looking for you," said Hicks.

"What for, Jarvis?" asked Sam.

"I've got another tip for you: A fellow named Raymond Maples was over at the Roi-Tan a while ago. I believe you've got him on your list?"

"What makes you think so?" asked Sam.

"He seems to think so, Ranger," said Hicks. "I was in the Roi-Tan with him when we saw you ride into town. He acted real nervous and let it slip that you're looking for him."

"I am looking for him," said the ranger. "But it's not like you think. I only want to ask him the whereabouts of Sonny Blue and the Harper boys. I'm not out to arrest him for anything."

Jarvis Hicks grinned. "Well, he must have a guilty conscience about something. I thought I ought to come tell you how he's acting, in case he went nuts and started shooting at you." Jarvis Hicks thumbed over his shoulder toward the street beyond the barn door. "Turns out I just saw him split out of here like the devil was on his tail. But I figured I'd tell you anyway."

"Much obliged," said Sam. "So, you're back to hanging around at the Roi-Tan?"

"Oh, I'm not drinking though—well, not much anyway," said Hicks. "No, sir. I stay there to keep my eyes and ears open for any information that might be helpful to the law. I ain't forgot what you did for me, Ranger."

"What about the peddler you shot?" Sam asked. "And what about the rancher, Gunderson?"

Jarvis Hicks shrugged. "Loman Gunderson is too busy nursing his foot. The peddler, Benfield, is still here. I can tell it ain't over between him and me. But there's nothing more I can do about it. I tried to apologize for shooting him, even though I was in the right. What more can I do? He *did* try to go for that hide-out gun in his shoe top, whether he admits to it or not."

"Stay out of his way as best you can," said Sam, "and keep Sheriff Tackett apprised of the situation. If you and him throw down, you better make sure the whole town sees it's self-defense. You don't want to wind up on the bad end of a rope again over him. I might not be here to stop it next time."

"Thanks, I'll do the best I can," said Hicks. "I don't want to shoot nobody ever again. All I want to do is live in peace, maybe make up for some of the wrongs I've done over the years if I can." His expression turned troubled. "But you know something, Ranger? I never knew trying to live right was so damned hard to do. No wonder some folks won't even attempt it."

"How's that, Jarvis?" Sam asked.

"Seems like when I was a no-good sonuva— Well, you know how I was, everybody and their brother was my friend," said Jarvis. "Now, I go around trying to say something good to folks, like 'God bless you,' or 'Hope the Lord takes a liking to you,' or something along that line, they can't get away from me quick enough to suit 'em, it seems like. You'd think I milked skunks for a living."

The ranger smiled. "It's just taking folks some getting used to, Jarvis .... They all knew you when you was no good. If you've truly changed your ways, it's like they've got to get to know a whole new person. Give it some time, folks will come around once they see you're really on the right track. Who knows? You might even serve as a good influence on some of them."

"Well, that's what I'm hoping for, Ranger. See, it's hard to feel what I feel inside and not be able to tell others about it. There's times I feel just like a preacher. Something good happened inside me, Ranger! I get so happy, so joyous thinking about it ... I can't keep from shouting about it to the world."

"Well, be careful shouting to the world, Jarvis," the ranger said. "Sometime the world doesn't want to hear about something good. I hate to say it, but lots of folks are suspicious of anything good—they get so used to bad things, they seem to trust bad more than they trust good." The ranger stopped himself from saying any more on the subject. "Anyway, that's the way it looks to me sometimes."

Jarvis scratched his head. "I never thought about it, but now that you mention it ... folks search the sky more often for a storm than they do for good weather. I know that's how I always was. I reckon one reason I was such a no-account was because I never saw anything good coming anyway." He paused for consideration, then said, "Ranger, you've given me a lot to think about."

Sam raised his hat and rubbed his shirtsleeve across his forehead. "Well, while you're thinking about it, I've got to get going. I need to pick up some staples before I head out." He turned toward the front doors.

"Uh, Ranger?" Jarvis said, sounding a little uncertain of himself. "I've been doing some praying since the other day. Would you mind if I prayed for you now and then?"

Sam stopped and looked him up and down. "Why on earth would I mind you praying for me, Jarvis?"

Jarvis shrugged. "I don't know, Ranger, but I've found some folks get real touchy about it when I mention it."

"Not me, Jarvis," said Sam. "Pray for me anytime you feel like it. I need all the help I can get."

"I saw Sheriff Tackett on my way here," said Jarvis. "He told me what happened to Maximus and his bride out there. Are you going after the man who done it?"

"First, I'm bringing in her husband's body," said Sam. "Then I'll see what I can do about catching the killer!"

"It's him, ain't it, Ranger?" Jarvis said in a guarded tone, as if the walls of the barn might hear him. "I know it's him. It's Carlos the Snake."

The sound of Jarvis Hicks's voice gave Sam pause. "Yes, I believe it is, Jarvis, by all accounts."

"I knew Carlos the Snake was involved the minute I saw you ride into town," Jarvis, said, a fearful look coming to his face.

"Oh? What made you think so?" Sam asked.

"I just *knew* it. I've had nothing but bad thoughts about it ever since I told you about him the other day, Ranger. I wish you could leave him be, let somebody else go after him."

"But the fact is I can't, Jarvis," said Sam. "I don't get to pick and choose. I have to take my work the way it comes to me."

"Just this once I bet you could," said Jarvis, his voice sounding more urgent as Sam turned back toward the door. "I can only see bad things coming out of your hunting Carlos the Snake."

"See, Jarvis," said the ranger, "there you go thinking only of the bad."

"I can't help it, Ranger. I hate saying it, but I can see him standing over your body." Jarvis's voice trembled. "I never had anything like this come to me before—but I see it, Ranger. I see that picture plain as day. Don't go after him, Ranger. I'm pleading with you."

"Take it easy, Jarvis," Sam said, speaking calmly, seeing how excited he'd become. "I've had those kind of thoughts before. Any man who wears a badge has seen those pictures in his mind. But the pictures always pass, Jarvis. They have to, else I couldn't do my job."

Jarvis rubbed his forehead with a shaky hand. Looking at him, Sam realized that the man might be in bad need of a drink.

"How do you stand it then, Ranger?" Jarvis asked, relenting in his attempt to dissuade Sam from doing his job. "Don't it trouble you, seeing that kind of picture?"

Sam managed a tired smile. "Not for long, Jarvis. I replace it with another picture. I see me stopping men like Carlos the Snake from hurting anybody else. Now that's a *good* picture, if you want to look at something good."

Jarvis let out a tense breath and shook his head slowly, getting the ranger's message. "Lord, I'm trying, Ranger .... I sure am trying."

"Stay with it then, Jarvis," said Sam. "It'll get better for you." He turned and left the livery barn.

"Lord, I hope so," Jarvis Hicks whispered, bowing his head.

Within the hour Sam had washed his face and neck in a bucket of water and taken on water and food for his ride back onto the desert floor. On his way out of town, riding a big buckskin and leading a team of horses on a lead rope, Sam sidled over to Sheriff Tackett, who stood on the boardwalk out front of the doctor's office. "How's the woman?" Sam asked.

"She's coming along as well as can be expected," Sheriff Tackett replied. "She asked for you .... I told her you was getting ready to go after Maximus's body. She tried to get up off the cot, said she was going, too. The doctor had to talk her down." Tackett looked out across the simmering desert floor, then back at the ranger. "I sure wish I could be more help to you on this, Sam."

"You're needed here, Sheriff," said Sam. He nodded back toward the livery barn where he'd last seen Jarvis Hicks.

"Jarvis is pretty jumpy. I expect it's from not drinking as much as he used to."

"Not as much?" Tackett gave him a bemused look. "From what folks are telling me, he ain't been drinking at all. The bartender at the Roi-Tan said he'll buy a shot of whiskey and sit it in front of himself when he comes in there and starts preaching to people at the bar. But he said Jarvis's glass ain't been touched when he leaves. Peculiar, don't you think?"

"Preaching, huh?" said Sam. "Well, if that's his way of fighting his devils, I reckon it doesn't do any harm. Is there a minister around here? Somebody he can talk to, get some things off his chest?"

"Naw," said Tackett, "there's been no minister here since Reverend Koss's wife ran off with a teamster, and Koss burnt his church to the ground.

There's a meeting every Sunday in somebody's home ... but those Christian folks ain't going to welcome old Jarvis, leastwise none of the men are. I reckon they'd be afraid for their wives and daughters."

Sam sighed, understanding. "Is that peddler going to be any trouble?"

"Naw," said Tackett, "I don't think so. I'm keeping a pretty close eye on him. He made some threats, what he's going to do to Jarvis and all. But I'm hoping he'll meller down after a while. Meanwhile, I just figure on keeping the two separated best I can. I used to think Jarvis was a handful when he was a drunk and a rounder. But now that he's found the Lord, I don't know what in the world to do with him."

Sam shook his head, drawing the buckskin and the lead-rope horses toward the middle of the street. "See why I don't like working in town?" he said.

Carlos the Snake watched the distant rise of dust draw closer across the broad rolling belly of the desert basin. He'd kept himself hidden a good two miles behind the ranger, the woman, and the two prisoners. And he'd managed to follow them without so much as raising dust. Once the exhausted party had ridden into Halston, the distant town looking like nothing more than a thin black smear on the horizon, Carlos had rested his horse in the slim shade of a low rise standing against the afternoon sunlight. He'd sipped warm water from his canteen, fingered the three big rifle cartridges in his pocket, and waited. Come nightfall, Carlos planned to slip into town unseen. In the morning, he would see what he needed to do to get to the woman.

Scanning the horizon, he first caught sight of a black wavering stick figure coming in his direction when the hot whir of wind picked up the risen dust and spread it slantwise upward into the sky. Carlos smiled to himself. That was quick. The lawman had taken no more time than he needed to drop off his prisoners and the woman. Now here he came in the hottest part of the day. "You're making it easy for me, lawman," Carlos murmured, squinting into the swirl of heat. "That ain't like you."

Carlos took his time capping his canteen and looping it over his saddle horn. He drew the big Remington rifle from his saddle boot, took one of the brass cartridges from his pocket, and slipped it into the rifle's breech. He snapped the rifle shut. Then he ran a hand along the barrel, took the sighting sticks from the saddle boot, and brushed his boot back and forth in the sand, clearing himself a good shooting spot.

A few minutes passed as Carlos made adjustments on the rifle sights, raising high for an eight hundred yard to a thousand yard shot. This was pushing the Remington to its limits. Carlos knew that the closer he allowed the ranger to get, the better his chance of hitting him. But the ranger had a big rifle, too. Carlos wasn't going to take any chances, not with only three cartridges left.

When the thin black figure bobbed up and down within range, Carlos made himself comfortable with the rifle butt in place against his shoulder and settled in for the shot. He centered his sights on his target, took a good breath, let it out evenly. Then he stopped breathing, seeing his sights stop stone still before his eyes. He squeezed the trigger back slowly, letting the sound of the shot come as a surprise to him.

Beneath the deafening roar of the Remington, Carlos's shoulder jolted back with the recoil. A full second seemed to pass. Then, before him, the black stick figure turned limp and melted like wax down the horse's side. As Carlos stood up with the cross sticks and rifle in his hand, he saw the riderless horse go off to the left. In a sudden rise of dust, he caught a vague glimpse of another animal speeding off in the opposite direction, a lead rope whipping in the air.

"And that's that," Carlos said aloud, opening the Remington and flipping out the spent cartridge in its halo of smoke. *"Adios,* lawman." He walked back to his horse, slipped the rifle and cross sticks into the saddle boot, then mounted and rode away.

CHAPTER 9

By the time the ranger came upon Raymond Maples lying in the hot sand, the gaping wound in the outlaw's chest was covered with a dark red froth of blood. Maples wheezed through his shattered lungs and wiped a blood-soaked bandanna across his lips. "How the hell ... did you get in front of me?" Maples asked, his voice raspy and weak. He watched the ranger step down from the buckskin and walk over to him, the big Swiss rifle in one gloved hand, a canteen in his other.

"It wasn't me who shot you, Raymond," Sam said, gazing warily off at the distant hill line, "so don't raise that pistol at me."

In Raymond Maples's bloody right hand a Colt lay cocked and ready, his finger across the trigger. "I don't know ... if I could raise it if I wanted to," Maples said, his words ending in a bloody cough. "I cocked it ... for buzzards."

"Then ease it out of your hand," said Sam. "I'll keep the buzzards away. I've got some water for you. Can you drink?"

"I'll try," said the wounded outlaw. "I've never been ... shot this bad."

Sam stooped down, and held the canteen to Maples's blood-crusted lips, cradling the back of his head as the man sipped from it. No sooner had Maples swallowed, then he coughed the water back up, pressing the wet bandanna to his lips. "Aw, hell ... this is a rough way to go, Ranger!"

"Take it easy, Raymond," Sam said. ""I'm going to sit with you through it." He gave Maples another sip. This time, Maples managed to keep it down. "I wish you hadn't gotten spooked and run out of Halston," Sam said, his voice low, sympathetic. "I wasn't out to get you, Raymond."

"Well, damn it," said Maples, with regret, "you mean ... this was all for nothing?" His bloody hand gestured with the bandanna toward the gaping chest wound.

"Yep. I'm sorry to have to tell you," said the ranger, "but all I wanted was some information on Sonny Blue and the Harpers."

"That damned Sonny ... I oughta known his name would play into me getting killed someday. I had nothing but ... bad luck riding with him."

"I know," Sam said. "Now take it easy, save your breath."

"Why?" asked Maples, "I ain't apt ... to get up and walk away from this!" He left the pistol lying in the dirt, raised his bloody hand and let it fall limply onto his chest. "Who done this, then?"

"I'm pretty sure it was a man they call Carlos the Snake," said Sam. "Ever heard of him?"

"Hell no," Maples coughed. "Sad ain't it ... I'm killed by a man I never wronged. Why'd he do it?"

Sam winced and looked away for a second. Then he said, "To be honest, Raymond, I believe he thought you were me."

"Lord God," Raymond Maples sighed, "it just gets worse as you go. I hate hearing that."

"I'm sorry, Raymond, but you asked," said the ranger. "This man is on a vengeance trail, after some men who killed his folks years ago."

"Well, by God, if that don't beat ... it all to hell," said Maples, his voice growing weaker, his eyes starting to look more distant and cloudy. "I'm just an ... innocent bystander? After all I've done?"

"I reckon," Sam said gently.

"Damn ... vengeance killer. They always ... cause something like this. I never was the kind to hold ... a grudge, myself."

"That's to your favor, Raymond," said Sam. He looked off

again toward the distant hill line. "Somebody kills a man's folks I expect it's safe to say he's going to take revenge on them. But it seems like somebody always gets hurt that had nothing to do with it. He killed Halston's undertaker, and nearly killed the man's new wife—" Sam stopped talking as he looked back down at Raymond Maples and saw the outlaw's dead hollow eyes staring blankly into the sun. He reached out with his fingers and closed Maple's eyes. "Well, anyway, you get the picture, Raymond," Sam whispered.

It took three days for Darcy Tennison to regain her strength and get back on her feet. As soon as she was able, Sheriff Tackett and Jarvis Hicks accompanied her to her deceased husband's funeral parlor. In the preparation room at the rear of the large clapboard building, Earl Blume was busily at work, cleaning the body of an old miner who'd died of a rattlesnake bite and lay a week inside his overheated shack before being found. It was customary for an undertaker to lock the door to the preparation room whenever the room was in use. But in their nervous haste, Earl and his young son, Little Herman, had both forgotten to do so.

When Sheriff Tackett opened the door and the smell of death billowed out, Darcy gasped and turned away, her hand going over her nose and mouth. Jarvis Hicks shrank back a step, jerked a clean handkerchief from his shirt pocket, and threw it up to his face. But then, seeing Darcy Tennison sway as if ready to faint, Jarvis quickly put an arm around her waist to steady her, and held his handkerchief over her nose. "Easy does it," Jarvis said to her.

"Lord have mercy, Earl!" said Tackett. "Why ain't this door locked?"

Seeing Darcy Tennison, Earl Blume's eyes grew wide above the wet towel tied around his face. He threw a bloodstained cloth over the naked dead miner. "Fan harder!" Earl said over his shoulder. At the rear door, young Herman stood waving a large hand fan out the open door, a wet towel also tied around his face.

"I'm sorry, ma'am!" Earl said to Darcy, stepping around the preparation table, wiping his gloved hands up and down on his long black apron. "I— I wasn't expecting anybody!" His voice was muffled by the wet towel. He pressed the three intruders back out into the hall and said over his shoulder to Herman, "Keep fanning!" Then he quickly closed the door, and gestured Darcy, Tackett, and Jarvis Hicks toward the front of the building.

"My goodness," said Earl Blume, "this is terrible! What you must think of me! I told Herman to lock that door—that is, I'm pretty sure I did." Stripping the gloves from his hands and dropping them to the floor, Earl pulled the towel down from across his mouth and stepped forward. He dragged a wooden chair from against the wall for Darcy to sit in.

"That's quite all right, Mr. Blume," Darcy said, having been introduced to Earl and his son Little Herman while she was still under the doctor's care. "I must remember to knock in the future." She shot a glance at Tackett and Jarvis, then touched a corner of the handkerchief to her watery eyes. "This will serve to remind me to always make certain the door is locked when I'm with one of our guests."

"Guests?" Jarvis gave Sheriff Tackett a bemused look.

"Yes," said Darcy. "That's how Maximus told me he refers to the deceased who are brought here. Isn't that so, Mr. Blume?"

"Well, yes, ma'am, he did. Max always tried to act like death was just one more obstacle a person had to surmount. He always tried to lessen the grief of the loved ones, the way the departed would have wanted him to—"

"That's fine, Earl, just fine," Tackett cut in, uncomfortable with the line of conversation. "Max was a good undertaker ... there's no two ways about it." Tackett's attention went to Darcy. "Did you just say you're going to be using the preparation room?"

107

"Yes," said Darcy, lifting her chin. "I'm certain my husband, Max, would want me to run this business—at least to keep it going until some other mortician might come along and take it over. That's only prudent business, wouldn't you agree?"

The three men looked at one another in surprise. Sheriff Tackett said, "But, ma'am, you just saw what goes on back there. That's no kind of work for a young woman like yourself to be doing—"

"Nonsense, Sheriff," Darcy said, cutting Tackett off. "Where I grew up, there were no funeral parlors. We simply prepared our dead and buried them."

"'Well, yes, ma'am"—Tackett blushed—"that's true for those of us living out away from town in these parts as well. Folks with land to be buried on and kinfolk around always attend to one another. But in a town like this we've got lots of folks who own no land to be buried on. We also have lots of folks passing through. They could be strangers from anywhere in the country. Our undertaker looks after them, cleans them up, gets them properly buried. It's as much a public necessity as it is a funeral service. In some towns the barber does it."

"I think I understand," said Darcy. "Max told me a lot about how the business works. I believe I can handle that."

Tackett winced a bit. "Ma'am, these deceased can be in some tough condition. Some of them are found out on the desert and brung in wrapped in a blanket. Some of them are killed in gruesome terrible ways. These are not friends and family, ma'am. They're *customers* is what these dead people are." He looked at Jarvis and Earl, asking for their approval. "Yes, ma'am, these are paying customers, in a sense."

"I see," said Darcy, with restraint. "It's acceptable for a woman to handle the dead out of kindness, but not acceptable if she gets paid for it. That seems to be the general thinking about anything a woman does."

"Well I don't know about that," said Tackett. "The thing is, being a mortician ain't exactly the sort of thing you'd expect to see a young lady like yourself doing."

"Well," said Darcy, "like I told you, Max and I had already discussed it. I had agreed that I would help him run this business." She wasn't about to mention how grimly she had anticipated working side by side with her husband. But that was when Max was alive. Her situation had changed dramatically since then. Now that Maximus wasn't going to be here, there was nothing she could do but run this business and support herself until a better opportunity came along.

"In fact," Darcy added, casting a glance at Earl Blume, the wet towel hanging down beneath his chin, his shirtfront wet above the bib of his long apron, "I see no reason why I can't begin work immediately."

The three men looked at one another stunned, the rancid smell of death still lingering around Earl Blume. "Ma'am, you still need some rest!" Sheriff Tackett protested. "You can't just jump back there and commence working in that terrible stink."

Ignoring Tackett, Darcy looked at Earl Blume. "Mister Blume, what would Max be doing about now, if he were here?"

Earl Blume felt the other two men's eyes on him, looking to him for some sort of solution. "Uh—" Earl stalled for a moment, then asked quickly, "What is today? It's Wednesday, correct?" A broad grin of relief came to his face. "Yes, of course it is! It's Wednesday. That was always bookkeeping day for Max!" He looked from one to the other of the two men, making sure he'd done his job well. "Yep, that was ole Max all right! Every Wednesday, rain or shine. You couldn't drag him away from his paperwork! I used to say to him sometimes, 'Max, why don't you put that off till—'"

"Good," said Sheriff Tackett, cutting him short. "There now, ma'am"—he turned to Darcy—"if you really want to take part in the business and do as your husband would do ... this is what he would be doing today." He spread a hand in gesture toward the oak rolltop desk in the corner of the room. "Let Earl and his boy handle the back room for a while, until you get all your strength back anyway. Maybe by then, you'll come to your sense— I mean, take a look at this business a little closer."

Darcy looked skeptically at the oak desk, then back at Sheriff Tackett as she stood up from the chair and handed Jarvis Hicks's handkerchief back to him. "Bookkeeping day, eh, Mister Blume?"

"Yes indeed, ma'am," said Earl, feeling the men's eyes on him again, "every Wednesday, just like I said."

Darcy looked at the men in turn, their expressions revealing nothing. "Then I suppose I better roll up the desk and get to it."

"There now, that's the way," Tackett said, accompanying her to the desk, pulling the chair from beneath it for her. "You just make yourself to home here, ma'am .... Let Earl help you get situated."

"Thank you, Sheriff," Darcy said, lifting the rolltop and looking at the well-organized pigeonholes and labeled file drawers. She raised the front cover of a leather-bound account ledger and smoothed it open. "I'll just see what I can make of things here."

"Yes, ma'am, you take your time," Tackett said, breathing a sigh of relief as he looked at Earl Blume and Jarvis Hicks. Sheriff Tackett backed away from the desk, looked at Jarvis Hicks again, and nodded toward the door.

Outside the funeral parlor, Sheriff Tackett swabbed his brow with his palm and placed his black Stetson down firmly on his head. He let out another relieved breath and said to Jarvis Hicks, "I'm glad that's over with. Can you imagine her wanting to do something like that?"

"I hope you don't think you stopped her doing anything she's got planned to do, Sheriff," Jarvis replied.

"I hope it'll stop her long enough to think about it some," said Tackett. "That's the best I can do. If she wants to go ahead and handle a bunch of stinking swollen-up corpses, I reckon I can't really keep her from it. At least, I won't be there to see it, like we just would have if Earl hadn't come up with that bookkeeping idea."

As they stepped away from the building and down into the street, Jarvis shook his head and smiled. "Do you think she fell for that, Sheriff?"

"You saw it, didn't you?" Sheriff Tackett responded.

"I saw her go along with it," said Jarvis, "but she wasn't tricked. She saw right through it."

"Oh? What makes you so sure?" Sheriff Tackett quickened his pace across the wheel-rutted dirt street. "It sounded pretty good to me."

"I suppose it might've," said Jarvis, "if she doesn't know the day of the week." His smile grew wider. "Today's Thursday, not Wednesday."

Tackett considered it for a second, not seeing what difference it could make. "You sound like you think it's all right, her wanting to be an undertaker."

Jarvis shrugged. "I can't say there's anything wrong with it. Now that I've come to follow the Lord and learn his ways, I have to see all people as equal in every regard, no matter what their race, or if they're a man or a woman, or if they're a Presbyterian, or a Mormon, or if they—"

"Hold it." Sheriff Tackett stopped in the street and turned facing him, a perplexed expression coming to his face. "Don't you have something you ought to be doing, Jarvis?"

Jarvis shrugged again. "You told me to stick close to you, Sheriff ... remember? You said that peddler, Benfield, is drunk and on the prod, making threats against me. I'll go if you want me to though." He started to turn and walk away, but Sheriff Tackett stopped him.

"No, that's all right, Jarvis, you stay with me. Just keep the religious talk to yourself, if you don't mind. I get tired of hearing it."

"I don't know why, Sheriff," said Jarvis. "It's just the gospel truth. And after all, if the truth won't set a man's spirit free, what will? The Bible says clearly that if a man wants to know the Lord—"

111

"Don't start, Jarvis," Sheriff Tackett warned him. "I appreciate the Bible as much as the next man. But I don't like having it quoted at me."

"I don't know enough Bible to quote a lot of it yet," said Jarvis. "But I think it's my duty to tell people what it says."

"Then I expect somebody besides that peddler will be shooting you before long," said Sheriff Tackett. "Then you can be cleaned up and buried by a woman undertaker ... see how that suits you." They stepped up onto the boardwalk out front of the sheriff's office.

"I don't know why it bothers folks so much, hearing what the good book's got to say," Jarvis ventured.

"I'll tell you why," said Tackett, rolling his eyes upward for a second, keeping himself under control. "Because all a man is doing who's quoting the Bible to you is reminding you that he knows more about God than you do!"

"Well, don't he?" Jarvis said.

"That ain't the point," Tackett fumed. "It's just his way of making himself feel good." Tackett threw open the door and stepped inside, Jarvis right behind him. "If a man wants to hear a sermon, he'll go to church." Tackett wagged a finger in the air for emphasis. "Nobody wants to have the errors of their ways pointed out to them, leastwise not whilst they're enjoying a drink at the bar, or trying to gamble, or taking care of their wants."

"So, you're saying I've been doing wrong? Trying to tell people about the Bible and how we ought to all try to live right and love one another?" Jarvis Hicks sounded hurt by Sheriff Tackett's remarks.

Tackett took deep breath and settled himself down. "What I'm saying, Jarvis, is that you're getting on everybody's nerves with your newfound religion. So take it easy. Besides, these people all know you and what a four-flushing, two-bit scoundrel you was before. Why should they listen to you all of a sudden? For all they know, you ain't changed any. Tomorrow they might find out it was a big put-on."

"It's no put-on, Sheriff, I swear it ain't, as God's my witness," Jarvis said quietly, shaking his head. "Lord strike me down dead, if I'm making this up."

"I'm not saying it is a put-on," Tackett replied. "I'm just saying for all folks know, it could be. Or, it could be that you've lost your rabbit-assed mind, going around telling everybody they ought to love one another! That's crazy and you know it. Everybody luuuv one another?" Tackett said in a mocking tone. "That ain't even natural, Jarvis, for people to go around loving one another. I know the Lord said it is, but he never seen the likes of people nowadays. You'd have to be a striped-back, raving fool to love everybody. So think about it before you go telling it to folks. There, that's what I'm saying."

Jarvis thought about it for a second. "I see what you mean, Sheriff. Why should they believe I'm a changed man just because I say I am. What right have I got to be no-account all my life, then expect everybody to take me at my word?"

"Well, don't go letting it upset you too much, Jarvis," said Sheriff Tackett. "Just slow down on folks a little."

"No, you're right, Sheriff," said Jarvis. "The Bible says a man is judged by his works. All these people have ever seen is me gambling and whoring and whooping it up. That's all the works they ever saw out of me. All my religion is to them is just talk. Well, from now on, Sheriff, everybody's going to see my works. I aim to show everybody what the Lord can do when he takes over a man's spirit."

"Aw, hell," Sheriff Tackett grumbled as Jarvis turned and rushed out the door. "Why can't I learn to keep my mouth shut till this idiot winds down?" he asked himself.

Outside on the dirt street, at the hitch rail out front of the Halston Bank, a black-and-white paint horse, wearing a worn-out saddle, stood with its head lowered.

Inside the bank, the horse's owner walked to the counter and looked through the ornamental iron bars. He stared right past the young teller, who asked, "May I help you, sir?" The teller looked with disdain at the long gray hair, the week-old beard stubble, the seedy clothes. But his sour expression managed to hide itself when the cold green eyes turned sharply into his.

"I'll see that man right there," the stranger said, nodding past the teller.

"I'm sorry, sir," the teller said, "But our president, Mr. Trumbough, cannot be disturbed right now. Is there something I can—?"

"I bet he can be, if you try hard enough," the stranger said in a gruff tone, cutting the young man off. "Tell him Galt is here. Tell him right now." His voice grew stronger, more demanding.

The teller reeled slightly from the smell of stale rye on the man's breath. But before he could turn and say anything to the bank president, Victor Trumbough rose up from his desk. He'd heard the raised voice and stepped forward to investigate.

"Is there a problem, Gerald?" he asked the teller, buttoning his coat across his thick stomach.

"Oh, no, sir." Gerald Bratcher remained composed, smiling at the bank president. "This gentleman asked to see .... I told him it was impossible at the moment." Gerald stepped to the side as Victor Trumbough moved closer and cocked his head for a better look at the man.

"My goodness," Trumbough whispered to himself, looking at the haggard face, "Bristoe?"

"In the flesh," the man said, a slight mirthless smile coming to his tobacco-stained lips. "Bet you thought you'd never see me again, eh?"

"But he said his name was Galt," the teller interjected, looking confused.

"That was just to get his attention," the stranger said, staring past the confused teller at Trumbough. "Well, *Victor,* are you going to invite me in?" As he spoke, putting a mock emphasis on the name *Victor,* he raised a big, worn-looking Colt pistol from its holster and raised it toward the clerk.

Gerald Bratcher gasped, but then breathed in relief when Bristoe flipped the gun backward in his palm, laid it on the counter, and shoved it forward. Still, Gerald shied back a step as if the pistol were a coiled rattlesnake. He glanced at Trumbough for guidance.

"Take it, Gerald," said Trumbough, giving the teller a grave look, "and hold it for Mr. Bristoe, please, while I step through the door."

"Yes, of course, sir," Gerald replied. He picked up the pistol and held it in his hand, his thumb across the hammer, as Trumbough went over to the tall barred door and slipped his key into its lock.

As he opened the door, Bristoe took a step forward. But Trumbough stepped through the door quickly and pulled it shut behind himself, feeling the latch catch securely.

"Perhaps we'd be more comfortable talking out here," Trumbough said, gesturing toward a wooden chair sitting beside a small desk in a corner.

Bristoe grinned and chuckled under his breath.

"Yeah, I reckon *you* would at that." As they walked to the corner desk, Bristoe said, "What's wrong, *Victor?* Do you think I'd rob your bank, an old buddy like me?"

At the corner desk, Trumbough offered him the chair with the sweep of his hand as he said, "Either say my name correctly, or don't say it at all."

Bristoe refused the chair and replied, "You don't really want me to say your name correctly, do you, Victor?"

This time there was no mockery in Bristoe's voice, so Trumbough let the question pass. He lowered his voice to keep from being overheard by Gerald Bratcher, who stood staring intently from behind the counter. "What can I do for you, Bristoe?"

Bristoe took his time, rubbing his beard stubble, then said,

"What's it been? Two years? Three?"

"It's been three," said Trumbough. "Last time, I recall telling you never to come here again."

"I know," said Bristoe, "and believe me, I ain't here because I want to be. There's men on my trail wanting to kill me." He saw the lack of concern on Trumbough's face. "Not that they're going to be any real problem. I'm as quick as ever."

"Oh? Then what brings you here?" Trumbough stood with his feet a shoulder-width apart. His big hands hung loosely at his sides, loose but ready, as if at any moment he might need to defend himself.

"Hellfire!" Bristoe's grin widened; he spread his rough hands, shrugging. "Money brings me here. What else would? I'm broke and need a stake to get me on down the trail." He looked Trumbough up and down. "You do want me to get on down the trail, don't you?"

"I can't shell out to you every time the bottom drops from under you," said Trumbough. Yet, even as he spoke, his right hand slipped into his trouser pocket. "Aren't you able to support yourself? Don't you work?"

"Sure," said Bristoe. "I always was a good gun hand, don't you recall? Trouble is, I got this problem with my elbow. It affects my shooting." He rubbed his right elbow as Trumbough looked on.

Catching his meaning, Trumbough said in disgust, "You're a drunk, is what you're telling me."

Bristoe laughed. "It's a fact—shooting and drinking don't mix. But I just can't seem to do one without the other anymore," he said. "Nobody likes hiring a drunken gunman. Would you?"

Trumbough didn't answer. Instead, he said, as he drew a roll of dollar bills from his pocket and licked his thumb, "If you don't sober up, I suspect whiskey will soon kill you, one way or the other. But that's your derision to make."

"Yeah, that's the same thing some fellow told me last night in the saloon here ... some sort of preacher, I guess he was. Said he was kicking the bottle himself. Kept a glass of whiskey in front of him while he preached at me. Kind of funny I thought." Bristoe chuckled. "Said he wanted to pray for me, you believe that?"

"That was Jarvis Hicks, it sounds like," said Trumbough, counting out bills on the thick money roll. "You might do well to listen to him."

"I drink to forget the war," said Bristoe, watching greedily as Trumbough counted out the crisp new bills. His voice lowered secretively. "We both know how bad war memories can be."

When Trumbough made no response as he peeled back a hundred dollars from the roll, Bristoe added, "Don't forget now, the more money I get, the farther I can get from here."

Trumbough had stopped peeling back the bills. But while considering Bristoe's words, he stared at him for a second, then peeled off two more twenties. "Here, make good with it .... That's the last you'll ever get from me." Trumbough shoved the money in Bristoe's hand.

As Bristoe folded it and put it away, Trumbough turned, walked quickly to the counter, reached out to the teller, and took the pistol from his hand. He walked back to Bristoe, twirling the Colt in front of him, discreetly keeping Gerald Bratcher from seeing him do it.

When the Colt stopped twirling, the barrel was less than an inch from Bristoe's belly. Looking down at it, Bristoe saw that it was cocked, and that Trumbough's finger was across the trigger. Then, Trumbough smoothly uncocked it, flipped it sideways, and shoved it down into Bristoe's holster.

"Don't ever come back here, drunk or sober," Trumbough said, his voice louder, and Gerald Bratcher heard his threat. Trumbough's hand pulled open the lapel of his suit coat, just enough to show Bristoe the handle of the pistol he wore in a shoulder harness. "Don't forget, I've got war memories, too."

"You're threatening me?" Now Dan Bristoe's voice also rose. But he responded with a harsh laugh. Looking past

Trumbough, Bristoe said to Gerald Bratcher, "Hear that, boy? Your boss here just threatened my life." His eyes flashed back to Trumbough.

"Don't ever try pushing me again, *Mister Trumbough*," he said, giving Victor Trumbough's name sarcastic emphasis. "You've only been showing the good folks of Halston the smiling side of your face. You don't want me telling these people what your other side looks like."

Gerald Bratcher listened and watched, wide-eyed.

"You're drunk and crazy, Bristoe. Now get out!" Victor Trumbough stalked forward threateningly.

Dan Bristoe was forced backward, yet he only gave up ground a step at a time, his hand poised near his pistol. "I'm going, Trumbough!" Bristoe pointed a stiff finger. "But don't ever threaten me again unless you stand ready to make it good. I'm leaving here come morning on the trail west. If you've got something to settle with me, you know where to find me."

After Bristoe left, slamming the door behind him, Victor Trumbough stood in the middle of the floor, staring after him for a moment, his big fists clenched at his sides. When he turned and walked back to the counter, Gerald Bratcher stood stunned, having never heard his boss raise his voice to anyone before. Trumbough trembled with rage. Without looking Gerald Bratcher in the eyes, he said, "I have some things to take care of tomorrow, Gerald. If you'll come in early, I'll help you get the day set up before I leave."

"Yes, sir, Mister Trumbough," the clerk said. "I'll get here bright and early." He paused for a moment, then said, "Sir? You're not going out to meet him in the morning, are you?"

"What?" Trumbough hadn't given Bristoe's challenge another thought.

"He just said he'd be on the west trail tomorr—"

"No, of course not," said Trumbough, cutting the clerk off, dismissing such a notion. "The man is a drunkard on his last legs. I shouldn't have said anything he could take as a threat. Forget what you heard, Gerald. It was an ugly incident. Nothing more will come of it."

"Yes, sir, of course, sir," said Gerald.

CHAPTER 10

Carlos the Snake slipped into Halston late at night through a back alley. On his way to town, he'd searched out the body of the man he shot and realized that it wasn't the ranger. Maples's body had been dragged over to the side of the trail and thinly covered with sand and a few rocks someone had scraped together. His name had been crudely carved onto a scrap of deadfall juniper that stood jammed down between two rocks. It didn't take but a moment for Carlos to get the picture.

There were three sets of hoofprints coming from town. Two of the sets were large—a wagon team, Carlos concluded. He'd thought immediately of the big expensive hearse sitting out there on the desert floor. The third set of prints belonged to a saddle horse.

Carlos could almost visualize the ranger stepping down on this spot, finding this man's body on his way out to bring in the hearse. He could be mistaken about it being the ranger dragging the body from the trail, but he didn't think so. Either way, Carlos had to ride on into Halston. He had unfinished business here. Before coming to town, he'd stopped and slipped the big rifle, saddle boot and all, beneath a large rock just off the trail.

The streets of Halston were empty except for a couple of drunken buffalo hunters who stood arguing over a whiskey bottle. From the glow of light above batwing doors of the Roi-Tan Saloon, Carlos heard the tired sound of a late-night piano. He veered his horse to the hitch rail and stepped down, taking a guarded glance back and forth along the dirt street.

Vengeance

Carlos saw only one drinker at the bar when he stepped inside. The man stood leaning against the bar with his shoulders slumped forward above a shot glass and a half-full bottle of rye whiskey. In a rear corner, a piano player sat bowed low over the keyboard, playing a slower version of "The Rose of Alabama." The bartender, seeing the newcomer flash a glance at the piano, called out to the piano player, "Ed, why don't you let that thing cool off a spell? Ain't nobody wants to hear music this time of night—nobody with any sense anyway."

The piano player nodded with a mouthful of short cigar and softened his playing, but still didn't stop. "The man loves his work, I reckon," the bartender said, giving Carlos a shrug. "What can I get for you, stranger?"

Carlos looked the lone drinker up and down as he took off his gloves and shoved them behind his gun belt He noted the salt-and-pepper beard stubble, the run-down boots, the worn, but well cared-for Colt slung low in a tied-down holster. "Same as he's having," said Carlos. "This round is on me."

The lone drinker turned his bloodshot eyes to Carlos and said in slurred voice, "No, you don't, mister. I pay for my own ... and yours, too." He looked at Carlos with an expression of drunken contempt. "This a celebration night for me." He picked up his shot glass and tossed back a gulp of rye.

"You heard him, stranger," said the bartender, setting a shot glass in front of Carlos and filling it from the lone drinker's bottle. "Never argue with a man who's celebrating, I always say." The bartender sounded tired of dealing with drinkers all day.

"Much obliged then," Carlos said to the man, raising the glass in a loose salute. He drank the shot in one deep swallow and set the glass down. "What are you celebrating?" he asked.

The drinker gestured for the bartender to refill both glasses, saying, "Keep 'em coming, Rudy." Then he looked at Carlos and added, "I'm celebrating getting out of this shit-hole of a town, is what I'm celebrating."

He passed a cold glance at the bartender. "I've only been here a few days, but I hate every rotten sonuvabitch I've met here so far. If the world was a pig, this town would be its hind end." He tossed back his drink in affirmation. The bartender rolled his eyes upward in contempt and moved away, wiping a bar towel in a wide circle atop the bar.

Seeing the bartender's reaction, the drunk called out, "I hate everybody here except ole Rudy." He poured his glass full, sloshing rye over onto the bar, then raised the dripping glass toward the bartender. "Here's to you, Rudy Mackintosh! The best barkeep in town."

"Yeah, yeah." The bartender waved him away. "Here's to you, too, Dan Bristoe, the best *drunk* in town."

The man roared in drunken laughter, then tossed back his drink, not at all offended.

"Bristoe?" Carlos turned his full attention to the man, now that he knew what he'd already suspected. "You're not *the* Dan Bristoe are you? Dan Bristoe the gunfighter?"

Bristoe wiped the back of his hand across his lips, then let his hand drop near his pistol butt. "If I am, what of it?"

"Whoa now," Carlos said, smiling, spreading his hands in a show of peace. "I have nothing but respect for you, sir. In fact, I came all the way here looking for somebody like yourself, if your gun's for hire, and you want to make some serious money."

"Big money, ha!" Bristoe scoffed. He pulled out a wad of money from his shirt pocket—money from Victor Trumbough—and flashed it back and forth. "Do I look like I'm hurting for cash? This is money earned for straightening out a few cattle rustlers up in the high country. They won't be doing any more cross-branding. You can count on that." He gave Carlos a drunken wink. The bartender murmured something sarcastic under his breath and shook his head. He slung the bar towel over his shoulder and walked farther away, leaving the two alone at the bar.

"In that case," said Carlos, keeping his voice low, just between the two of them, "I suppose you wouldn't be at all interested in these ...?" He let the question trail as he raised a few gold coins from his vest pocket and spread them on the bar top.

"Well, now." Dan Bristoe's eyes perked up, and his voice also lowered, sounding less slurred. "I'm never too flush to turn down shining gold. I always say a man ain't interested in gold is a man who ain't interested in life."

"I always say that, too." Carlos smiled. He watched Dan Bristoe hover over the gold coins. Carlos felt his stomach crawl as he saw Bristoe pick up a coin and fondle it, then lay it down. "I know where there's a fortune in these buried. All I need is a partner I can count on to help me go get them."

Bristoe raised a skeptical brow. "This isn't one of them hidden treasure deals, is it? Because I've known too many men went looking for buried treasure, never found a dime."

"No," said Carlos, "this is a sure thing. I saw it with my own eyes. It's there for the taking."

"Then why you looking for a partner? Why not keep it all for yourself?" asked Bristoe.

"Believe me, if I could I would," said Carlos. "I know where it's buried. It's near the ruins of an old Spanish mission across the border. I could get it myself. But I'd have a hard time getting back here with it. There's too many cutthroats and bandits between here and there. I'd rather settle for half, and have a good gunman guarding my back."

"That's good thinking on your part." Dan Bristoe grinned. He'd been sizing up Carlos. The man seemed to have a sharp hard edge to him. He was dressed for the desert and armed for trouble. Yet, here he was, needing a gunman, somebody like himself, Bristoe thought. He chuckled to himself, hell—some things never changed. "Who are you, mister?" Bristoe asked.

"I'm Andrew Thorp," Carlos said, as naturally as it were really true. "I want to leave come sunup, if you're interested in coming with me."

123

"Not so fast, boy," said Bristoe, trying the word *boy* out on him, seeing how the young man stood for it. *That's how it's done*, Bristoe reminded himself. Push the man a little at a time, pretty soon you let him know who's the top dog. "I need to know some more about this gold, how it got there—how you know about it, and so forth."

"And you will know, sir," said Carlos, catching on to the word *boy* right away, but knowing what Bristoe was doing, and willingly letting him. "First thing tomorrow, when we hit the trail, I'll tell you everything. Then, if it doesn't sit well with you, you can turn it down. How's that?" He watched Bristoe's bloodshot eyes as he tried to consider it. "But you won't turn it down," Carlos tossed in quickly. "I can promise you that"

Bristoe looked him up and down, feeling like his luck was about to change. No more squeezing money from old friends who would pay just to get rid of him. "I'll tell you what, boy," said Bristoe, "let's ride to where I got a campsite." He snatched the bottle of whiskey from the bar and palmed a cork into it. "It'll be morning soon. You can cook us some breakfast whilst you tell me all about it."

"Sounds fair to me," said Carlos. "I'm ready when you are." He raised his drink, finished it, set the shot glass down, and stepped back from the bar.

Outside on the boardwalk, a gunman named Gil Willet had been watching Carlos and Dan Bristoe through the dirty window. Seeing they were about to leave, he backed away. He then slipped down onto the dirt street, unhitched both horses from the hitch rail, and hurried, leading them over to a dark alley, where four more men sat atop their horses waiting for him. "He's coming out, Ferrel!"

Willet said in an excited voice, hitching Carlos's and Bristoe's horses to a downspout on the building beside them. "There's another fellow with him!"

"All right, boys, get out there and get ready," said Nort

Ferrel, swinging down from his saddle. "We'll see where this other man stands before we start this ball rolling."

The other men hurried and stepped down with him, quickly wrapping their reins around another downspout. "I want to be the first to put a bullet in him," said a young cowboy named Joey Earles. "After all my cousin Rowdy was one of the ones he kilt."

"Don't worry," said an older cowboy named Chester McAllister. "They'll be plenty of shooting to go around. Bristoe might be a drunk, but don't forget he killed three of our best men." Chester slid a sawed-off shotgun from inside the blanket roll behind his saddle. He broke it open, took two loads from his pocket, and shoved them into the barrels.

"Yeah, but he ambushed them," said a man named Denver Sipes. "It might be a different story altogether, him having to face somebody straight up."

"If Bristoe's such an easy kill," said Chester McAllister, "how come it took five of us to come looking for him?"

Sipes didn't answer. Instead, he drew a rifle from his saddle boot, levered a round into the chamber, and left it cocked. He asked Nort Ferrel, "Where do you want me, Nort?"

"Stay wide of him with that rifle. Just make sure he don't make a run for it. He runs like a rabbit, I heard. Chester, be careful you don't hit us with that scattergun. Don't know why you brought that damn thing anyway."

"I brung it because it puts a stop to anything and everything that gets in front of it," Chester snapped. The shotgun barrel drifted toward Nort Ferrel as Chester spoke.

"See? That's what I'm afraid of," said Ferrel, nudging the double-barrel away from his stomach. "Be careful with it!" Then Ferrel said in a low voice to the other men, "The rest of you keep a good half circle with me. We'll all take him at once, soon as I tell him why."

"Don't tell him nothing," said Chester. "Let's just shoot him and be done with it."

Ralph Cotton

"No," said Nort Ferrel, "we're not heathens. Besides, I want him to know he's dying for killing some Bar H men."

Chester McAllister shook his head. "Anything you say, Nort. Let's get it done."

When Carlos and Dan Bristoe walked out onto the boardwalk, the first thing they noticed was that their horses were gone. The gunmen had taken position in the street. Carlos, seeing the dark figures gathered in a half circle, instinctively slapped his hand to his pistol butt. At the center of the half circle, a voice called out, "Hold it, mister. This ain't got nothing to do with you! He kilt some of our drovers up north of here. You can step back inside. This ain't your fight."

Carlos let his eyes move from man to man, hearing the distinct click of a cocking shotgun to his right. "This man is a friend," said Carlos. "So, this is my fight." He had no time to consider the irony of his situation. All of a sudden, he was willing to risk his life for that of a man he'd sworn to kill. Carlos was determined beyond reason that no one was going to deny him his vengeance. Beside him, Dan Bristoe stood stunned by Carlos's words. He barely managed to switch his whiskey bottle from his right hand to his left.

"Friend?" said a voice from the circle of dark figures in the street. "Hell, that whiskey sot, back-shooting sonuvabitch ain't had a friend since his ma spit him out in the dirt—"

The voice was cut short beneath the blasts of gunfire coming from Carlos's pistol. Before anyone could respond, a bullet sliced through Chester McAllister's chest, causing him to jerk sideways as he pulled both triggers on the sawed-off shotgun. The double blasts of buckshot ripped through Nort Ferrel and Denver Sipes, ripping Ferrel's head from his body, taking Sipes's left arm off at the shoulder. Yet, even as Sipes turned screaming in the street, blood spewing from his stub of an arm, a shot exploded wildly from his rifle before a bullet from Carlos's Colt silenced him.

126

Dan Bristoe's pistol had just cleared leather as Carlos's Colt worked its way from right to left in one long streak of blue-yellow fire. Gil Willet went down as he managed to get off a shot. But the bullet went wild and blew a hole in the big glass window of the Roi-Tan. Willet let out a loud grunt and collapsed dead in the dirt. At the end of the streak of gunfire, the street fell silent, except for the sound of a frightened horse nickering in the alley across the street. Then a sobbing arose from the dirt street as Joey Earles raised up onto his knees with his pistol wobbling in his bloody hand.

"Bristoe! You bastard! You killed my cous—"

One last shot resounded along the dark street. Joey Earles's body slapped backward onto the ground, hard enough to raise dust. Then Carlos opened his smoking Colt, punched out the empty cartridges, and reloaded as he looked back and forth in the dark. From the other end of the street, a hound began barking loudly. Lamps began to glow above storefronts. Dan Bristoe stood speechless, letting his half-drawn pistol fall back into his holster.

"Did you say you wanted to cook us both some breakfast while I explain this deal to you?" Carlos asked in a quiet voice.

Bristoe swallowed a dry knot in his throat, and said, "It would be my pleasure, Mister Thorp."

"Call me Andrew," said Carlos.

But as the two started to step down to the sheet, behind them Rudy cocked the shotgun he'd snatched from under the bar. "Both of you hold it right there!" Rudy said, his voice shaky, but resolved. "You ain't going nowhere till the sheriff gets here."

"Hellfire, Rudy," said Bristoe, "it was a fair fight. You know it was. We walked out here. They called us down."

"I know it was fair," said Rudy, "but damned if you're walking away leaving this mess for me to explain!"

"You see where I put the last man who pointed a shotgun at me," said Carlos.

127

"Yep, but I've felt lucky all day," Rudy said. He leveled the shotgun, taking aim from four feet away.

"Everybody freeze!" Sheriff Boyd Tackett's voice boomed as he came to a slippery halt in the blood-slick street. "Hands in the air, all of you! Rudy! Shotgun on the ground! Let's move, boys! I ain't in no mood for it!"

"It was a fair fight," Carlos said over his shoulder.

"It always is!" Tackett shouted. "Now raise your hands, or I commence shooting!"

Dan Bristoe eased his hands upward, still holding the whiskey bottle, saying to Carlos, "Go on, Andrew. He'll see we ain't to blame here!"

"That's right, mister," said Sheriff Tackett. "If you ain't in the wrong, I'll soon know it, and you'll be on your way."

"He's telling the truth, Sheriff," said Rudy. "It wasn't these men's fault. I watched them walk out, then I heard the shooting. This bunch was waiting for them. I heard one say Bristoe here killed his cousin."

"Is that right, Dan Bristoe?" Tackett asked, stepping forward, taking the Colt that Carlos let dangle on the thumb of his upheld hand. "You've shot somebody else's cousin? Seems like that was why those boys tried to kill you over in Summit when I was sheriff there."

Lifting Bristoe's Colt from his holster, Tackett noted that the barrel was cool. It hadn't been fired. But Tackett wouldn't mention that right now.

Bristoe shrugged. "Cousins are a problem in my occupation."

Tackett turned, facing Carlos and gestured for him to lower his hands now that the Colt wasn't in them. "What about you, mister? Whose cousin did you kill?"

"He's my partner," Bristoe butted in. "Name's Andrew Thorp. I'm lucky he was with me, too. Look out there ... imagine what that scattergun would have done to me."

Tackett's gaze went across the grisly scene in the street. "I can see it." He turned and stepped down from the boardwalk.

Behind him, Jarvis Hicks came running, with a lantern held above his head. Behind Jarvis, other men came running, some shoving their nightshirts down into their trousers. "Everybody stay back!" Tackett warned. "Especially if you're barefoot! You don't want to step in this mess."

"Oh, no!" Jarvis Hicks said, stooping down over Nort Ferrel's headless corpse. "This one never knew what hit him! His whole head's gone ... nothing left but a streak of bone and—"

"Shut up, Jarvis, we can see!" Tackett shouted. "If you want to help, some of you men get busy and get these bodies out of the street before sunup. This looks bad on Halston, something like this happening. At least keep all the womenfolk from having to see it."

"What you mean, Sheriff," said Loman Gunderson, limping up behind the gathering crowd on a hickory walking cane, "is that this looks bad on you." He pointed his cane for emphasis. Then he said to the townsmen, "Remember all this when it comes election time. This is what happens when you get the wrong man wearing a badge."

"What are you doing back in town, Gunderson, looking for a bullet in your other foot?"

"I came to town last night, if it's any of your business, Tackett."

A big man with a slick shaved head stood beside Loman Gunderson. Using his cane as a pointer, Gunderson tapped the man on his thick chest. "Everybody listen up! This is Dutch Cull. He's the man I'll personally be backing for sheriff come election."

"Damn you to hell, Gunderson," said Sheriff Tackett. "Go somewhere and hang yourself." He looked at Dutch Cull. "Howdy, Dutch, I haven't seen you since Tombstone."

"I liked to have died in Tombstone," the big man said. He gestured a thick hand toward Loman Gunderson as he continued speaking to Tackett. "No hard feelings here, I hope."

"Naw," said Tackett, "I don't blame you for Loman Gunderson's actions. This blowhard idiot can't see when it's time to back off and take his losses. Did he tell you who shot him, and why?"

"Nope," said Dutch Cull.

"It was that young ranger who has become a friend of mine, the one who killed all the Junior Lake Gang."

"You mean Sam Burrack?" Dutch Cull said, his voice turning a bit wary.

"Yep, that's who I mean. Gunderson got feisty wanting to lynch a man—Sam aired his boot out for him."

"Naw-sir," said Dutch Cull, giving Gunderson a strange look, "he never mentioned that at all."

"I bet he didn't," said Tackett. "This is one of those small-town problems that an outsider ought to avoid getting involved in if he can. Do you get what I'm saying, Dutch?"

"I'm starting to," the big man said.

"All right then, good luck to you," Tackett said, ending his conversation with Dutch. He turned back to Bristoe and Carlos, who still stood waiting on the boardwalk. "Both of you come on. Let's go to my office where we'll have some privacy. Tell me who these men are and what this was all about. Then you're free to leave." He looked at Rudy, who'd backed into the door of the Roi-Tan. "You come along, too, Rudy, you're the witness."

"Aw hell, Sheriff," Rudy protested, "you know how thirsty a crowd gets, something like this happens. I'll lose money!"

"Not as much as you'll lose if I close you down, drag you by the ear, then stall you around all day before I get to you." He motioned Rudy forward with his hand. "Now come on like you've got some sense .... I'll have you back here before they get the street cleaned."

CHAPTER 11

Like the rest of the sleeping townsfolk, Darcy Tennison had been awakened by the exploding gunfire. She had rolled out of her bed, gripped by fear. Her thin cotton sleeping gown trembled with her racing heartbeat. She could not force herself to dress and go see what the shooting was about. Instead, she'd remained in her room above the funeral parlor cringing in terror beside her bed, her hands clasped to her ears, for what seemed like a long time.

Then, long after the gunfire had ceased, she slowly summoned up her courage and coaxed herself to her feet. She picked up her housedress, lying across the chair beside her bed, and put it on. Without knowing what had gone on outside, Darcy knew that in all likelihood, she would soon hear a knock on her door, and her services would be called upon. She was right. By the time the knock came, she had composed herself and was ready for it. Earl Blume had told her that much of her business would arrive in the middle of the night, at her back door.

Darcy heard the second knock as she descended the stairs with a glowing lamp raised in her hand.

"I'm coming," she called out, her voice sounding shrill and shallow to her as she hurried along the hall to the preparation room.

Before entering the preparation room, she turned the wick high and bright in the lamp. "Who is it?" she stopped long enough to ask before opening the back door.

"It's me and Little Herman, ma'am," Earl Blume said, his voice sounding excited. "We brought in some business."

He continued as Darcy opened the door and looked into the two stark-white faces in the harsh glow of the lamplight. "Miss Darcy, we got enough work to keep us busy all night. There's five dead men here!"

"Five! My goodness, what an earth ...?" Her voice trailed off.

"A gunfight that you wouldn't believe, ma'am!" said Earl. "Two of them was shot by their own man!"

Darcy didn't want to hear the details. She saw the dried blood on Earl and Little Herman's shirts and hands—two ghouls in front the night's hunt.

Earl jerked his head toward the buckboard wagon in the alley behind him. Dusty boots stuck out from the rear of the buckboard, their toes pointed upward at the black sky. "The town pays two dollars a head for cleaning these wretches up and putting them in the ground." He offered a tired smile. "I ran for a buckboard soon as I heard the shooting. It pays to be on your toes, I always say."

As Darcy heard the excitement in Earl's voice, she also noted how his hands quivered ever so slightly. Beside him, Little Herman looked blank and grim, a smear of dried blood on his chin. "My, my," Darcy said, turning, setting the lamp on a bare table, "then let's get them inside." She stepped over to where a canvas stretcher stood folded, leaning in the corner.

"Here, ma'am, let me and Herman get that," said Earl. "You hold the lamp for us, if you would please."

Without responding, Darcy stepped back and picked up the lamp again. She followed the father and son outside and watched them spread the stretcher out on the ground beneath the rear of the buckboard. "I better prepare you for this, ma'am," Earl said, seeing Darcy turn and raise the lamp for a closer peep at the dead men. "One of them took a close-up shotgun blast that—"

Darcy's gasp at the sight of the headless corpse caused Earl to cut his words short. "Sorry, Miss Darcy, I should have warned you sooner," Earl said. "This is what the sheriff was trying to explain to you about the condition some of these folks are in. It's not a pretty business, I'm afraid. I suppose if it were, everybody would be doing it. You go on back inside, ma'am. Little Herman and I will make out."

"Nonsense, I'm fine," Darcy said, quickly collecting herself and taking a step back from the buckboard. "I must accustom myself to this sort of thing. This is how I make my living now."

"Yes, ma'am," said Earl. "I use to have to tell Little Herman the same thing back when he was reluctant to handle the dead. But look at him now. He just wades in and takes a-hold, like an old hand at it."

"Yes, I see," said Darcy.

As Earl and Little Herman dragged the first body from the buckboard and laid it on the stretcher, Darcy looked at the smear of blood left behind on the rough wagon planks. It dawned on her that at a time like this, the business she ran was nothing more than a street-cleaning service.

"I'll go set up one of the folding preparation tables," she said, "so we can both work on one at the same time."

"You just as well set up two more," said Earl. "Little Herman will do as well as we would on this job. These men are going straight into the boxes anyway. The sheriff didn't say if he'd want their photographs or not. Maybe you'd like to go ask him while Herman and I take care of the cleaning up," Earl suggested.

"No, but thank you, Earl," said Darcy. "I'm sure there's no hurry. I'll go ask after we get things in order here."

Once the other two preparation tables were in place, Earl Blume locked both the front and rear doors to the room. Because of Darcy's presence, Earl discreetly gathered three towels and draped them across the corpse's privates before the cleaning began. Both he and Darcy blushed and avoided one another's eyes until his covering task was finished. Then, in moments, the three were busily at work, each with a bucket of soapy water and a washcloth in his or her hand.

Little Herman stood on a chair in order to reach the grisly blood-streaked body of Denver Sipes, with its arm and part of its shoulder missing. Darcy stepped back from her task and wrung out her wet rag, inspecting the scrubbing she'd just given Nort Ferrel's headless corpse. She ignored the queasiness in her stomach as she looked at Earl and Little Herman. They went about their work methodically, their wet washcloths moving in slow, circular motions against soft dead flesh.

With the windows open to let in fresh air, the cool breeze brought with it insects from the night, which circled and lighted on the dead until the swat of Herman or his father's hand sent them circling away. Darcy watched a blowfly swing in from above the glowing lamp. For a moment, it crawled across the dead face of Denver Sipes, then careened upward and landed on Little Herman's lip. The boy blew it away, wiped a wet hand across his lips, and continued working.

Suddenly, Darcy had difficulty breathing the smell of strong soap mixed with the coppery odor of blood. She felt the room tilt slightly, and she said in a weak voice, "Perhaps now I'll go ask the sheriff about photographs."

Seeing the flushed look on Darcy's face as she walked quickly to the door, Earl Blume dropped his washrag into the bucket and followed her out into the hall. "Miss Darcy, are you all right?" he asked.

Darcy noted the slight quiver in his voice as she turned facing him. "Yes, Earl .... I just needed to get out and get some fresh air. It's almost dawn. I'm sure the sheriff won't mind me dropping by."

"No, ma'am," said Earl, "Sheriff Tackett won't mind at all. Most likely he's spent the rest of the night questioning the men who did this shooting."

"Very well then," said Darcy. "I won't be long."

"Uh, Miss Darcy," said Earl as she hurried toward the front door.

"Yes, Earl?" she asked, her hand on a shawl hanging on a coat tree beside the door. She took the shawl, shook it out, and swung it around her shoulders.

"I just want to tell you, ma'am, that it's not unusual for a person to feel like you do ... about handling a mess like we've got back there."

"Oh?" Darcy stood listening, sensing there was more to come.

"Yes, ma'am .... The fact is, I still get real nervous and ill from it myself sometime."

"Just sometime, Earl?" Darcy asked.

"Well, to be honest, ma'am," he continued, "I never have gotten real comfortable doing this work the way some people do. Little Herman doesn't seem to mind at all ... neither did Maximus. But some of us are cut out for this kind of work, some aren't. I just wanted you to know, you'll be all right here. You get used to it, sooner or later."

Darcy searched his eyes for a second until Earl was forced to look away from her gaze. "Earl," she said gently, "if this makes you ill and nervous, why on earth have you continued?"

Earl blushed a bit, saying, "Miss Darcy, sometimes a person has to force themselves to do something they're not cut out for ... just to make a living. I came here needing a job to support me and Little Herman. This was the only one open. So I took it. I try to make myself adjust to it. Sometimes it causes me troubled dreams and keeps me nervous and jumpy all the time. But no job is perfect." He offered a forced smile.

"I see," Darcy said. "Perhaps we can talk more about this later on." Then, dismissing the subject for the time being, she turned and left.

She took her time walking toward the dim lamp glow in the window of the sheriff's office She breathed the cold morning air in deep, cleansing her lungs of the smell of blood, of soap, and of the loss of urine and excrement that sudden death had brought upon its victims. How in the world would she ever get used to this? How did anybody get used to this and somehow manage to keep their sanity? *More importantly,* she asked herself, *why on earth would anybody want to force himself to get used to it?*

She pictured Earl Blume's, quaking lips, his strained smile as he'd tried to tell her everything was going to be all right. *Yes,* she thought, *this kind of encouragement from a man whose hands trembled constantly as if stricken by the palsy.* Well, she didn't know how much more of this she could take. One thing was for sure, she wasn't going to spend her life doing something she had to force herself to do. She would close the business and board up the building first.

Darcy's thoughts were so distracted by the dead and the dilemma they'd brought to her life, that she failed to knock first on the sheriff's door before stepping inside. She realized what she'd done only when she looked around and saw the three pairs of eyes looking at her. "Excuse me," Darcy said quickly, "I didn't mean to—" She stopped short and started to back out the door.

"No, please, come in, Miss Darcy," said Sheriff Tackett, flagging her inside with his hand as he stood from the edge of his desk. "We're finishing up here. Have a cup of coffee. I'll be right with you."

Seeing that the sheriff wasn't going to introduce the two men standing in front of his desk, Darcy thanked him a with a tight nod of her head and walked to the coffeepot on the stove. She listened as she poured herself a mug of hot black coffee and stepped away, taking a position for herself away from the men.

Sheriff Tackett continued as if Darcy wasn't here. At first, he'd had a suspicion that something wasn't right about Dan Bristoe's new partner, Andrew Thorp. Yet, after questioning both the men, he found Thorp to be cooperative and courteous to a fault. Knowing Bristoe to be a hired gun, Tackett wasn't at all surprised that these men had come to town to kill him. What had surprised the sheriff was the fact that five men lay dead in the street, yet Dan Bristoe's pistol hadn't even been fired. Granted, two of the men had been shot by one of their own. *But still ....*

Tackett looked the two men up and down, not wanting to concentrate all of his attention on Andrew Thorp. When he'd first begun questioning them, he asked who'd drawn and fired first. Now after an hour and half of questioning, he asked in an offhand manner as he refilled their coffee mugs, "Which ones did you shoot, Bristoe?"

Before Dan Bristoe could answer, Andrew Thorp cut in. "What difference does it make? Things happened so fast, Sheriff, I don't think either one of us knows who did what. The main thing is, they started it. Now we're alive ... they're not."

"He's got a powerful point there, Sheriff, you've got to admit," said Dan Bristoe. "Now, as much as we enjoy drinking coffee with you ... it's time we got on down the trail. Me and my partner has important business to attend to, and all this coffee has taken the edge off my whiskey glow." Bristoe patted the bottle of rye he'd shoved inside his shirt.

Then he turned his attention to Darcy Tennison, saying, as he touched his fingertips to the brim of his ragged hat, "Besides, I don't like to keep this young lady waiting." He paused as if waiting for an introduction. When none came, he cleared his throat and looked back at Sheriff Tackett for permission to leave.

"Yep, you two go on," said Tackett, realizing that this Andrew Thorp wasn't going to say anything more about the shooting than he already had. Tackett picked up the two men's Colts from atop his desk and handed, them over. "I hope you're leaving Halston, Bristoe. Don't forget, I loaned you some traveling money. Now I expect you to do some traveling."

Ralph Cotton

"I ain't forgot, Sheriff," said Bristoe. Three days earlier, before Dan Bristoe had gone to Victor Trumbough for money, he'd put the touch on Sheriff Tackett for seven dollars to get his horse shod and ready for the road. Tackett had considered the seven dollars a good investment in keeping the peace in Halston.

As the sheriff and Bristoe spoke to one another, Carlos the Snake looked closely at the woman, recognizing her. As soon as his holster belt was buckled, he adjusted it on his hips and said to her in a polite tone of voice, "Ma'am, since nobody is going to introduce us, I'm Andrew Thorp. And who might you—"

"I never introduce men while I'm questioning them, Thorp," Tackett butted in. "Miss Darcy, this is Andrew Thorp and Dan Bristoe ... they're just leaving."

"It's my pleasure, ma'am," said Carlos the Snake, liking the idea that he knew her from their encounter in the desert, but that she had no idea in the world that he was the man who'd come within a hairsbreadth of killing her.

Their eyes met, and although she neither realized nor sensed any recognition of him, Darcy felt an icy sensation run down the length of her spine, so strongly that it must have shown on her face.

"Miss Darcy, are you all right?" asked Sheriff Tackett.

"Yes ... I— That is, it's been a long night. The Blumes and I have been cleaning up the corpses, and I ...." She let her words trail away, not knowing if it was the right thing to say in front of the men who'd done the killing.

Seeing both Bristoe and his partner look at him with questioning glances, Sheriff Tackett said, "Miss Darcy here is our new undertaker ... and the only *woman* undertaker I bet any of us has ever seen."

The two men looked surprised, but only for a moment before Bristoe said, "Not me. I knew a woman undertaker up in Creed. But she become one when she tired of whor—"

138

He caught himself and quickly changed his words. "That is she worked at one of the saloons there, singing, dancing and whatnot."

Darcy's face reddened; she looked down at the floor.

Sheriff Tackett seethed. But he kept his temper in check and said, "Miss Darcy had the funeral business thrust upon her. Some murdering skunk killed her husband—who was a fine man, I don't mind saying. We're putting the word out all around, to help catch the scoundrel."

"Someone killed your husband, ma'am?" Carlos the Snake said in a sympathetic tone. "I'm terribly sorry to hear that. I certainly hope the law brings the killer to justice."

"Thank you, Mister Thorp .... Yes, I'm certain the law is doing all it can."

"That's right, ma'am," Sheriff Tackett cut in, speaking to Darcy Tennison, but giving the young gunman a dark glance. "I can't say that I'll be riding out looking for the killer myself—somebody has to stay here and keep a hand on things. But the ranger, Sam Burrack, is on this situation. Anybody who knows the ranger, knows that he gets who he goes after."

"Is that right?" said Carlos the Snake, taking a strange pleasure in what was going on, listening to people talk about him. "I can't say that I ever heard of him. Must really be something, huh?"

Sheriff Tackett didn't answer. But looking at the way this stranger's eyes had locked onto Darcy Tennison made the sheriff uncomfortable. "Unless you've got something to add about the shooting last night, Andrew Thorp, you two are free to go."

"Sounds good to me," said Dan Bristoe, half turning toward the door. "Come on, partner, let's get our knees in the wind."

But his partner didn't give him a glance, his eyes still riveted on Darcy Tennison. "It's too bad I got to leave, ma'am," he said to her. "I'd love to stay and see if I could be of any help."

"That's kind of you, Mister Thorp .... Perhaps you'll come

back this way soon. If so, I will look forward to welcoming your help most sincerely!" She'd had no idea she was about to say such a thing. But upon saying, it she suddenly realized how strongly attracted she was to this man. It was as if they had met somewhere in the past, though she knew better. She blushed, feeling their eyes on her, wondering what these men must think, her having only just lost her husband. Yet, strangely enough, she felt no guilt, no shame.

Sheriff Tackett stood stunned, more so than Dan Bristoe or his new partner. Carlos the Snake said with a guarded smile, "Ma'am, I will be delighted."

After a silent pause, Tackett shook his head as if to clear it, then said, "All right, you two. I said we're finished here. That means go on, get out of here." He stepped forward and swung the door open. The two men left, Dan Bristoe stepping outside quickly, but his partner taking his time, giving Darcy Tennison a lingering gaze.

As soon as Tackett closed the door behind the two men and heard their boots move down off the boardwalk, he turned to Darcy, saying in a shocked voice, "Ma'am, pardon me for saying so ... but these are not the kind of men you can be sociable with. The least thing said, they might take it the wrong way."

"Thank you, Sheriff," Darcy said, "but I know very well what I said, and how I meant it. I do hope to see Mister Andrew Thorp again."

Tackett just stared at her, not knowing what to say. "Well, I have to admit, Thorp is a polite, likable sort. But don't forget, all you've been through of late, I'm certain your thinking ain't as clear as it ought to be just yet ...." He let his words trail off, not sure of exactly what he meant to say.

"Tell me, Sheriff," Darcy said, filling the silence that the sheriff allowed to come between them, "do you feel a person should spend their life doing something they hate, simply to make a living?"

Tackett let himself consider it, then shrugged and said, "No, not if they have a better choice. Some people have to take what's there for them, I reckon. But if a person has a say in it, I believe they should do what makes them most happy."

"So do I, Sheriff," Darcy said, gazing out through the dusty window into the dim golden dawn. "So do I."

CHAPTER 12

Carlos the Snake and Dan Bristoe found their horses among those the townsmen had gathered from the alley and taken to the livery barn. No sooner than the two had mounted and rode out of Halston, Dan Bristoe began drinking from his bottle of rye and pumping his new partner for more information. After what had happened, Dan Bristoe was as curious about his new partner as he was about the gold they were going in search of. "I can see you were too young to have been in the war," Bristoe said, "so where did you get so damn good with a gun?"

"I grew up along both sides of the border," Carlos said, feeling free to tell this man whatever suited him, now that they were out of Halston. "My father taught me to defend myself as soon as I could lift a pistol." Carlos looked back through the early morning sunlight toward Halston. The town had grown smaller behind them. The more distance they put between themselves and Halston, the better Carlos the Snake liked it. "He was a tough man, my pa," Carlos added, watching Dan Bristoe's eyes for any spark of recognition. "His name was Tom Bannion. Does the name ring a bell for you?" Carlos let his hand drift to his pistol butt, ready in case Bristoe made a sudden move for his gun.

"No, I can't say that it does." Bristoe shrugged and shook his head, giving it little thought. "Any reason I should have heard of him?"

"He fought for the South, down along the border," Carlos said, letting out only a little at a time. "He wasn't a regular though. He rode guerrilla."

"So did lots of folks, I reckon," said Bristoe, showing no sign of realizing they were talking about a man he'd helped kill years ago. "I rode guerrilla along the border myself. But that's all water under the bridge. We lost, they won, the hell with it. Better luck next time is all I can say." Dismissing talk of the war, he asked, "What about this gold? How far are we going to have to go to get it?"

"Not too far," said Carlos.

"Well, I sure as hell hope not," said Bristoe, the whiskey slur back to his voice now after a few drinks from the bottle. "I always say, gold is far more fun to spend than it is to look for." He laughed at his own words, then gigged his horse forward into a trot for a few yards, wobbling drunkenly in his saddle.

He called back over his shoulder, "Come on, partner, you're moving too slow." Laughing out loud, he reined his horse off the trail and toward a collapsed tent lying in the sand beside a blackened circle of stones surrounding a campfire. "Damned if I ain't drunker than a blind hoot-owl all over again."

"Is this your campsite?" Carlos asked. Beyond the collapsed tent, Carlos saw strewn whiskey bottles amid other sordid piles of debris. Above the garbage and bottles, a swarm of blowflies droned and hummed.

"Yep, such as it is," Bristoe said, stopping his horse and stepping down from his saddle. "Climb down and make yourself to home." He staggered a little as he walked over to the tent, flipped up one corner of it, and picked up a canvas bag covered with grease stains. "I've got a quarter of dried elk, some meal for flapjacks, and some beans in a tin somewhere here. Alls you got to do is help me gather some mesquite and get a fire going. We'll eat like kings here in a few minutes." Even as Dan Bristoe searched through the canvas bag, he managed to hold on to the bottle of rye.

Carlos stepped down from his saddle and looked at Dan Bristoe, the man weaving in place, too drunk for too long to remember the taking of two human lives years ago in the old Spanish mission. But Carlos remembered. As he stood watching this drunkard rummage through the canvas sack, he pictured his father and mother as he had seen them that last day. He also pictured himself as a young boy riding terrified away from the mission in a cloud of dust. There was something about the taste of the dust that day that he had never forgotten. He could still taste it if he let himself.

"Why don't you sit down and take it easy, Bristoe?" Carlos heard himself say. "I'll fix us some breakfast." He uncinched the saddle from Bristoe's horse and pitched it to the ground, giving the drunken outlaw something to lean against. "There, now rest yourself, Bristoe. You won't be in any shape to ride if you don't go a little easier on the rye."

"I always handle my liquor," Bristoe slurred, hugging the bottle protectively. "That was my celebration party last night, in case you didn't know it." He staggered over to his saddle on the ground and dropped down against it.

"Yeah? What were you celebrating?" Carlos asked, scraping together a pile of unburnt twigs and remnants in the gray circle of ashes.

"I was celebrating getting out of that pig-patch"— Bristoe chuckled—"and for finding the money to celebrate on." He threw back a shot of rye and wiped his mouth. "It pays to know people across this country ... people who'll put out some hard cash to keep your mouth shut."

Carlos paid closer attention now. "Who do you know in Halston that was willing to give you money, Bristoe?" Carlos asked.

Bristoe spread a sly, drunken grin. "Only one of the biggest, most-respected men in town," Bristoe boasted. "He and I rode guerrilla together back in that war you was talking about. He's still hiding from what he was back then. I just remind him of it now and then, when I run short of cash."

"Who are you talking about, Bristoe?" Carlos asked, his voice a bit demanding.

"It wouldn't be fair of me to tell." Bristoe chuckled again, under his breath. "I don't know when I might need to put the touch on him again."

Seeing the intense look on his new partner's face, Bristoe felt uncomfortable all of a sudden, even in his drunken condition. He'd said too much, he thought. He didn't want to say anything that could put him on bad terms with Victor Trumbough.

Carlos stared at him for a moment as if trying to read his thoughts. Then he said, "It's the sheriff, isn't it?"

"The sheriff? Boyd Tackett?" Bristoe blinked his drunken bloodshot eyes. "What made you think that?"

"I heard him say he's known you for a long time. You might as well tell me, Bristoe," Carlos said, his voice beginning to sound menacing.

Bristoe wasn't about to mention Trumbough's name. So he shrugged, saying, "All right then, yeah, it's Tackett. Me and him rode together .... Why's it so all-fired important that you had to know it?" Something abort his new partner had Bristoe feeling edgy.

"I'll explain it all to you later, *mi amigo,*" Carlos said with a slight smile. "I want you to be sober enough to understand every word."

Bristoe took a long swig from the bottle of rye. "Suit yourself then. I'm going to take a little shuteye while you fix breakfast. Be sure and wake me when it's ready," Bristoe sank down, his back against the saddle, and pulled his hat brim low across his forehead.

"You can count on it," said Carlos.

While Dan Bristoe collapsed into a drunken stupor, Carlos finished building a small fire. He found a blackened skillet beneath the tent and cooked some of the dried elk he'd carved from the quarter of meat. He didn't bother making any flapjacks. He'd decided he wouldn't be here that long. His first thought had been to play Dan Bristoe along for a couple of days, and find out whatever Bristoe could tell him about the men who'd killed his family. But it was clear now that Bristoe's mind was too pickled by alcohol for the man to be of any help. Besides, Carlos kept picturing the face of the young woman back in Halston.

Over an hour had passed when Dan Bristoe felt a sharp kick in his ribs. "Wake up, Galt," Carlos said, standing above him, a halo of harsh sunlight circling his head and shoulders.

"Who?" said Dan Bristoe, shielding his squinting eyes with his forearm. "What did you call me?" His voice was full of whiskey and sleep. He felt another sharp kick.

"I called you, 'Galt'," said Carlos. "That's your real name isn't it? Calvin Galt? That's the name you went by when you rode with Wolf Avrial." As he spoke, Carlos continued planting short sharp kicks in the waking gunman's ribs.

"Hell no! I never went by that name—" His words were interrupted by the toe of Carlos's boot. "Hey, damn it!" he shouted, "Cut it out! What's wrong with you anyway?"

"Nothing's wrong with me, Galt, you murdering snake," Carlos said in a low growl. "Nothing that killing you won't cure." He kept kicking, short and pointedly.

"Hold it!" Dan Bristoe tried scooting out of range, but Carlos stepped forward, still kicking. Bristoe made a grab for the pistol at his waist, but the holster was empty. "Just wait a damn minute!" He threw both hands up in a show of peace. "All right, maybe I was Calvin Galt at one time, but in the war! So what? You're too young to have any grudge with me! I never done anything to you!"

"You killed my ma and my pa, Galt," said Carlos. "My pa was Tom Bannion—you and Avrial's men killed him when he refused to tell you where some stolen gold coins were buried. The coin I showed you in the saloon is one of those coins." As he spoke, Carlos watched the bloodshot eyes for any sign of recognition. He saw none.

"I admit my name's Calvin Galt. But you're crazy as hell if

you think I killed your ma and pa. Far as any Tom Bannion goes, I never heard of him. I already told you that, didn't I?"

"You're lying, Galt. My pa was a hard-riding, fast-shooting Southern guerrilla rider. You couldn't have rode along the border and not have heard of him."

"Boy, I don't mean to dim your opinion of your pa—whoever he was—but I wouldn't know him from a pig in a rut. Every ole boy I ever met back then was hard riding, fast shooting. So that don't make your pa anybody special."

Carlos kicked him again, this time harder. Calvin Galt rolled over onto his side, gasping for breath, his arms wrapping around his stomach. "Make no mistake, Galt, I'm going to kill you either way," said Carlos, lifting his pistol from his holster and cocking it slowly. "Nothing's going to change that. I just figure since you're dying, you might want to come clean ... admit what you did, that you killed my ma and pa."

"Ha! What for?" The drunken gunman spat and picked up the bottle of rye from where it lay shoved into the front of his grimy shirt. "So's you can feel better about what you're doing? Dang it, boy, I've gunned down more folks than you got fingers and toes."

Uncorking the rye whiskey, he threw back a long drink, then said, "God ain't got time to hear my apologies, even if I was of a mind to make any. If you've got killing to do ... get it done. I always figured on going to hell someday. But as far as me killing your folks goes ... I don't remember it one way or the other."

He cast the empty bottle aside and let out a whiskey belch. "So there's all I've got to say on it." He slumped back in the hot sand with a strange smile on his face. "Now do your worst, you sorry sonuvabitch."

The first three shots seemed to hit him all at once, one in the crook of each arm, the third in his right knee. Dan Bristoe rolled sideways writhing in the sand, unable to even clasp a hand to his wounds. But he managed to rise above the pain long enough to curse at Carlos and say, "Damn you! Is that the best you've got? Hell, no wonder somebody killed your pa ... if he was as weak as you are!"

Three more shots exploded, one smashing his other kneecap, the other two hammering him in the chest. Bristoe struggled, his cheek down in the sand, his legs and arms useless. Blood spouted from his chest wounds. He said, in a gasping breathless voice, "That's more like it ... but you're still pretty damn puny." Through a red watery veil he watched Carlos the Snake punch the spent shells out of his smoking Colt and take his time replacing them.

"It'll get better," Carlos said, cocking the pistol, taking close aim at Dan Bristoe's right ear. "I've got all day."

When the ranger heard three distant explosions on the trail ahead, he only slowed the big hearse and listened. But when three shots more erupted, then paused, the ranger reined the team of horses down to a slower walk and stared off through the swirl of heat and sunlight. In the amount of time Sam considered it would take to reload a six-shot Colt, the firing resounded again, deliberate and steady. Sam could almost visualize a man firing at targets, tin cans or bottles. Counting six shots, Sam waited through another pause, then heard six more steady shots.

"Some folks have bullets to spare I reckon," Sam said to the wide sky above him. He slapped the reins to the wagon team and brought the horses into a quicker pace. The ranger picked up his rifle from where it leaned against the seat beside him. As the hearse rolled on, he laid the rifle across his lap.

It was nearly an hour later when Sam noticed the clump of tent canvas flapping in the hot breeze, just off the trail up ahead. High up in the sky, Sam saw the wide lazy circle of a buzzard, and it prepared him. Rather than rein the hearse over into the sand and chance getting it stuck, Sam stopped the team and stepped down with his rifle in his hand. He untied the saddle horse from the rear of the hearse and led it behind him, making sure if something happened, he wasn't going to be left afoot out here in the hottest part of the day.

Walking over to the clump of canvas, Sam heard the drone of flies and saw the dark bloodstains. Above him, the buzzard had been joined by another of its species. Together, the big scavengers swung down into a lower shorter circle. Sam raised his bandanna up across his nose and stepped closer, already knowing what lay beneath the bloody canvas. He reached out with the tip of his rifle barrel and flipped the corner of the canvas over.

"Lord have mercy," Sam whispered to himself, staring down at the bullet-shredded corpse. "I hope you were already dead when most of this happened."

Only one of corpse's bloodshot eyes remained in its socket. The eye stared away at an odd angle. Beneath the remaining eye there was little left of the man's face. The nose and the chin had been shot away, leaving only an open bloody cavity of gore and bone fragments. Sam swallowed the bile rising in the back of his mouth and stepped to the side, looking at the ground where hoofprints led off across the desert floor.

Sam backed away from the macabre scene, took a canteen of water down from his saddle, opened it, and took a sip. Instead of drinking the tepid water, Sam only swished it around in his mouth, then spit it out.

This was the work of a madman, Sam thought to himself, capping the canteen and looping it back on his saddle horn. Waiting for his mind to adjust itself to the horrible sight on the ground, he looked beyond the collapsed tent at the debris and empty whiskey bottles, trying to get a picture of what had gone on here. Nothing came to him. He had a gut feeling that this was done by the same man who had killed the young mortician and pinned the woman down with the long-range rifle.

"Carlos the Snake," Sam whispered, "is this your handiwork? Is this where vengeance has led you?" He stood in silence for a moment, as if expecting a reply. Then he let out a long breath. Regardless of who had done this, Sam knew there was nothing he could do about it now. He had to get the hearse back to Halston.

Sam slipped his rifle back into his saddle boot. He tied his horse's reins to one of the larger rocks surrounding the campsite, then stooped down to his task of gathering the shredded body up in the stiff canvas. Pulling the bandanna higher up across the bridge of his nose, Sam lowered his sombrero brim on his forehead to offer better protection from the swarming flies.

Once the body was wrapped securely in the canvas, Sam took a lariat from his saddle, uncoiled it and looped a turn around one end of the bundle. He tied the other end of the rope to his saddle horn and dragged the body twenty yards to the hearse. When he'd loaded the body inside the hearse, Sam closed the glass windows to keep the flies out. At the rate he was traveling with the big heavy hearse, it would be late night before he arrived in Halston. But he wasn't about to hurry the horses in this heat.

Climbing up into the driver's seat, Sam cast one last long glance out across the desert. He whispered under his breath, still talking to Carlos the Snake, "You're on a tear right now, but you'll slip up soon enough. When you do ... it'll be time to cure whatever sickness is making you do this."

CHAPTER 13

It was deep in the afternoon when Carlos rode into Halston, leading Dan Bristoe's horse behind him. Before riding in, he'd taken the big rifle, boot and all, from his saddle and slid it back beneath the same rock where he'd hidden it the last time before going to town. Now, his shadow and the shadows of the horses stretched long in the falling sunlight as Carlos sidled up to the hitch rail out front of the sheriff's office. He stepped down from his saddle and spun both sets of reins around the rail.

On the boardwalk, Sheriff Tackett stood listening to Jarvis Hicks talk about his newfound outlook on life. Tackett looked relieved to see somebody ride up. Jarvis Hicks had worn him out, talking steadily all afternoon. But upon recognizing Bristoe's horse, Tackett realized something was wrong.

"Excuse me, Jarvis," Tackett said, raising a hand to silence Hicks for a minute. Then the sheriff turned his attention to Carlos the Snake. "Where's your partner, Thorp?" Tackett asked, watching Carlos slap dust from his chest with his hat brim.

"That's what I'd like to know, Sheriff," said Carlos, almost forgetting for a second that he'd said his name was Andrew Thorp. He gestured toward Bristoe's horse. He shook out his hat and placed it back on his head. "Dan got drunk and wandered off this morning after we left here. I went looking for him, but all I found is his horse."

"Most likely he passed out and fell out of his saddle," said Tackett. "Did you scout around good for him? In heat like this, he might have crawled under the nearest shade."

151

"Yes, I did," said Carlos. "But I don't really think he fell out of his saddle. Take a look at this." He reached, out and rubbed a gloved hand down the sweaty horse's withers, then held it up for Sheriff Tackett to see. It was streaked with horse sweat and dark blood.

"Yep, I see what you mean," said Tackett, he and Jarvis Hicks both stepping down from the boardwalk for a better look. "Anyway, I was just speculating. I've seen Dan Bristoe pretty drunk over the years, but I've never known him to fall off a horse."

"Yeah, I know," Carlos said, fishing for any information he could find. "Dan told me you two are old buddies from years back."

Tackett looked a little bewildered. "I wouldn't go so far as to say we were ever friends. We've known one another for quite a while."

"Don't worry, Sheriff," said Carlos, watching Tackett's eyes, "I won't be telling anybody."

"I hope not," said Tackett, "since there's nothing *to* tell."

"We've all got our secrets, eh, Sheriff?" said Carlos, dismissing Tackett's words.

"Look, Thorp," said Tackett, "just so's we both understand one another—"

"Now this looks strange to me," Jarvis Hicks cut in, before Tackett could finish speaking. Hicks rose up from where he'd stooped down and inspected the long streak of horse sweat and blood down the horse's foreleg.

"What looks strange?" Tackett asked.

Jarvis Hicks looked back and forth between the two of them, then for some reason decided not to say any more right then. He rubbed his wet thumb and finger together, feeling the grit of sand in the sweat and blood. "This whole thing, is what I mean." Jarvis shrugged.

Sheriff Tackett just stared at him for a moment, then said in exasperation, "Well ... yes, it does all seem strange, Jarvis.

That's what we were talking about."

"Sorry," said Hicks, stepping back onto the boardwalk out of the sun.

"What's wrong with him?" Carlos asked quietly, keeping it between himself and Sheriff Tackett.

"He's drying out from a long drunken spree," Tackett replied, equally as quiet "Pay him no mind." He looked the dusty young man up and down. "Come on in out of this heat—you look like you could use some cool water."

"Much obliged, but I need to get these horses looked after first," said Carlos. "I'm going to pick up a fresh mount and get on the trail. If Dan's out there hurt, I want to find him. I figure you'll be wanting to ride along with me."

"Then you figured wrong, Thorp," said Tackett. "I'm sorry, but I've got prisoners to look after. Maybe Jarvis here will ride out with you."

Thinking quickly, Carlos said, "No thanks, I don't need one drunk searching for another out there."

"You bet you don't," Jarvis Hicks murmured as he and Tackett watched Carlos walk away toward the livery barn.

Tackett gave Jarvis Hicks a curious look. "What got into you all of a sudden?"

"I don't believe a word he just said about Bristoe," Hicks whispered, still casting a wary eye in Carlos's direction.

"Oh, really? What happened to all that newfound trust in your fellow man you've been burning my ears with?"

"I still mean what I've been saying, Sheriff, but this is a whole different thing. That man is up to no good. I can feel it."

"Want to tell me what it was you started to say a while ago, before you stopped yourself?" asked Tackett.

"There was no sign of any blood on the saddle, Sheriff," said Jarvis Hicks. "Didn't that strike you as odd? Or did you even notice it?"

"Never you mind what I notice or what I don't notice, Jarvis," Tackett said, a bit irritated as he turned to the door of the office. "I've had your mouth yapping at me so much today, I'm surprised I can remember my own name."

"Well, I don't see how something could happen to cause Bristoe to get blood all down his horse's side, yet not get any at all on the saddle, do you?"

Before opening the office door, Tackett turned and said to Jarvis Hicks over his shoulder, "First of all, nobody has said anything happened to Dan Bristoe. The blood could have came from any number of places. Bristoe could have shot an elk."

"You don't believe that, Sheriff, and neither do I," Jarvis said. "That man has done something to Dan Bristoe, and we both know it."

Sheriff Tackett let out an impatient breath and said, "I'll tell you what I know, Jarvis: I know that last night that man killed five men who tried to ambush Bristoe."

"The way I counted, he only killed three," said Jarvis. "Two of them were shot to pieces by one of their own."

"All right then," said Tackett, "he killed *three* men. But he faced five men. Either way, does it make sense that he'd risk his life for Bristoe, then do him harm?" Tackett shook his head. "No, I don't think so. That would be mighty hard to sell to a judge, even if I believed it myself. And I'm not telling you what I believe, one way or the other. A lawman don't go around revealing what he thinks." Tackett opened the door and stepped inside, Jarvis Hicks following him.

At the livery barn, Carlos turned the two sweaty horses over to Stanley Baggs, who in turn handed the reins to young Willie Burns. Willie frowned and grumbled under his breath.

"I'm only leaving one horse here," Carlos said, gesturing toward Dan Bristoe's horse. "You can corral this one for an even trade. Feed and water the roan here. I'll be back for him ... and I'll want a fresh horse for the trail tonight. Are there plenty in your corral?"

"There's nearly a dozen good horses out there to pick from,"

Vengeance

said Stanley. Then, recognizing Dan Bristoe's horse, he said, "I know who this animal belongs to. What are you doing bringing Bristoe's mount here for a livery swap?"

"Bristoe was my partner," said Carlos, taking out money from his vest and paying for Stanley's services in advance.

"What do you mean he *was* your partner? Is Bristoe dead?" Stanley asked, as Willie Burns took the horses and walked away with them.

Carlos looked Stanley Baggs up and down. "I don't know if he is or not. You ask a lot of questions for a stable hostler."

Stanley tilted his chin up at a jaunty angle. "I'm not just a stable hostler—I'm also the deputy sheriff here in Halston. So I ask what I think needs asking." He took a badge he'd cut from a piece of roofing tin out of his shirt pocket as he spoke. He flashed it, then put it away. "A man shows up with another man's horse, it's my *job* to ask questions, mister."

"Sorry, Deputy," said Carlos, going along with the man. "I meant no disrespect But the fact is, I've already told the sheriff that I think something happened to Dan Bristoe. I'm going back out to the desert tonight and see if I can find him."

"All right then," said Stanley Baggs, with an elevated air of authority, "I'll ride along with you, see if I can help."

"Much obliged," said Carlos, not wanting to appear to be turning him down. "But the sheriff seems to think both of you are needed here to watch some prisoners. He told me so."

"He's talking about the Glovers," said Stanley Baggs.

"The Glovers?" Carlos asked. "You mean Stevie Boy and Mudcat Glover? They're in jail here?"

"Yep, Ranger Sam Burrack brought them in. Do you know them?" Stanley eyed him suspiciously.

"No, but I've heard of them," Carlos said quickly. "Some real bad ones from what I hear."

"Yes, they are. But the ranger figured me and Sheriff Tackett could handle them whilst he rides out to bring in a funeral hearse that got stranded out there."

155

"I see," said Carlos. "It sounds like you men have had your hands full here. Don't worry about Bristoe, I'll find him." So that was who the two prisoners were he'd seen out there with the ranger. The Glover brothers. A couple of no-account criminals. They could work into his plans very well, Carlos thought.

"Yep, our hands stay full here," said Stanley Baggs. "Law work never stops. A fellow named Gunderson has half the town down on Sheriff Tackett. I'm the only man here will do anything to help him."

"Is that a fact?" Carlos asked. "You mean your sheriff couldn't even raise a posse if he needed to ... him with a bad arm?"

"It's a damn shame, but it's true," said Stanley. "I'm going over to the jail in a few minutes to watch about those bummers while the sheriff gets himself some supper."

"This town is lucky to have men like you and Tackett," said Carlos. "I suppose the sheriff's an old hand at upholding the law? Probably been a lawman all his life?"

"Ever since the war," said Stanley, eagerly answering any question Carlos asked. "The fact is, Sheriff Tackett was a war hero. So he can handle most anything thrown at him, I expect."

"Is that right, a hero, huh?" Carlos looked impressed. "I suppose he rode for the stars and bars? A good ole Southern boy?"

"Yep, he sure was. My pa rode for the Union though. So would I have, if I'd been old enough at the time."

"I see." That clinched it for Carlos. Sheriff Tackett was the man Bristoe had been talking about. "Then I'm surprised you and the sheriff get along so well ... him riding for the South, you having a Union pa."

"Aw-heck, mister," said Stanley Baggs, "that war is old history, far as I'm concerned. I know there's still some who carry a grudge. But if you ask me, they're plumb crazy, too, after all this time. Let bygones be bygones is what I say."

"Yeah," said Carlos, "I suppose you're right." He leveled his hat on his brow and turned to walk away. "I think I'll get some supper myself while you tend the horses. Just leave the roan and a fresh mount saddled and ready at the corral."

"They'll be ready and waiting, said Stanley Baggs. "If you see the sheriff, tell him I'll be there directly. I want to help him all I can."

"If I see him, I'll sure tell him." Then, without looking back, Carlos said in a whisper, "You've done plenty for him already." He walked out of the livery barn and headed back toward the sheriff's office.

From her front window, Darcy Tennison watched him. She'd seen him lead two horses to the livery barn moments earlier. Now she watched him start back across the dirt street. Her heart raced in her chest.

On her way to the door, she snatched a sun bonnet from the coat tree in the corner. Hurriedly, she put the bonnet on and tied a bow beneath her chin, her fingers shaking with excitement.

As she rushed, preparing to meet the man in the street and pretend it was by coincidence, she chastised herself for allowing the sight of him to make her feel this way. For an instant she thought about her dead husband. But then she quickly pushed the sight of Maximus's face from her mind. She took a deep breath to calm herself as she opened the door and stepped out into the dusky evening light.

Carlos saw her and he smiled slightly to himself. When she stepped down from the boardwalk out front of her funeral parlor, he stared straight ahead as if he hadn't seen her. He even quickened his pace, making sure if she had come out to see him, she would have to hurry, before he'd gotten too far past her. "Mister Thorp?" Darcy called out. "Is that you?"

Carlos half turned, slowing down a step, but not stopping until he made sure he looked surprised at the sight of her. "Yes, indeed, it is, ma'am," he said, stopping now and lifting his hat from his head.

"I didn't expect to see you again so soon," Darcy said, walking up closer.

Ralph Cotton

"No, ma'am. And I didn't expect to be back so soon ... but my new partner, Dan Bristoe, has disappeared on me out along the edge of the desert. I came to report it to the sheriff."

"Oh, my, that's too bad," said Darcy. "I hope he's all right."

"The sheriff feels like he might have gotten drunk and fallen off his horse," said Carlos. "So I suppose I best get to hunting for him come morning. The desert can kill a man real quick."

Seeing the distant look come upon Darcy's face, Carlos said quickly, "Ma'am, forgive me ... I shouldn't have mentioned something like that, so soon after you losing your husband."

"That's all right, Mister Thorp," Darcy said, lowering her eyes for a second as if in respect for the dead. Then, surprising herself, she looked Carlos in the eyes and said, "Maximus and I weren't as close as one might think. We weren't typical newlyweds." Seeing the curious look on his face, Darcy added quickly, "What I mean is—"

"Ma'am," said Carlos, raising a hand to stop her, "you don't need to explain anything to me. I realize that people get married for lots of different reasons."

"It doesn't always have to be because they are head over heels in love, does it?" Darcy asked, at a complete loss as to why she was suddenly confiding in this man, in the middle of a dirt street, in a strange town she'd been forced to accept as her home.

Yet something drew her to this man, something deep and powerful. She felt as if he knew more about her than anyone had ever known about her—knew her in ways no one had ever known her. And she felt as if she knew him from some distant place, where they had only met briefly for a while before drifting apart.

"No, Miss Darcy," Carlos said, stepping in closer to her, looking deep into her eyes, seeming to read her thoughts and to understand them, "it doesn't have to be like that. But you have to admit, that would be a good thing to have happen to a person, wouldn't it?"

158

She didn't speak for a moment. Then she said without pretense or shame, "Who are you, Andrew Thorp? Why do I feel like I've known you my whole life?"

"I don't know," he said softly, "but I feel the same way. I felt it the second I first laid eyes on you."

"My husband—" She stopped, hesitated, then continued. "I didn't feel this way toward Maximus. I know this is crazy, but I've never felt this way in my life."

"Neither have I," Carlos said. "Now the question is, what do we do about it?"

They stood in silence, Darcy reading the question in his eyes. She had never wanted a man so badly in her life. Yet, she shook her head slowly and whispered, "I can't ... it's too soon."

"You're right," he said, "it's too soon. I'm sorry." He took a step back from her, half turned, slowly, still staring at her.

"No, wait," she said, seeing him start to walk away. "Don't go, please."

Now it was Carlos who shook his head. "I have to. We both know we shouldn't be doing this." He raised a hand as if to keep her from following him, then slowly moved away. When he had gone a few yards, Darcy backed up a step, turned, and hurried back to her funeral parlor, having a hard time breathing. Once inside, she leaned against the front door and stripped the bonnet from her head. She stood catching her breath for a moment, letting the bonnet fall from her hand to the floor. What on earth was wrong with her?

After a few minutes, when her knees felt stronger, she walked to the washroom where a pan of clean water sat atop a oaken stand. She scooped up cool water with her cupped hands and held it to her face. She felt feverish. Bowing over the pan, she raised more water in her cupped hand and poured it over her neck. She had to get out of here, that much was clear to her. If she didn't leave soon, she was certain she would lose her mind.

CHAPTER 14

Darkness had crept across Halston by the time Carlos watched Stanley Baggs walk along the street toward the sheriff's office. Baggs held his head high, his tin badge hanging on a string looped around a button on his shirt.

As soon as Carlos saw Sheriff Tackett step out of the office and head for the restaurant on the next corner, he hurried to the far end of the alley, where he'd stood watch from within the shadows. He then ran along the back of the row of buildings until he reached the rear door of the livery barn.

Looking around and not seeing the other hostler, Carlos moved quickly into the corral. He threw two dusty saddles atop two rangy-looking livery horses and led them to where Stanley Baggs had left Carlos's horses tied outside the corral. Baggs had fed, watered, and rubbed down Carlos's big roan. The roan appeared rested and ready, in spite of its hard day in the desert heat. Beside the roan, Carlos inspected the fresh livery horse Stanley had saddled for him. The animal was a big black gelding that looked fit enough. Carlos gathered the reins to all four horses and led them to a hitch rail behind the sheriff's office.

Inside the sheriff's office, Stanley Baggs sat on a wooden stool directly in front of the Glovers' cell. A rifle lay across his lap. He stared at the Glovers, barely blinking.

Stevie Boy Glover stared back for a second, then let out a breath and rubbed the back of his neck in frustration as he began pacing the floor in his stocking feet.

"Lord God! I hate it when he sits there like that," Stevie Boy said to his brother. "It ain't natural! He looks like a corpse with its eyes left open!"

"Yeah, come to think of it," said Mudcat, getting into the conversation now, "or like Uncle Luke after he come riding home fast that night and snagged his chin on a low branch." Mudcat laughed. "Uncle Luke never was himself after that.. He just sit and stared ... sometimes called out the name of that old dog that had been dead for years."

"That wasn't funny," said Stevie Boy, putting on a serious expression. "Uncle Luke couldn't help it. Doctor said he had brain damage."

Mudcat laughed again, nodding toward Stanley Baggs. "Well, can't you see a resemblance? Looks like Stanley here's got lots of headroom to rattle around in."

"I heard that," said Stanley Baggs.

"I don't care if you did hear it—it's the damn truth, Stanley," said Mudcat. "Look how you're getting on Stevie Boy's nerves."

"Sheriff Tackett said keep a close eye on yas," said Stanley Baggs with determination, "and that's what I'm doing."

"This must be what hell is like," Stevie Boy said. He rubbed his neck some more and continued pacing.

"Stanley, put yourself in our boots for just one damn minute," said Mudcat. "How would you feel knowing you was soon going to hang ... and that one of the last stupid faces you was ever going to see on this earth, was yours?"

Stanley Baggs said, unblinking, "I wouldn't done nothing to get hung for in the first place. Then I wouldn't have to worry about it."

"He's got a point there, Brother Mud, you have to admit," said Stevie Boy. Then Stevie Boy stopped pacing and gave Stanley Baggs a dark evil look through the bars. "But I want you to always remember what I would have done to you, Stanley, if I could just have got my thumbs in your eyes for a couple of minutes."

Stanley Baggs swallowed hard, seeing the crazed glint in Stevie Boy's eyes. "There's no call for that kind of talk. We was just having a conversation here."

"Yeah, but I just want you to think abou—" Stevie Boy cut his words short as they all looked toward the squeaking sound of the door opening. Carlos stepped inside without knocking and walked straight toward Stanley Baggs.

"Hey, hold it!" said Stanley. "You can't come over here. Sheriff Tackett said don't let nobody near the cell! These men are dangerous." Stanley had started to rise from the stool, the rifle held across his chest. But he sank suddenly and dropped the rifle, clasping both hands to his throat. Carlos's hand had streaked around from his side, wielding a big knife. The Glovers had both winced at the sight and sound of the knife slicing deeply, leaving a wide red gash behind.

Carlos stepped back from the spray of blood as Stanley Baggs writhed on the floor.

"Lord, mister," said Stevie Boy Glover, "I hope you ain't come here mad at us!"

"Shut up, Stevie Boy," Mudcat snapped, "can't you see he's here to spring us?" He turned, grasping the bars tightly with both hands, and saying to Carlos, "That's it, ain't it? You've come to bust us loose?"

Without answering, Carlos stepped over to the desk, rummaged through the large drawer, and took out the cell key. Mudcat grinned at Stevie Boy. "I told you, didn't I?"

"Brother Mud, when you're right you shine like a star." Stevie Boy grinned back.

On the floor, Stanley Baggs had ceased his struggle. His body lay limp in a wide dark pool of blood.

"Come on, hurry up," said Carlos, stepping quickly over to the cell door, plunging the key in the lock and turning it. "I've got two horses for you out back. Stay off the black though, he's mine."

"Sure thing!" Stevie Boy leaped through the open cell door,

letting out a muffled whoop of delight. "Thank you, Jesus!" he squealed. But behind him, Mudcat stepped out a little wary, looking Carlos up and down.

"Who are you, mister?" Mudcat asked in a cautious tone. "Why are you doing this?"

But Carlos had already started for the door, his pistol drawn now, waving the two men toward him. "Never mind who I am. Are you coming or not?"

"What the hell's wrong with you, Brother Mud?" Stevie Boy reached back and smacked Mudcat atop his head. "Damn right we're coming along, mister! Let us get our boots and arm ourselves first." Stevie Boy took a quick turn toward the gun cabinet in the corner.

"No, forget the boots and guns! Let's go!" said Carlos, his thumb cocking the pistol in his hand, almost pointing it at Stevie Boy. "We don't have time."

"Whatever you say, mister!" Stevie Boy hurried forward in his stocking feet as Carlos opened the door for him. "Come on, Mud! We're free men!"

But Mudcat, in his haste, slipped in the pool of blood on the floor and slid down right beside Stanley Baggs's body. "Damn it all!" Mudcat felt the warm blood seeping through his clothes. He desperately flung himself to his feet, his wet socks still slipping beneath him. Bowed over, he steadied himself for a second with one hand on Stanley Baggs's chest. In the waist of Stanley's trousers Mudcat saw the bone handle of a big LeMat pistol. He snatched it and shoved it down the back of his trousers beneath his loose shirttail.

"I'm not telling you again," said Carlos, standing at the door, Stevie Boy already outside and headed around the corner of the building.

"I'm coming, damn it!" shouted Mudcat. "This stupid hostler has bled all over everything!" He spread his arms to show the wet blood covering him. "See?" Then he slipped again, righted himself, and raced past Carlos through the open door.

"What the hell's taking you so long?" Stevie Boy hissed, already around back, seated on one of the horses, waiting for Mudcat and Carlos the Snake.

"I slipped in blood and liked to not got up," said Mudcat, snatching the reins from Stevie Boy's hands and leaping on the waiting horse. Beside them, Carlos stepped atop the black gelding, with the reins to his roan wrapped around its saddle horn. Mudcat took a quick look at the big black gelding and the sturdy desert roan. Then he shot a glance at the rangy old horses beneath him and his brother.

"Get moving," Carlos demanded, stalling back, putting the Glovers ahead of himself.

"You don't have to ask twice, mister," Stevie. Boy said, his voice shaking with excitement and gratitude. He punched his heels to the horse's sides and sent it racing along the back alley out of town.

"Me neither," said Mudcat, seeing how Carlos sat staring at him in the darkness. "Much obliged, mister, whoever you are." He gigged his horse and took off behind his brother. Carlos held his horse back for a second, watching the Glovers ride away. Then, before spurring the black gelding forward behind them, Carlos cocked the pistol in his hand and fired two shots into the ground.

"Aw hell, they're onto us!" shouted Stevie Boy, hearing the shots above the thunder of their horses' hooves. "Ride hard, Brother Mud!"

"I'm riding as hard as I can, damn it!" Mudcat screamed, gaining ground on Stevie Boy. As Mudcat's horse came alongside Stevie Boy's, Mudcat shouted, "Stop hollering at me! I'm a nervous wreck already!"

"Where is he?" Stevie Boy asked, not looking back, but staying low in his saddle, racing straight ahead in the darkness.

"I don't know!" said Mudcat. "They might have shot him back there!" He tossed a glance back over his shoulder into the darkness. "I don't see him anywhere!"

"Well, God bless that wonderful man, is all I can say!" shouted Stevie Boy.

Jarvis Hicks was the first to arrive at the sound of gunshots. He ran from the Roi-Tan Saloon to the edge of the alley beside the sheriff's office. He heard the sound of horses pounding away from town, but he also noticed that the door to the sheriff's office was standing wide open. Instead of running toward the sound of the fleeing horses, Jarvis ran up on the boardwalk and into the office.

"Oh, my God, Stanley!" he gasped, seeing Stanley Baggs's pale face with its startled expression, and the pool of blood surrounding him. Jarvis crept over to the body, looking all around, and seeing the open door to the Glovers' cell. As Jarvis stepped closer to Stanley's body and stooped beside it, he heard the sound of running boots coming from all directions behind him.

"In here!" Jarvis called out in a loud voice. "Stanley's dead! The Glovers have broke jail!"

In seconds, Jarvis Hicks stood up amid a throng of townsmen who drew into a tight half-circle around Stanley's body.

"Lord have mercy, look at his face," said one of the men. "Somebody caught him completely by surprise! Poor Stanley."

"Yeah," said Loman Gunderson, speaking to all the men, but keeping his eyes fixed accusingly on Jarvis Hicks, "I'd say poor Stanley must have seen that somebody he trusted had just nearly cut his head off."

"What are you trying to say, Gunderson?" Jarvis Hicks demanded, standing up from the body, and turning to face Loman Gunderson. "That I had something to do with this? You troublemaking, sorry fool! We all know how Stanley was. He was a good man, but he was a little slow. I can see Mudcat and Stevie Boy talking him into unlocking the door for some reason or another. Then they got their hands on a knife and cut his throat to buy themselves some time .... That was the end of it."

165

"Nice try, Hicks." Gunderson sneered. "But if that was the case, why'd they go shooting pistols on their way out of town? Maybe to warn you? To tell you to hurry up and come on?"

"You rotten, pompous—" Jarvis Hicks advanced with clenched fists.

Beside Gunderson, Dutch Cull stepped forward, and stopped halfway between his boss and Jarvis Hicks, stopping Hicks. "You heard him," said Cull. "Now back off before I screw my thumb in your ear."

"Hold it, hold it!" said Sheriff Tackett, muscling his way through the crowd toward the sound of heated voices. He immediately shoved Jarvis Hicks back an arm's length from big Dutch Cull.

Then he turned to Cull, saying, "Everybody simmer down here." He stared into Cull's eyes just long enough to let the big man know he would take no guff off him.

Finally Tackett turned, looked down at Stanley Baggs's body, and shook his head sadly. "Dang it, Stanley. You never harmed a soul in your life. All you ever wanted was to be a peace officer. Now look what it got you."

"Well, that's just real touching, Sheriff," Loman Gunderson said, sarcastically. "But it ain't going to bring this poor idiot back to life ... and it sure ain't going to catch the ones that killed him!" Gunderson looked around at the other men for support, saying, "Gentlemen, it's times like these we need a sheriff we can count on!"

He spread a hand toward Dutch Cull. "Now if Dutch here had been wearing the badge, I doubt if any of this would ever have happened. Someone in our midst, whose name I won't mention"—he paused long enough to cast a skeptical glance at Hicks—"has freed two killers! This is the sorry condition our town has sunk to."

Sheriff Tackett took his forearm out of the sling as Gunderson spoke. Working his stiff fingers open and shut, Tackett called out to the townsmen, "While we stand here jawing, the Glovers are getting away. I'm deputizing every man here who'll ride with me! Gather yourself a horse and meet back here in five minutes. I'll pass out rifles to those of you who have none."

"Save your breath, Sheriff," said Gunderson, "nobody here's foolish enough to ride with you." He looked around at the crowd. "See, men ... when we wanted to hang a no-account snake, he stops us, even allows his friend the ranger to assault me with a pistol. Now that he needs us to go out and do his job for him, it's a different story!"

"Mister Gunderson's got a point there, Sheriff," said one of the townsmen. "Why should we do your job for you? You treated us like a band of thugs when we came to hang Jarvis." He cut a quick look at Jarvis Hicks, adding, "No offense, Jarvis."

Jarvis Hicks seethed, looking at Loman Gunderson's satisfied expression. "Gunderson, you smug turd! If I wasn't on the road to salvation, I'd whip you blind with a shovel handle." He looked at Sheriff Tackett. "I'm riding with you, Sheriff. If the rest of these men don't want to support the law ... let it be on their consciences."

"Thanks, Jarvis," said Sheriff Tackett, "but I want you to go get Earl Blume and our new undertaker and get Stanley looked after. I'll be all right going after the Glovers."

"But you can't leave me here with *this* turd on the warpath," said Jarvis Hicks, thumbing at Loman Gunderson.

"Yes, I can," said Sheriff Tackett. He turned to big Dutch Cull, saying, "Dutch, I know you work for Gunderson, but I also know you're a man of honor. I want your word that nothing's going to happen to Jarvis here while I'm gone."

"You're asking an awful lot, Sheriff," said Cull, looking troubled by such a request.

"That's right, I am," said Tackett, "and I wouldn't ask if I thought you wasn't man enough to keep your word once you give it."

"Just one damned minute, Sheriff!" Gunderson barked. "This man works for me! He does what I say! I say fetch, and

167

he runs and brings back a stick. Keep your nose out of my business!"

"Really? Ain't fetching the sort of trick you train a dog to do?" said Tackett. He gave Dutch Cull a look that told Cull where he stood with Loman Gunderson.

"Go ahead, Sheriff," said Cull. "I'll see to it nobody lifts a finger against Hicks while you're gone."

"What?" Gunderson's face reddened with rage. "How dare you, sir! Consider yourself fired as of this minute!"

"Fair enough," said Dutch Cull, with a faint trace of a grin. "Does that mean I can forget running for sheriff come election?"

"You can forget running for anything in this town, ever!" Gunderson bellowed.

"If you're out of work, Dutch," said Sheriff Tackett, "it just so happens I could use a deputy for a couple of days."

"It'd be an honor," said Dutch.

Tackett stooped down, unlooped the tin star on the string from Stanley Baggs's shirt button, wiped it clean, and stood up. "He'd be happy to see you wear this, Dutch," said Tackett. "I'm in a hurry right now, so consider yourself sworn in."

"Sure thing, Sheriff," said Cull.

Loman Gunderson stood leaning on his hickory cane, watching in shocked disbelief. Seeing the badge pass from Tackett to Dutch Cull, Gunderson exploded. "I'll be double-blue-dog damned! I brought you here to run against this man, not work for him!"

"Life takes strange twists sometimes," said Cull. "Now, if you'd be so kind, step back all of you. Give Jarvis and me some room here. This is still a working sheriff's office. Let us do our jobs."

Loman Gunderson made a strange shrieking sound under his breath and limped through the dispersing men, banging his cane on the floor.

At the rear of the crowd, Maurice Benfield grumbled under his breath. He hadn't forgotten about Jarvis Hicks's shooting him, and he wasn't about to. He didn't care how many deputies were looking out for Jarvis Hicks—first chance he got, he was going to put a bullet in him.

"Wait a minute, Gunderson," Benfield said as Loman Gunderson limped toward the door. But Gunderson didn't stop until Benfield had followed him outside and down off the boardwalk.

"Mister Gunderson!" Benfield called out, louder this time.

"What is it, peddler?" Gunderson asked gruffly, turning on his cane to face Benfield.

"I think you and I have a common interest," said Benfield. "We both want to see that rat Jarvis Hicks with his head full of bullet holes, don't we? If so, sir," Benfield added, hooking his thumbs in his lapels, "then I am your huckleberry."

Gunderson ducked slightly, and looked back and forth at the passing townsmen. "For God sakes, man, keep your voice down. You heard what that big Dutchman said. He's looking out for Hicks!"

"He's not going to stop me from killing Hicks," said Maurice Benfield, "not after what Hicks did to me. I've just been biding my time,"

"Well, then by all means," said Gunderson, "go on and kill him."

"Like you said, it won't be easy, with Dutch Cull looking out for him. As soon as I kill him, I'll have to make tracks fast as a jackrabbit. Traveling costs money, Mister Gunderson. I'm sure you realize that."

"I see," said Gunderson. He considered it for a second, rubbing his chin. Then he said, as if coming to a decision, "Come with me, Mister Benfield. I think we both need a drink."

CHAPTER 15

Stevie Boy and Mudcat Glover had pushed their spent horses until both animals stood on shaky legs, their breath heaving deep in their chests. Still, the two brothers had only gone a little less than a mile from Halston. "Damn it, Brother Mud!" said Stevie Boy, jumping down from his saddle in fear that his horse was about to fall beneath him. "This ain't going to work out at all." He held the reins to the staggering horse, looking at it in disbelief. "I'm afraid these horses are about to have a stroke on us!"

"I bet it wouldn't be the first for either one of them if they do," said Mudcat, stepping down beside his brother, his horse swaying in place, its breath rattling and wheezing. "Nothing against our newfound friend, but damn if he'll ever pick another horse out for me." Mudcat looked back in the darkness as he spoke. "You reckon he really did get shot back there? I ain't seen, heard, nor smelt him since we heard those two pistol shots."

"I don't know," said Stevie Boy, "but something's up. We heard those two shots, then not a damn thing since. That ain't natural, if you ask me."

"Well ... here we are," said Mudcat, with a disgusted toss of his hands, "stuck on the edge of the desert with two horses that should of been dead before last Christmas. Both of us barefoot, neither one of us knowing whether to stand up for a fight, or duck down and take cover."

"Well, we for sure can't stand up to fight," said Stevie Boy, watching his horse falter almost down onto its knees before catching itself. "We ain't even armed! That's something else we need to consider real hard if we ever find ourselves in this kind of situation again."

Mudcat's hand drifted back and touched the butt of the big pistol under his shirt as he listened to Stevie Boy talk. He started to mention the gun to his brother, but before he could speak, the sound of Carlos's voice rose softly from the darkness as he stepped the black gelding forward, leading his roan. "You're sure complaining a lot for two men who were about to face hanging charges."

The sound of Carlos's voice startled Stevie Boy, but only for a second. He recovered and said, "You had us worried there. We thought they must've shot you."

"As you can see, they didn't," said Carlos, moving his horse closer, looking down at them. He offered no explanation for the two shots they'd heard.

The Glover brothers looked at, one another, bemused. Then Stevie Boy said, "So, I reckon that means they're hot on our trail?"

"That would be my guess," Carlos answered in an offhand tone.

The Glovers looked at one another again as Carlos circled his horses slowly around the two worn-out animals standing spraddle-legged in the sand. "Looks like we're going to have to share horses with you," said Mudcat.

"No, I don't think so," said Carlos. "I don't like sharing my horses, especially if there's somebody dogging my trail."

"Don't you sure enough?" said Mudcat, his voice going cold, his jaw tightening, beginning to see that there was something in the works here. "Well, by God, this is one fine time to let us know. Do you reckon you could have found a couple of horses any more ready to die than these two?" He gestured toward the exhausted animals.

Carlos spread a tight, evil smile. "Maybe ... if I'd had more time to look."

171

Mudcat felt his neck burn red beneath his shirt collar. He wanted to jerk the pistol from behind his back and shoot this man dead. But that would came soon enough He needed to bide his time for now. A shot could send the two good horses bolting away in the darkness.

"Not that Brother Mud and myself are ungrateful for what you've done," said Stevie Boy, cutting in, "but you have to admit, these two horses are about as bad as anything—"

"Shut up, Stevie Boy," said Mudcat. "Can't you see we've been put in a jackpot here?" In the darkness Mudcat's eyes cut from his brother back to Carlos. "What is your game here, mister? What does me and Stevie Boy have to do to get ourselves out of here alive?"

"I hadn't really planned on that happening" Carlos said coldly, slipping his pistol up out of its holster, taking his time cocking it. "To tell you the truth, I was surprised you both didn't trip and break your necks from the jail to the alley." He let the pistol barrel rest across his lap, pointing loosely between the brothers.

"That's real funny, mister," said Mudcat. "Who the hell are you, anyway? What's behind all this? If you're going to kill us, we have the right to know!"

"The right to know?" Carlos shook his head slowly. "I always wonder where people get notions like that." The pistol bucked once in his hand and Stevie Boy flew backward, the reins to his horse flying from his hands.

"Brother Mud ...!" Stevie Boy pleaded as he hit the ground.

Mudcat had already made a grab for the pistol behind his back, but Carlos's second shot lifted him backward off his feet before he could swing the gun around in defense. Mudcat hit the ground and rolled once to the side, feeling the impact of the bullet only an inch beneath his heart. The world turned watery and cold in a flash of a second, and Mudcat felt himself drifting off into a far greater darkness than he'd ever known.

Just one shot, Lord! Mudcat prayed silently, concentrating all of his strength on the pistol in his hand beneath his back.

He saw the black figure step down from the horse and walk toward him slowly, only one arm visible at its side. The other arm must be pointed out at him ready to fire another shot, Mudcat thought, his brain closing down even as his mind fashioned the idea. Well, he wouldn't have that.

Carlos stopped only a couple of feet back from where Mudcat lay in the sand. This was all working out just right for him, he thought, squeezing the trigger. The sheriff would track the horses this far. Carlos would be waiting. He would kill the sheriff, leave all three bodies lying here, and ride away. Once his horse's hooves hit rocky ground and shook anyone off his trail, the town of Halston would have to settle for what they found: a dead sheriff who'd caught up to two jailbreakers. What could be more simple?

But as Carlos's pistol exploded, he saw not only the streak of flame lick from his pistol barrel into Mudcat's chest, but the same streak of flame come licking back at him. The shot from Mudcat's pistol lifted him onto his tiptoes and spun him sidelong onto the sand.

There, you sonuvabitch .... Mudcat said to himself as he felt himself sink lower and lower into the cold blackness surrounding him. *That's for Stevie Boy ....*

On the ground, Carlos struggled, blood running between his fingers as he squeezed the wound in his right side. He felt blood running down his back from where the bullet had ripped through him. He tried reaching a hand back to inspect the wound, but he couldn't reach it.

He managed to stagger to his feet, and saw that in the excitement the only horse left standing amid the carnage was his big roan. The others, even the worn-out wrecks the Glovers had been riding, had all scattered during the shooting. Carlos stumbled over to the roan, leaned against its side, and rummaged through his saddlebags. He took out an old shirt and ripped it into long strips. He had to slow the bleeding, or he wouldn't last long enough to do what he'd set out to do.

* * *

Less than a mile back, barely outside the Halston town limits, Sheriff Tackett had heard the shots, and could make no sense of it. His first fear was that perhaps the ranger had circled on his way back to town and run into the fleeing outlaws. But that thought quickly vanished. There was no reason in the world for the ranger to have done such a thing.

Tackett's next thought was that some innocent party had been traveling to Halston from that direction and run into the outlaws. In that case, he dreaded what he would find on the trail ahead. He heeled his horse to a quicker clip, but still at a cautious pace, his eyes warily scanning the darkness ahead.

The first thing Sheriff Tackett found, as he neared the spot where Carlos had killed the Glovers, was one of the worn-out horses lying gasping in the middle of the trail. He stepped his horse wide of the animal and started to go around it, telling himself there was nothing he could do for it. He wasn't about to risk shooting the poor animal and let the Glovers know how close he was to them. Yet, before he could ride on, he heard the horse's terrible gasp for breath and its pitiful whinnying. He stopped his horse and dismounted from his saddle.

"Whatever happened out here, it ain't none of it your fault, is it, ole hoss?" He spoke soothingly as he walked over to the horse, drawing his pistol from his holster. Looking down at the animal, he recognized it as an old buggy horse that had once belonged to the preacher. Before the preacher had left town, he'd turned this horse and another old buggy horse over to the livery barn for safekeeping until someone took pity and offered the animals a home.

"My goodness gracious!" Sheriff Tackett said in a low, soothing voice. "Whoever made a run for it on you surely had no long-range plans in mind." He cocked the pistol and leaned down close to the horse's forehead, shielding his hand behind the pistol hammer to protect himself. The horse tried weakly to raise its head from the sand. But failing to do so, it dropped its cheek back to the dirt with a pleading whimper.

"Sorry, old hoss," Tackett whispered. "Dang it, I hate doing this." Then he glanced away as he pulled the trigger and saw the shot explode in the darkness.

In a moment, Sheriff Tackett was back atop his horse. He took a second to collect himself, raising his hat and running his hand back along his damp hair. "Whew," he whispered, letting out a tight breath. "That made no sense, taking these poor old horses to make a getaway."

He heeled his horse forward, mindful that whoever was up ahead had a pretty good idea of how far back he was. With one horse down, they wouldn't be able to make a run from him. He knew they would be ready for him somewhere along the trail. "Let's get it done," he murmured to the horse beneath him.

Less than a quarter of a mile ahead, Carlos had heard the single pistol shot. While he had no idea what the shot was about, he had a pretty good hunch about who'd made it. He'd hurriedly wrapped the strips of cloth around himself as best he could, and drawn them tight and tied them. He hoped the crude bandage would slow the bleeding until he could get help. Loss of blood already had him feeling weak and dizzy as he lay flat behind a short, single stand of mesquite and listened to the muffled sound of hooves coming closer through the sand.

Fearing the loss of blood would soon cost him his consciousness, Carlos shouted, "Stop right there," as soon as he saw the sheriff ride into view in the pale moonlight. He forced himself to his feet, his pistol raised and cocked at the sheriff.

Tackett watched the man stagger out in front of him as he drew up on his reins, bringing his horse to an abrupt halt. "Thorp?" said Tackett, hearing the slurred voice and seeing the man's difficulty staying on his feet. "It's me, Sheriff Tackett!"

"I know who it is now ... but you weren't Sheriff Tackett back then. Not the day you ... murdered my ma and pa."

"Thorp, what the blazes are you talking about?" Tackett saw the blood on Carlos's chest. "Hey, you're hit. Take it easy. We'll get you—"

"What was your name back then?" Carlos demanded, his voice sounding shaky but determined. "Was it *Vernon* Tackett? Or is Tackett even your real last name? What is it, *Vernon?* Tell me now before I send you to hell."

Tackett's hand had managed to pass close to his pistol butt, yet he could see the man had the drop on him. Now he began to get the picture as Carlos staggered closer, the pistol steady and fixed, in spite of his otherwise weakened condition.

"I get it now," said Tackett. "You're Carlos the Snake."

"That's me, all right," said Carlos. "Now who were you? Back then, when you did what you—"

"Hold on," said Tackett, cutting him off. "If you think I had something to do with your family's death, you couldn't be any more wrong! I never knew your folks!"

"Then ... how do you know what I'm talking about?" said Carlos.

"It's something I heard from a man back in town. He heard about it from a Mexican fellow named Cochio! Revenge turns a man into a mad dog! Don't you think people start hearing about it, when a man goes on the vengeance trail?"

"Shut up, Vernon! You'd say anything to save your hide! Bristoe told me who you are! You can't lie out of it!" Carlos's eyes had turned cold and glazed.

"Bristoe," Tackett said flatly. "If you believe anything Bristoe would say, you're more desperate for vengeance than I thought." As he spoke, Tackett inched his hand closer to his pistol butt, yet he saw little hope of clearing leather and getting a shot off before Carlos would. "Can't you see that this has made you too blind to listen to reason? You're ready to kill anybody—all it takes is the word of a fool to make you pull the trigger!"

Carlos felt himself growing more and more unsteady. He didn't have a moment to waste. "So long, Vernon," he said.

"Wait!" shouted Tackett, making a grab for his pistol.

But Carlos didn't wait, and Tackett didn't get the pistol up in time to help himself. The shot from Carlos's pistol flipped him backward from his saddle and dropped him facedown in the sand as his horse spun and bolted away.

Carlos barely managed to stay on his feet, staggering away from the trail to where he'd tied the roan to a low, scrub juniper bush. The coppery smell of blood caused the roan to toss its head and nicker nervously as Carlos approached. "Easy, boy," Carlos whispered, falling against the horse and grabbing the saddle horn for support. He forced himself up into the saddle and slumped forward onto the roan's neck. "Let's go, boy," he murmured, taking the reins in his hand and turning the roan back toward town. "Halston is the only choice I've got."

Darcy Tennison had sent Earl and Little Herman home for the night, after the two of them had helped her clean up Stanley Baggs's corpse. She'd managed to keep a steady hand and had needed very little help in sewing up the deep gash across Stanley's throat. Earl Blume had even commented on how well she'd done. She'd thanked him and gone on about her task, having to close Stanley's eyes more than once as they continued to seep open while she washed his dead face.

Darcy kept her hands from trembling until Earl and Little Herman Blume were out the back door. Then, she walked very calmly, yet woodenly, out of the preparation room, purposefully keeping herself from looking at Stanley Baggs's pale bloodless body. She went straight to the desk in the office, unlocked it, jerked up the rolltop cover, picked up the bottle of whiskey she'd hidden there earlier, and pulled the cork from it. "Medication," she said to herself. She held her breath, turned the bottle up and took a long swallow.

No sooner than she'd lowered the bottle from her lips and stood it on the desk, she heard the door to the preparation room creaking open. She gasped as she stepped into the hall and felt

177

Ralph Cotton

the body fall against her.

"Help me," Carlos whispered, his voice too low to be understood, "I'm bleeding ... bad." From across his shoulder the heavy saddlebags fell to the floor. Darcy heard the jingle of gold coins. But she paid no attention.

"Oh, my God, Andrew Thorp!" She sank to the floor with him, at least breaking his fall, the two of them coming to rest with his head in her lap. She raised her hands and saw the dark blood. "I have to go get the doctor!"

"No doctor," Carlos said weakly. "Don't leave me. Please... you help me."

"I will, of course I will," she said. "But we need the doctor. He knows more about what to do—"

"Get the bleeding ... to stop," Carlos whispered, his face partially buried in her lap. "But please ... no doctor right now. The law... thinks I killed a man. They might be ... coming for me."

Darcy struggled from beneath him. Seeing the dark smear of blood in the hall behind him, all the way from the preparation room, she gasped again. But then she got a grip on herself and struggled to her feet, the floor slick with his blood. "You're right, we've got to stop the bleeding fast! Here, try to help me get you on your feet," she said. "We've got to lay you down somewhere so I can get to the wound. You can tell me what happened later."

Outside on the street, Jarvis Hicks held a bright lantern up with one hand and waved it back and forth slowly. He and Dutch Cull stood watching the big hearse roll in from the far end of town. A dog bounded from its spot beneath the boardwalk and ran out barking and lunging at the hooves of the horses until Sam reached down with the long wagon whip and cracked it above the dog's head. The dog spun and raced away, seeming to scoot across the dirt with its tail tucked between its legs.

"Thank God," said Jarvis. "It's about time he got back." He began walking quickly forward to meet the hearse, Dutch Cull staying close beside him, scanning the darkened alleys on both sides of the street.

178

Sam Burrack saw the worried look on Jarvis Hicks's face in the glow of the lantern, and he reined the team of horses down as he pulled back on the long wagon brake. "Where's the sheriff?" Sam asked, as if having sensed that Tackett was the cause for Hicks's concern.

"Ranger, you can't believe how glad I am to see you," said Hicks, gesturing the ranger down from the driver's seat. "We've had a jailbreak—your prisoners are gone! Sheriff Tackett went after them alone! We've heard some shooting awfully close to town a while ago. But so far we haven't seen nor heard anything from the sheriff."

Sam wrapped the reins around the brake handle and secured them with a half-hitch. He sprang down from the hearse, walked forward, and ran a safety trace from the horses to a hitch rail alongside them. "And nobody went with him? Why, because they were my prisoners ... no concern of the townsmen?"

"Something like that, Ranger," said Jarvis, "except the Glovers did kill poor ale Stanley Baggs. Sheriff Tackett is having trouble with Gunderson and some of his cronies over everything." He jerked a thumb toward the big gunman beside him and continued. "This is Big Dutch Cull. Gunderson brought him here to cause Tackett some problems come next election—'course Gunderson wasn't counting on Dutch and Tackett knowing one another. Tackett made him a deputy. Dutch is looking out for me while Tackett's gone."

"Mmmm-mmm." Sam shook his head. Then he looked them both up and down and said, as he started walking toward the livery barn, "I've heard of you, Cull. I'd rather have you on Tackett's side than agin him."

"I've heard of you, too, Ranger," Cull replied. "I reckon I could say the same thing. Gunderson left out a few details when he hired me .... I wouldn't have come here otherwise. I want you to know, I'm game for whatever you and Tackett need done here."

"Much obliged," said the ranger, still walking. He cut a

glance toward the funeral parlor just in time to see a lamp in the upstairs window go dim. "I won't bother her with this tonight, Jarvis. But come morning, give her back her hearse, and tell her there's a body in it!"

"Whose?" said Jarvis Hicks, giving the hearse a quick glance.

"Best I can make him out, it's that drunken old gunslinger, Dan Bristoe," said the ranger. "He's gotten pretty ripe in all the heat. Open that door with your face covered!"

"So, you're going after Tackett, tonight?" Jarvis Hicks asked, looking at the ranger, seeing the worn-out look on his face.

"Yep," said the ranger, "if he locks horns with Stevie Boy and Mudcat out there, tomorrow will be too late." As Sam spoke, he looked off to the southwest, where a thin glow of light flickered, then vanished. "I believe we've got a storm moving up from old Mex to boot."

"I can ride with you, Ranger," Big Dutch Cull offered, "but the sheriff did make it plain he wanted me here."

"I understand, Cull," said Sam. "Suppose one of you could rustle me up a cup of coffee? Make sure it's strong enough to float a pistol."

At the funeral parlor window, Darcy Tennison watched the ranger and the other two men walk toward the livery barn. She stood back in the dark-ness of the room and stared through the lace curtains, her hands wet with Carlos's blood. She bit her lower lip in contemplation for a moment. Then she turned, picked up the pan of water from the stand beside the window, and hurried back to the where the only lit lamp in the house still burned brightly, in the preparation room.

"Where's my ... saddlebags?" Carlos asked in a weak voice as she entered the room and closed the door behind herself.

"Don't worry," she said, "1 put them in a safe place." She set the pan of water down on a stand beside the preparation table.

"Did you look inside?" Carlos asked.

"No," Darcy said, too busy with his bleeding wound to look him in the eyes as she spoke, "but I didn't have to. It's full of money. Gold I would have to guess, from the weight and sound of it."

"Yes, gold," Carlos said, hearing the detached way she mentioned it. He laid back and let her go about her task. He had nothing to fear from her. She had no interest in his gold.

CHAPTER 16

Lightning had begun to twist and curl, seeming to walk across the lower planes of the sky as Sam Burrack left Halston on his big Appaloosa stallion. By the time he found the dead horse in the trail, a sheet of rain whipped sideways across the land, shining purple in the dark of night. Sam's first glimpse of the Glover brothers came in a flash of blue-yellow light. His hand had gone to his pistol butt instinctively at the quick flash of light across the faces of the dead men. But then he let his hand relax, stepped down from his saddle, and led Black-Pot around the area, seeing the blood on the ground dissipating rapidly in the sweeping rain.

In the next long flash of lightning, Sam saw another outline of a man lying facedown on the ground. He hurried closer and recognized Sheriff Tackett as he stooped and rolled the body onto its back. "Sheriff, it's me, Sam Burrack ... can you hear me?"

Tackett didn't answer, yet the ranger could hear a low rasping sound in his chest. He saw the blood on Tackett's side and tore his shirt open. The bullet had hit high in the sheriff's right ribs. Feeling behind Tackett's back, Sam could find no exit wound. Sam untied the bandanna from around his neck, pressed it to the wound, and laid Tackett's hand against it. Rain pelted hard and wind driven. "Don't worry, Sheriff, I've got you," Sam said above the rising wind and rain. "You just hang on. I'll get you back to Halston."

"Sam ...." Tackett whispered, as the ranger scooped him up in his arms and stepped over to lift him to the saddle.

"Yep, it's me, Sheriff," said Sam. "Don't try to talk right now." He put Tackett in the saddle and let him slump forward.

"It was him, Sam ...." Sheriff Tackett whispered, clutching Sam's sleeve. "It was Carlos the Snake ...."

"All right, Sheriff," said Sam, "I hear you. Now take it easy, let's get you back to town."

"He killed Baggs, and broke the Glovers loose ... just to get me out here—thinks I had something to do ...." Tackett drifted into unconsciousness, leaving his words unfinished. His clenched hand fell from Sam's sleeve.

But Sam got the gist of it. Carlos the Snake thought that Boyd Tackett had something to do with his family being killed. It figured, the ranger thought, climbing up, seating himself behind the saddle, his arms around the unconscious sheriff, holding the reins.

From what he'd seen of Carlos the Snake, the ranger knew the killer's rage was no longer directed only at those responsible for his family's deaths. Like any crazed animal, Carlos the Snake would grow more ruthless until he was stopped.

The ranger looked around in the rain and the darkness. By morning, the rain would have washed away all of the killer's tracks.

In Halston, through the sheriff's office window, Jarvis Hicks watched the storm blast the buildings along the boardwalks. Signs stood sideways on their chains; metal roofs chattered like an army of snare drums in the dartlike rain. "If he doesn't show in a couple of minutes, I'm going after him," Jarvis said without turning to face Dutch Cull.

But before Cull could respond, or Jarvis Hicks could say any more on the matter, he saw the ranger's big Appaloosa step up to the hitch rail out front of the doctor's office, the stallion stopping with its head bowed to one side against the weather. "It's them, Dutch," said Jarvis Hicks. "The ranger ... and he's got Sheriff Tackett with him."

183

On their way out the door, Jarvis grabbed a rain slicker from a peg on the wall and draped it over his shoulders. The two ran across the rutted rain-filled street, splashing muddy water up around them.

"Is he alive?" Jarvis shouted, bounding up onto the boardwalk beside the ranger, Cull only a step behind him. There was no sheltering overhang above the doctor's office, just a small canvas awning that offered little protection as it fluttered in the hard wind. Jarvis reached out and let the ranger shift some of Tackett's weight to him.

"Yep, he's alive, but he took a slug in the ribs," said the ranger, rain running down from the brim of his sombrero. Inside the dark office, a lamplight blossomed. "He's going to need some cutting to get the bullet out." Sam, Jarvis, and Dutch Cull watched through the rain-streaked door glass as Dr. Elwood Maxwell padded sleepily across the floor in a ragged pair of house slippers, his thin gray hair standing wild atop his head. "Hang on, Sheriff," Sam urged, looking at Tackett's pale wet face.

From a window on the second floor of the Halston Bonanza Hotel, Loman Gunderson and Maurice Benfield watched. The room was darkened behind them. Upon seeing the ranger step onto the boardwalk carrying Sheriff Tackett in his arms, Benfield had raised the rifle to his shoulder and taken aim, simply practicing. But Gunderson had no way of knowing his paid assassin was only getting himself a feel for the rifle. Gunderson had hurried forward on his cane and shoved the rifle to one side. "What the hell are you doing?" Gunderson had demanded. "Are you out of your mind?"

Maurice Benfield hadn't bothered to explain himself. He'd shrugged and laid the rifle aside. "I caught a peek in the lightning. Looks like your sheriff hit a hard spot in the trail," Benfield said, nodding out the window.

"Yeah? Then good for our beloved sheriff," Gunderson

said sarcastically. "I wouldn't mind seeing the whole lot of them rot in hell." Gunderson leaned forward, his nose almost pressed against the glass, trying to make out the figures on the boardwalk below. "There's that two-bit piece of punkwood now," Gunderson said, seeing Jarvis Hicks and Dutch Cull step up onto the boardwalk.

Maurice Benfield leaned down beside him, seeing the lamplight glow from inside the doctor's office dimly illuminate the faces at the door. "So it is .... Want me to put a bullet in him right now, while the ranger's got his hands full?"

"No, wait," Gunderson said quickly, as if Benfield might go ahead and start shooting any second. "We'll get Jarvis when Big Dutch isn't around. Believe me, we don't want Dutch on our backs. He's one of the deadliest gunmen in the west. That's why I hired him." He paused for a moment, then added, "Leastwise, I thought I had hired him." He looked embarrassed. "Who could have known he would turn on me like that? For two cents, I'd have him shot, too."

Benfield grinned. "I'm afraid two cents won't get it done, but I'm sure we could work up a figure we both could agree on if we tried."

"Not if it means I have to give you any more in advance," said Gunderson, his face taking on a firm expression. "I've already advanced you half of the hundred dollars you're charging to shoot Jarvis Hicks for me. You said yourself you never killed a man before. This is a little shaky if you ask me."

Maurice Benfield raised a brow, saying, "Any more shaky than it was dealing with Dutch Cull? As far as I'm concerned, Jarvis Hicks is as good as dead. Just let me find the right time and place where there's no witnesses. If you want to throw this hot-shot gunman, Dutch Cull into the bargain, it'll cost you an extra two hundred dollars—half now and the rest when I nail him."

"Two hundred dollars? My God, man! Are you insane?" Gunderson bellowed. "Nobody is worth that kind of money!"

"Oh, yeah?" said Benfield. "Then you go ask around, see how many takers you get when it comes to killing that gunman. If you really want him dead, two hundred's a bargain .... Of course, if you don't really want him killed, after him making a complete fool of you in public, then I reckon that's your concern."

Gunderson hissed to himself, "Sonuvabitch!" He rubbed his chin for a moment, looking down at the floor in contemplation. Then he looked back at Benfield and said, "All right then, I'll do it!"

He jerked a roll of bills from inside his coat and peeled off a hundred dollars. "But you better make damn sure I get my money's worth before all this is over." He shook his finger in warning.

Maurice Benfield smirked, snatching the money from Gunderson's hand. "Don't work yourself into a lather." He was beginning to like the idea of being a paid gunman, especially since he'd pocketed a hundred and fifty dollars so far, and hadn't yet shot anybody. He was almost grateful that Jarvis Hicks had tried to kill him in the first place, now that he was starting to see an angle in all this. "Besides, what would you do about it ... have me shot?"

In the preparation room of the funeral parlor, Darcy Tennison worked tirelessly throughout the night attending to Carlos's wounds while the storm raged. It was early dawn before Carlos came around. He'd passed out again no sooner than Darcy had gotten him atop one of the stiff wooden tables and undressed him from the waist up. She'd cleaned his wounds front and back and put a couple of stitches in them in hopes of stopping the bleeding. It had worked. When Carlos finally awakened, his stomach was queasy from loss of blood, but he felt stronger than he had the night before. The room was not swaying now. His thoughts were not as jumbled.

Looking around the room, able to think more clearly, he asked himself why on earth he'd come here, of all places. Yet, as he considered it, there was really no place else for him to go. He laid a hand on his chest and felt the soft clean bandages there. It struck him, that had he killed this woman back on the desert, he would have bled to death last night. "Does— does anyone know I'm here?" he asked, his voice still weak, but nothing like it had been before she'd attended to his wounds. He took note of his holster belt hooked on the corner of a chair back less than two feet from him.

"No," said Darcy, her fingers busily working, unfastening his belt "I told you we would talk some more after I got you taken care of. I didn't want to tell anyone you're here without your knowing it first."

"What are you doing?" Carlos struggled up onto one elbow and saw her pulling down his trousers.

"I'm getting these bloody trousers off you," she said matter-of-factly, "before they dry all the way to your skin. The last two men on the tables here, I had a hard time peeling their trousers off." She felt him trying to resist. "Don't worry, I'm getting more and more comfortable doing this ... although it is different, undressing a living person for a change."

"I bet." Carlos looked over at the body of Stanley Baggs on the table three feet to his right. It dawned on him that moments ago, the two of them had been lying here alone, the killer and his victim at rest in the same dark room. He saw the wide stitches in Stanley Baggs's throat, and had to look away. He saw the clean pair of trousers Darcy had draped across her shoulders. She saw the look on his face as he looked at Stanley Baggs.

"Is that the man they think you killed?" she asked softly, as if attempting to keep the dead man from hearing her. She pulled Carlos's trousers the rest of the way off his feet and dropped them to the floor. Then as Carlos watched her, she gathered the legs of the trousers, slipped them over his feet, and pulled up as far as she could. "Raise up some," she said, and Carlos did.

"You didn't answer me," Darcy said pulling the trousers all the way up to his waist. She began buttoning the fly. "Well, is it?" She directed a nod at Stanley Baggs's cold gray body, a hand towel lying across his privates.

Carlos let out a breath and sank slightly on the table. "Yes, it is. I'm not going to lie to you. The law thinks I'm the one who killed that deputy .... They also think I'm the man who killed your husband out on the desert floor." He studied her eyes, gauging how quickly he could reach out and grab the pistol if he needed to stop her cold.

"Oh ..." Her eyes went flat for just a second. Carlos could not determine what effect his words had on her. She looked down and asked him calmly without facing him, "And is it true? Did you kill this poor man?" Her eyes went to Stanley Baggs, then came to Carlos's and fixed there. "Did you kill my husband, Maximus?"

"Do you think I would be stupid enough to come here if I did something like that?" Carlos asked.

"Stupid enough, no." Darcy shook her head. "But brazen enough, I don't know. Maybe," she said. "The ranger said the man who killed my husband is on a vengeance trail ... searching out the men who killed his mother and father. If that's true, I suppose a person will go to great lengths to keep anybody from stopping him. If it was me after my family's killers, I know I would." She looked even deeper into his eyes. "But I wouldn't allow myself to kill innocent people."

"Neither would I," Carlos lied. "You've got to believe me, Darcy. I haven't killed anyone. I have just been in the wrong place at the wrong time. With the law, that's all it takes to get a man accused of something. I was searching for Dan Bristoe north of town when Sheriff Tackett's escaped prisoners ambushed me. They shot me and I managed to get away. I was riding the same trail as them and ran into Tackett. They killed the sheriff and rode away. But believe me, the law is going to accuse me of it, if I let them know I was anywhere around."

"Then what will you do?" Darcy asked.

"I've got to get healed some, and get out of here. I can't let the ranger know I'm here .... He won't even stop to listen to reason, not that one. He'll start shooting the minute he sees me. Will you keep me hidden here until I can travel? Can I trust you, with my life?" Carlos was ready to reach out for his pistol the second he saw the least flicker of resistance or distrust in her eyes.

Darcy hesitated, considering something. Yet, whatever was going through her mind, Carlos got the impression it had nothing to do with whether or not she would keep quiet about his being here. Something else was at work. "I have your word that you didn't kill Maximus? That it wasn't you who tried to kill me out there?"

"Yes, you have my word," said Carlos, "as God is my witness, I had nothing to do with—"

"Where will you go?" she asked, cutting his oath short.

Her question took Carlos aback for a moment. He studied her eyes, then said, "I don't know ... Mexico, somewhere where I can hide until I think it's safe. Why?"

Darcy sighed, leaning forward a little and checking on the bandaged wound, seeing where it was bleeding. But it bled just enough to keep itself clean of infection. "Good," she said, commenting on the wound without answering him. "Let's not wear you out. You get some more rest now. When you wake up, I'll have some hot soup for you."

Carlos watched her turn and leave the room, picking up the lamp as she went. Before she could close the door behind her, Carlos said, "Leave it open a little, please?"

"All right," she said. "It will be daylight soon anyway. Now go to sleep."

Carlos listened carefully until he heard Darcy's footsteps move down the hall, then he reached out, his chest thumping in pain, and tested how quick he could get the pistol into his hand if he needed it. He was in a peculiar situation here. But all he could do for now was wait things out and hope it all went his way. He still had men to kill. He wasn't about to let anything stop him.

In her bedroom on the other side of the large clapboard building, Darcy walked over and picked up a spare travel bag her late husband had left behind when he'd gone to bring her here from Montana. She opened it, turned it upside down, and shook out dust from inside. She walked over to the oaken dresser and picked up a handful of personal items she'd pur-chased since arriving in Halston. Outside the storm raged. She picked up a brush and hand mirror and laid them carefully in the bottom of the bag. Then she touched a finger to the corner of her eye and brushed away a small tear that had formed there.

"Forgive me, Max," Darcy whispered aloud, as if Maximus were alive and watching from every corner of the room. "I just can't stay here and do this."

The storm had spent itself and moved on in the gray hours of morning. By sunup, the streets of Halston were a long shallow puddle of water. The first wagon to try to make its way from the livery barn, ended up sinking a rear wheel almost to its axle in the deep sucking mud. Jarvis Hicks, Dutch Cull, and a handful of civic-minded townsmen made their way early to the stack of walk boards the town kept piled beside the mercantile store for such times as this. In a few minutes, the muddy streets were crisscrossed with walk planks running in every direction.

In the back room of the doctor's office, Sheriff Tackett lay in a narrow bed with his head propped up on a pillow. He had drifted in and out of consciousness throughout the night, ever since Dr. Maxwell had probed into his side, found the bullet, and removed it. The incision was long, high up on his back just under his shoulder bone. Seeing the ranger standing over him when he opened his eyes, Tackett said in a weak voice, still groggy with laudanum, "Sam, I knew ... if anybody showed up out there, it would be you come looking for me."

"Well, then I reckon you was right," Sam said. "But Jarvis Hicks was going to come ... Dutch Cull, too. So don't go feeling sorry for yourself, thinking you've got no friends." Sam offered a thin smile.

Tackett managed to return the smile, barely.

"Yeah, I could see Jarvis coming for me ... Dutch, too, now that he's not working for Gunderson. He's my deputy for now." There was a silence, then Tackett said, "I need to get up from here and get busy. This town's always got something going on."

"Whoa," said Sam, putting a hand down on Tackett's shoulder to keep him from getting up. "I didn't bring you all the way back here so's you can kill yourself busting loose all the doctor's handiwork back there. He said you're going to be flat on your back a few days, and out of the saddle at least a couple of weeks. So make yourself comfortable."

"But Sam, I got a job to do," said Tackett.

"You've got Dutch Cull pinned to a badge. I'll help him look after the town for you," Sam said.

"But what about going after Carlos the Snake?" Tackett asked. "Maybe I can't ride, but you can. He's got to be stopped, Sam! He's plumb loco."

"For now the storm's washed his tracks clean. But I'll get to him, Sheriff," Sam said. "Don't worry about that. He's now at the very top of my list."

Sheriff Tackett started to say more, but a quiet knock drew their attention to the door.

"Come in," said Sam. They watched the door open slowly and saw Victor Trumbough take his hat from his head and nervously run a hand along the side of his hair. "What can we do for you?" Sam asked, standing with his right hand resting at ease on his pistol butt.

"Sam, this is Mr. Trumbough, president of the bank here," Tackett said, his voice beginning to sound tired once again. "Mister Trumbough, this is Ranger Sam Burrack."

"A pleasure, Ranger Burrack," said Trumbough, yet Sam saw a distance in his eyes. He was clearly not here on a social call.

"Likewise." Sam nodded respectfully. "Then I'll just excuse myself while you two talk."

"No, please, Ranger," said Trumbough. "I'm here to tell the sheriff something very important .... I feel it concerns you as well."

Sam and Tackett gave each other a glance, both taking note of the grave expression on the banker's face.

"I—I heard what happened to you, Sheriff Tackett," Trumbough continued. "I'm afraid it might be my fault." He saw their eyes narrow on him in curiosity. "Yes, you see ... I believe it was me this Carlos the Snake was looking for. I felt I needed to tell you both about it."

Sam and Tackett looked at one another again. Then Sam reached out and pulled a chair from against the wall and put it close to the bed. "Sit right down here, Mister Trumbough. Tell us everything," said the ranger.

CHAPTER 17

When Victor Trumbough had finished telling Tackett and the ranger his story, he hung his head for a moment and raised a hand to his eyes. "I'm not proud of what I was back then," he said. "I was young, wild, and embittered by the war—not that it makes any excuse for what we did. But, so help me God, I've tried every way I can since then to make myself into a better man than what I was back then. I even changed my name from Vernon to Victor, as if that would make a difference."

"And knowing somebody in town here was befriending Dan Bristoe," said the ranger, "Carlos the Snake thought it was Sheriff Tackett here."

"I'm afraid so," said Trumbough, without looking up just yet. He reached inside his coat, took out a handkerchief and wiped his face. "But it wasn't that I befriended Dan Bristoe ... I was being extorted by him."

"All of you men were pardoned at the end of the war, Mister Trumbough," said Sam. "You didn't have to pay Bristoe a thin dime."

"His real name was Calvin Galt, Ranger ... and yes, you're right. There was nothing anybody could do about it, legally. But that wasn't my concern. It was the shame I couldn't bear facing. The truth is, I think I gave him money mostly just so I wouldn't have to see his face—a reminder of that terrible thing we did." Victor Trumbough lifted his eyes now and took a deep breath putting the handkerchief back into his coat pocket. "And now, after all these years ... that poor frightened child has become a man. He wants the people who killed his parents punished." Trumbough shot a glance back and forth between them. "How can anyone blame him?"

"Dang it," Sheriff Tackett whispered, having heard the details now from one of the men who had witnessed the killings, "you sure ain't made hunting Carlos any easier, Victor. If I was to catch up to him now, I reckon I'd hate to have to kill him, even after him shooting me."

"Whatever animal Carlos has become," said Trumbough, "there's no denying that me, Wolf Avrial, and the rest of our gang made him that way. I don't envy you your job, Ranger. I know you'll feel torn now, going after him, knowing why he's doing all this."

The ranger had stood listening in silence. But now he spoke up, saying, "It's not my job to judge whatever wrong has been done against the man. It's the wrongs he's done to others that puts me on his trail. I'm not hunting the frightened little boy whose loved ones was killed. I'll be hunting the killer that has cut short the lives of many good people who never harmed him."

"Yes, you're right of course," said Trumbough, nodding in agreement, then continuing. "After I gave Calvin Galt some money, I left the next morning and rode all day ... out to Cochio Santavia's spread. I went there to tell him something had to be done about Galt. But it was Cochio who told me about Carlos the Snake. That's how I figured it was me he was looking for when I heard what happened to you last night. Jarvis Hicks told me what happened to you. I'm sorry I didn't come to you sooner with all this. I suppose I hoped it would all go away. And it might real soon, when Carlos goes after Cochio Santavia. Cochio is ready for him. So are the men who work for him."

"What about Wolf Avrial?" the ranger asked. "Whatever become of him?"

"He's also a banker," said Trumbough. "In fact, he's the one who helped me get started here. He put up some of the money I needed. He's sort of a silent partner, you might say. He owns three banks of his own, spends most of his time traveling the world. Like me, he has to live with what he did. I suppose traveling is his way of dealing with it. But he's not a bad man, Ranger. He and I were a couple of the lucky ones. We managed to put that hateful war behind us." His eyes lowered. "Except for the shame we have to live with."

A short silence passed as each of them reflected on Carlos the Snake and the impetus for his killing spree.

Then Victor Trumbough stood up from his chair and said, "I must get back to the bank now, gentlemen." He looked down at Sheriff Tackett. "Again, Sheriff, I'm sorry for what's happened to you. If there's anything I can do ...." He left his words hanging.

"Much obliged, Victor," Tackett said. "I'm just glad you came to us. It might make things easier, catching Carlos the Snake."

The ranger stood in silence once again until Victor Trumbough left the room.

"If this don't beat all," Tackett whispered. "I ate a bullet that dang near killed me, because this man was once a no-good murdering guerrilla. Now he's a pillar of the community .... The boy whose folks he killed is out to kill him, and we're the ones not only supposed to protect him, but bring down this Carlos who was wronged in the first place!" He shook his head slowly, mindful of the pain in his back beneath the thin coating of laudanum dulling it. "I swear, Sam, I'm quitting law work. It just don't make sense sometimes."

"That's only because the people involved don't make sense sometimes, Sheriff," said Sam. "This is a case where you can't blame anybody for what they've done. But either way, your poor undertaker is dead. His young wife is now a widow."

"I know," said Tackett, "and either way, I'm still laying here with a bullet cut out of my back."

"Get some rest, Sheriff," said Sam. "I'll go tell Jarvis and Deputy Cull how you're getting along." He turned and left.

Outside, in the muddy street, Jarvis Hicks and Dutch Cull

Ralph Cotton

had just finished helping some townsmen lay walk boards from the hotel to the barbershop when they looked up and saw the ranger walking toward them along the mud-splattered boardwalk. "How's he doing, Ranger?" Jarvis Hicks asked as Sam drew closer.

"As well as you could hope for," Sam replied. His eyes went from Jarvis to Cull. "He wants you to stay on as deputy, Dutch, but he asked me to take over for him. No offense, but he figured you being new in town, and the way Gunderson's acting, it might be better this way."

"I understand, Ranger," said Dutch Cull. "I'll follow your orders. It's good to be working, whoever I'm working for." He looked back and forth between Jarvis and the ranger. "Folks think it's a big deal being a paid gunman. They don't realize how many slim weeks a fellow goes through from one job to the next. I know preachers and piano players who make more than I do, all things averaged out."

"Well, you're working now," Sam said with a trace of a smile. He turned to Jarvis Hicks. "How was the woman when you went to tell her the hearse was here?"

Jarvis scratched his head. "I don't know, Ranger. She's a hard one to figure out. Looked like she'd been up all night. Looked scared to death when she opened the door, even after she saw it was me, and I told her why I was there."

"She's been through an awful lot, Jarvis," said Sam. "It might take her a while to get her mind straightened out, losing her husband, nearly getting killed herself."

"Sure."—Jarvis shrugged—"I see how all that could make a difference in a person for a while. Anyhow, she said she'd get Earl Blume or his boy to move the hearse around back and take the horses to the livery barn. They must've, because the hearse is back there now with its tongue on the ground."

"You told her about the body in it?" Sam asked.

"Yes, but she didn't seem too concerned. Said she'd have Earl get to it when he got a chance. See what I mean about

196

her? One minute she acts scared to death, the next she doesn't have a care in the world."

"Did you tell her why I didn't bring her husband's body back with me?" Sam asked.

"Yep," Jarvis said with a bemused look, "but she didn't appear too concerned one way or the other. Like I said, she's a hard one to figure."

"Let's just be patient with her, Jarvis," said Sam. "Some things take time." As he spoke, Sam looked off toward the front of the funeral parlor just in time to see Darcy's hand move away from the curtain.

Inside the funeral parlor Darcy stepped back from the window and walked over to her bed, where she'd helped Carlos move to as soon as he was strong enough to walk. He'd insisted she bring his saddlebags and let him see them. He'd had her shove the saddlebags beneath the bed where he would be near them.

Now he lay with pillows behind his back, his color coming back, his voice stronger as he asked Darcy, "What's wrong? What's going on out there?"

"They suspect something," she said. "I'm sure of it. I saw the ranger and the other two talking .... The ranger looked over this way. He might have seen me looking out there."

"Take it easy, Darcy," Carlos said, seeing that she was getting too shaky, perhaps too much so to be trusted. "They have no reason to think I'd be here. This is probably the last place in the world they'd think to look for me. The storm wiped my trail clean. If we keep calm, everything will be all right I'll be able to travel in a couple of days. I could travel right now, if I had to."

"Then let's go right now!" she blurted out nervously. "Right now, before something happens that will stop us!"

"Calm down, Darcy." Carlos pushed himself up and sat on the side of the bed, pain starting to throb in his bandaged wound. "You're making this bigger than it is. You want out of here so bad, you're scared something is going to happen to make you stay."

Carlos had told her he would take her with him when he left. But he'd only half meant it. He needed her between himself and the law for now, but, he reminded himself, that this was the same woman he was ready to kill only a few days ago. He would tell her anything he had to, to keep her on his side. But then, as soon as he was through with her ....

"Yes, you're right, I am afraid," Darcy said. She stepped over in front of him and he put his arms around her waist and drew her against him, in spite of his pain. He felt the warmth of her stomach against his cheek, her hands as light as air on the back of his neck. "But I've got to get away from this town, Andrew," she said. "I'll do anything it takes to put this place behind me."

He closed his eyes and let himself drift in her warmth, the sweetness of her scent. Maybe he wouldn't leave her behind once he was through with her—maybe he wouldn't be *through* with her. Not for a while anyway, perhaps not for a long while.

"I— I could prepare the hearse. It would be comfortable for you," she said. "I could make up a story—tell my helper, Earl, to take care of things here while I take a short trip somewhere. Nobody would think anything of it. I'll tell him I need to go somewhere and think about what I want to do with this funeral business. Please, Andrew. I have to get out of here! You don't know what this place is doing to me."

Carlos thought about it, his eyes closed, his face resting against her. "I know a place near Circle Wells. We could ditch the hearse there ... ride the horses. I have some things to take care of over that way. Then we could double back on horses and hit the border."

"Yes! We could do that," Darcy said. "I have some money, not a lot, but enough for us to live well in Mexico, for a while anyway. At least until we find a way to support ourselves. Anything I do is better than this."

Carlos studied her eyes for a moment, wondering if she realized how much gold was in his saddlebags. Perhaps she had no idea what this amount of gold coins was worth. He liked the idea of her not knowing. Her innocence attracted him. When a silence passed, he said, "You might hear some things about me, Darcy, some terrible things."

"I know," she said. "I've thought it over, and I simply won't listen, not to any of it."

"You're certain?" Carlos looked up at her.

"Yes, I'm certain ... as long as you didn't kill Maximus, I don't care what you've done in the past. It's what we do in the future that counts."

"Yes ... I've always said that." Carlos closed his eyes and pressed his face to her stomach once again. "Tonight then," he whispered against her.

By late afternoon, the muddy storm water had either soaked down into the street or boiled upward into the hot sky. The ranger, Dutch Cull, and Jarvis Hicks stood on the boardwalk out front of the sheriff s office, looking down at the dried crusty mud stuck to the walk planks. The planks were starting to stick tight to the moist, but drying, ground. "By morning it'll be time to peel them up and restack them," Jarvis said. "Makes you sort of wonder why we bothered laying them down, don't it?"

Neither the ranger nor Dutch Cull answered. Instead, they turned and walked inside the sheriff's office. Dutch looked back at Jarvis Hicks, who stood gazing across the street toward the Roi-Tan Saloon. "You coming, Jarvis?" Dutch asked.

Jarvis wiped a hand across his lips. "In a minute, Dutch. I'm going to make a stop at the saloon, see who's been up to what around here." He grinned, seeing Dutch give him a look "Naw, I ain't going to drink. It's just that sometimes the habit of being in a particular place is just as strong as what you did while you were there. Does that make any sense?"

"No, not really," said Dutch Cull. "But it doesn't have to make sense to me, long as you know what you're talking about. I'll have some coffee boiled when you get back."

Across the street, from behind the cover of a stack of shipping crates, Loman Gunderson watched Jarvis Hicks walk along the planked street toward the saloon. Behind Gunderson, Maurice Benfield had just stepped out of the mercantile store, having shed his bowler hat for a wide-brim Stetson with a low flat crown, the kind he imagined a true gunman might wear.

"There he goes, alone!" Gunderson hissed, flagging Benfield toward the street with a nervous hand. "You'll never get a better chance than right now!"

But Maurice Benfield suddenly felt hesitant. "Take it easy, Gunderson. This ain't a good time."

"What the hell do you mean it's not a good time?" Gunderson snapped. "The street's nearly empty, he's alone! Step out there, kill him, and run like hell, while nobody's looking!"

"All right, just settle down," said Benfield, knowing Gunderson was right. A couple of quick shots would do it; then he'd get out of sight quick. But still Benfield stalled. He fidgeted with his holster, and adjusted his belt. He had every intention of killing Jarvis Hicks. But he didn't like the suddenness of this situation. He'd just put his new hat on and walked out the door. Now he was supposed to just jump out into the street—a muddy street at that—and start blasting away at somebody.

"Damn you, man!" Gunderson spat at him. "If you yellow out on me, I swear I'll—"

"Shut up, Gunderson." Maurice Benfield cut his employer off with a cold gaze, feeling himself get back into the frame of mind he imagined a killer should be in. "I'm going for him right now. Just keep out of my way and watch your mouth."

"Then you better hurry up," said Gunderson. "He's almost to the saloon."

"Don't rush me," Benfield warned. He stepped down slowly into the street and took a few steps along the walk plank. Jarvis Hicks was almost across the street on another run of walk planks. Instead of drawing his pistol and shooting him, Benfield called out across the twenty yards of soft moist dirt between them, "Hicks! Stop right there!"

Jarvis stopped quickly at the sound of Benfield's voice, and turned on the walk planks to face him. "Benfield?" Hicks looked stunned for a second.

Now Benfield wasn't sure what to do. His plan to shoot Hicks by surprise and take off running wasn't going to happen now. He hadn't even drawn his pistol. He'd had things worked out perfectly in his mind. Something had thrown his timing off. "You know why I'm here, Hicks! Let's get to it!" *Whoa,* Benfield thought, hearing himself, what the hell was he doing? He'd had no intention of saying something like that. His hand opened and closed on his pistol butt. He had to get control of this thing and get it done now that he'd tipped his hand. He rocked back and forth restlessly in his boots.

"Hold it, Benfield!" Jarvis Hicks said, spreading his coat open by its lower corners as if about to perform some sort of curtsy on the walk planks. "I'm not armed. You're not going to shoot an unarmed man, are you?" Hicks saw the baffled look on Benfield's face. "Especially one who's as sorry as he can be for what he did to you ... and wishes to God there was some way to make up for it?"

That seemed to stump Benfield for a second. He stopped rocking on his boots; his hand turned loose on his pistol butt. "Don't think I've forgotten that you shot me, Hicks! I'm still going to kill you for it!"

"Jesus!" Loman Gunderson grumbled to himself, seeing and hearing what was going on from behind the shipping crates. He reached over beside him and snatched up Benfield's rifle. He jacked a round into the chamber.

"I understand how upset you are," said Jarvis Hicks, his

Ralph Cotton

voice level and sympathetic. "I've tried every way I can to tell you I'm sorry. Have you ever stopped to think how lucky you are that you're still alive ... instead of going around thinking about nothing but killing me? That's the sort of thinking that'll destroy a person, Benfield."

Maurice Benfield gritted his teeth and felt perspiration bead on his brow. The man had a point, he had to admit.

"Did you ever think that maybe God spared you for some higher purpose in life?" Hicks continued. "Something besides filling your heart with bitterness and stalking around like some mountain panther, ready to spring down and kill?"

"You meant to kill me, Hicks," Benfield said, his voice carrying nearly the conviction it had to begin with. "I can't forget that. How can I?"

Jarvis Hicks turned loose of his coat corners and raised a finger, for emphasis, seeing that apparently Benfield was listening to him. That was good. "You forget by reminding yourself that you are *alive,* Benfield .... That by some miracle God saw fit to spare you from dying in that den of iniquity over a seedy, cheap gambling argument. The same as he saw fit to spare me from a violent hanging."

Hicks spread his hands reverently and raised his closed eyes to heaven. "Lord, let this man see through the foolishness that has blinded his heart! Don't cast on my soul the dying knowledge that was him killing me that sent him farther down that road to hell. Let him ask his heart, Lord, can he truly do something this terrible to a fellow man?"

"Maybe he can't! By God, I can!" Loman Gunderson shouted. Abandoning his hickory cane, he jumped from his cover into the street, missing the walk planks and sinking up to his ankles in clinging mud. He threw the rifle up against his shoulder, screaming as he fired.

"No!" shouted Maurice Benfield, standing on a wobbly walk plank halfway between the two men, looking back and forth frantically. On his right stood Jarvis Hicks, unarmed, his eyes raised to heaven in prayer, refusing to acknowledge the fact that a man was shooting at him. On his left stood Loman Gunderson, in the mud, the rifle blazing in his hands.

"God no!" Benfield shouted, unable to move, holding his hands out as if they would stop the bullets from whistling past him toward Hicks.

Amid the flurry of rifle shots resounding along the street, one lone pistol shot exploded from the boardwalk in front of the sheriff's office. Dutch Cull stood with his smoking Colt extended at arm's length. His one, well-aimed pistol shot caused the rifle fire to stop abruptly. Loman Gunderson fell sidelong into the mud, one foot coming up out of his dress shoe, his bandaged foot still stuck solidly.

"Damn it to hell," Benfield murmured to himself, glancing around, seeing faces appear in doorways and windows. Gunderson tried to claw his way forward on his belly, seeing Dutch Cull loom above him as the big man stepped down onto the walk planks and came closer. Dutch's pistol was extended and cocked, smoke still curling from its barrel. "I brought you here, Dutch Cull! I hired you to work for me! Now look what you've done."

Not sure whether or not the man had a pistol inside his coat, Dutch Cull said, "Lay still, Gunderson, or I'll shoot you again."

But Loman Gunderson was outraged that a man whom he'd brought here to work for him had betrayed him. As Gunderson's hand went inside his coat to clasp against the bleeding wound in his shoulder, he bellowed in a sobbing voice, "How can you do this to me? End up shooting me like a dog in the street!"

Dutch Cull heard his words, but was more interested in the hand going inside the coat. "It ain't that hard for me," he said, the pistol bucking in his hand. The shot silenced Loman Gunderson for good, seeming to hammer him facedown into the soft earth.

"Damn fool. The law ain't got time for all this who-shoots-who nonsense," Dutch Cull said under his breath. Holstering his pistol, he looked around at Maurice Benfield and past him at Jarvis Hicks. "Is everybody all right?" asked Cull.

Hicks and Benfield looked at one another before answering. Then Hicks said, "All right here, Dutch."

Benfield looked himself up and down quickly, carefully keeping his hands raised chest high. "Yeah, thank God, we're both all right," Benfield called out.

"See?" Jarvis Hicks said to himself. "All a man needs is good intentions .... God takes care of all the rest." He raised his eyes to heaven once again, in thanks, then walked the rest of the way across the planks to the waiting onlookers, who stood watching him wide-eyed.

"Here, let me give you a hand, Reverend Hicks," said a teamster, who was there making his weekly supply run from Halston to the Medallion Mine Company.

Jarvis took the man's rough hand and stepped onto the boardwalk.

"You shouldn't make fun, Albert Wrensee," said a woman to the teamster, chastising him. "This is a serious matter of the spirit happening here."

"Ma'am, I wasn't poking fun at all!" said Albert Wrensee. He reached a hand up and dusted Jarvis Hicks's shoulder. "I meant *Reverend* in the most serious sense." He turned tearful eyes to the gathering crowd. "I seen what happened out there. A man tried killing him .... He neither pleaded not retaliated. Instead, he prayed! Prayed and trusted the Lord ... with bullets whizzing past him. If that ain't faith, I'll eat my shaving brush!"

Jarvis Hicks looked at Maurice Benfield, seeing him hurry across the walk planks and come running up to him.

"Jarvis, I'm sorry," Benfield pleaded with tears in his eyes. "I swear to God, I'll never do nothing like that again." He shot a glance back over his shoulder toward Dutch Cull, who walked slowly across the walk planks. Behind Dutch came the ranger, taking another run of planks, but headed in the same direction.

"Take it easy, Maurice," said Jarvis Hicks. "Everybody saw what happened. You've got nothing to worry about. I only hope and pray that this has all taught you something."

"It has, brother!" Benfield raised a hand toward the onlookers, saying, "Folks, I want all of you to know, that whatever bad things I might have said to any of you about this man ... I take it all back. What this man has shown me is far more important than the fact that he tried to kill me only a few days ago...."

As Benfield went on talking to the crowd, Dutch Cull and Sam came up beside Jarvis Hicks. "See, Ranger?" said Hicks. "I trusted the Lord, and the Lord saved me. Now do you believe that I'm a changed man?"

"I never said I didn't believe you in the first place, Jarvis," said the ranger beneath the sound of Benfield's voice addressing the onlookers. "But I expect if anybody here *didn't* believe you before, they sure ought to now."

As the townsfolk and lawmen stood listening to Maurice Benfield tell how Jarvis Hicks had shown him the errors of his ways, Darcy Tennison heard it from a distance as she led the team of horses from the livery barn along the back alley by the funeral parlor. From the boy at the livery barn, she'd learned that Sheriff Tackett was still alive, in spite of having been shot and left for dead. But she wasn't about to mention this to her new friend Andrew Thorp, not now anyway. The sooner she was out of this town, the better. She wouldn't risk telling him anything that might change their plans.

CHAPTER 18

"Did you find out what all the shooting was about?" Carlos asked Darcy Tennison as soon as she stepped inside the rear door to the funeral parlor.

"I didn't get close enough to hear everything," said Darcy, "but someone tried to kill a fellow and one of the deputies shot him."

"One of the deputies?" Carlos searched her eyes. "Any word on the sheriff yet?'

"Not that I've heard," Darcy lied. "After the storm last night, it could be a day or two before anybody travels that road and finds his body. We won't have an easy time of it ourselves. The hearse is not the best wagon for road travel." Seeing the hesitancy come into his eyes, Darcy added quickly, "But it will do until we get to where we can leave it somewhere and ride the horses."

Carlos saw the way she'd ducked her eyes slightly when he'd asked about the sheriff. "Are you sure you're telling me everything?" he asked.

"Of course." Seeing his suspicion, Darcy purposefully returned his steady gaze. "What reason would I have for *not* telling you everything?"

He nodded, convincing himself she was being honest "All right," he concluded, "it'll be dark soon. It's going to be tricky, traveling on wet ground of a night. Are you up to it?"

"Yes," said Darcy, "I'm ready to go." She smiled. "I've been ready to leave since the minute I arrived here."

* * *

Outside, Little Herman Blume elbowed his way through the crowd and looked down with a faint smile at Loman Gunderson lying dead in the mud. He peeled off his cloth cap and looked around the street, as if expecting to see more bodies.

The ranger watched Herman let out a sigh and put his cap back on his head. "Want to go tell your dad and Miss Darcy that we have need of their services here?" Sam asked.

Little Herman looked at him. "I can handle him myself, if somebody'll help me heave him up onto a buckboard."

"I think you best go get your dad," said Sam.

Little Herman seemed to sulk a bit as he turned and made his way back through the crowd.

For the next few minutes, the crowd listened to Maurice Benfield ramble on tearfully about faith until a townsman edged up beside Sam and Dutch Cull and asked, "Shouldn't one of the undertakers be here by now?"

"Any minute now, I'm sure," said Sam, looking off toward the funeral parlor. His eyes went from the funeral parlor to the doctor's office where Sheriff Tackett lay recovering from his surgery. "If you'll stay here for a minute, Dutch, I'll go tell the sheriff what happened. He'd be anxious to know."

Dutch Cull nodded in agreement.

Sam walked the planks to the doctor's office, but once inside, Dr. Maxwell told him that Tackett was fast asleep, having been given a strong dose of laudanum only moments before the shooting started. "He's doing fine," the doctor said, speaking softly outside the door to Tackett's room, "but let's let him sleep as long as he can."

"Good then," said the ranger, speaking just as softly. "I'll come back after a while and fill him in on everything."

Back on the street, Sam noticed that no one had yet shown up from Tennison's Funeral Parlor. "What's taking so long?" he asked Dutch Cull.

Ralph Cotton

"Beats me," said Dutch. He nodded toward Jarvis Hicks and Maurice Benfield, the two men speaking almost at the same time, their arms looped across one another's shoulder. "If these two would settle down and stop preaching, I believe most of these folks would go on about their business."

Sam looked at Benfield and Hicks, then back at Dutch Cull. "Let them go till they get it all out of their systems, I reckon," Sam said wryly. "I'd rather hear them preaching than shooting at each other."

"Yep." Dutch Cull spit and ran a hand across his lips. "Religion can do strange things to a fellow. I hope it never befalls me."

Sam and Dutch stood quietly watching until soon the crowd had all but broken up and left. Still no one had come to remove Gunderson's body from the street. A few yards down, tied to a hitch post out front of the Roi-Tan, sat Loman Gunderson's one-horse buggy.

"Give me a hand, Dutch," said the ranger. "Looks like I'll have to take him there myself." Together the two of them lifted Gunderson from the mud, carried him to the buggy and rolled him upward onto the passenger side.

Dutch Cull walked across the soft ground alongside the buggy as the ranger drove it to the back of the funeral parlor. After knocking a few times without getting an answer, Sam and Dutch started to turn away. As they did, they saw Earl Blume hurrying along the alley toward them, Little Herman trotting right behind him.

"Sorry I'm late, Ranger," said Earl. "I was eating supper with the widow Quincy. Little Herman found me. I'll get right out there now and move the body."

"Never mind, Earl," said Sam, "we brought him to you." He thumbed toward the buggy.

Earl saw Loman Gunderson's feet sticking out of the buggy, one in a muddy sock, one in a muddy bandage. "Much obliged, Ranger."

208

"Where's Miss Darcy?" Sam asked, seeing the fresh tracks of the hearse leading away along the alley, leaving an inch-deep rut in the mud toward the livery barn.

"She took the hearse over to the livery for a once-over. Said the front axle's squeaking something awful," said Blume. "I offered to take it for her ... but she insisted on doing it herself."

Sam nodded. "How's she doing, Earl? Is she getting over everything all right?"

"I don't know, Ranger." Earl Blume shook his head as he stepped over and looked down at Loman Gunderson's dead face streaked with mud. "One day she seems awfully quiet and hard to talk to, the next she's chipper as a squirrel." He stuck his key in the back door of the funeral parlor, unlocked it, and swung it open. Then he reached into the buggy, with the ranger and Dutch Cull helping him. The three of them hefted Gunderson's body up, carried it through the door and laid it on the preparation table next to where Stanley Baggs lay.

"Poor Stanley," said Earl Blume, shaking his head slowly. At his side stood Little Herman on his tiptoes, looking at the dead blank face in the failing evening light.

"He looks awfully blue," the ranger commented.

"That's because I haven't powdered him and made him up yet," said Earl. "His funeral is tomorrow. I like to fix them fresh at the last minute.... Seems like they look more natural that way."

"I see," said Sam, dusting his hands together as he and Dutch Cull stepped quietly to the back door. "Well, tell Miss Darcy howdy for me."

Outside, as they turned and walked away, Dutch Cull said in a lowered voice, "Don't, know why, but those places always did spook the hell out of me."

Sam stared straight ahead as they walked along. "Did they bury Dan Bristoe today, Dutch?"

"I don't know, but I doubt it, the ground so wet and all," Dutch replied. Seeing a studious expression on the ranger's face, he added, "Want me to go back and ask?"

"No, that's all right. I was just curious. I'll ask Earl later if I need to," said Sam. "Tennison's Funeral Parlor is a busy place all of a sudden." They walked on silently in the long thin shadows of late evening.

Two hours later, after a supper of beans from a tin and dried beef warmed on the stove in the sheriff's office, the ranger stood in the glow of the oil lamp beside Sheriff Tackett's bed and told him what had happened in the street.

"I swear, Sam," Tackett said when the ranger finished, "I feel awful having to impose on you this way. I know how you hate being cooped up in a town."

"Think nothing of it, Sheriff," said Sam. He poured cold water from a metal pitcher into a glass and handed it to Tackett.

The sheriff sipped, then said, "So Gunderson kept on till he managed to get himself killed." He shook his head. "I hate hearing that, even though the man was causing me so much trouble. It's a shame to see a man prosper the way he did out here, then watch his own pride and overhandedness ruin him."

"Not to speak ill of the dead, but he was a bully, a bully and a spiteful man," the ranger said. "We knew at the outset that somebody would die because of him. If it had to be that way, I'm glad it was him instead of some innocent party."

"Loman Gunderson meant well. He just didn't know how to live with his prosperity. Couldn't relax and enjoy his success, had to keep picking at something or somebody." Tackett sighed. "Either way, it's a dang shame," he said. "His daughter, Sara, needs to be notified."

"I'll send Dutch out first thing in the morning and tell her," said the ranger. "He can take Gunderson's buggy back to her. I expect she'll want to bring his body back to their spread for burial."

"That's my guess," said Sheriff Tackett, sipping his water. "His wife is buried there. Poor Sara, she's left all alone now, except for the family of Mexicans who work there."

Tackett seemed to consider things for a moment, then he said, "Do me a favor, Sam. Instead of sending Dutch out there, ask Jarvis Hicks to go."

The ranger eyed him closely. "Are you sure that's a good idea, after all the trouble Gunderson raised ... all of it starting over Hicks seeing his daughter?"

"I know it sounds like a strange thing to do." Sheriff Tackett offered a weak smile. "Old Loman will roll over in his grave from it. But I'm just looking out for everybody concerned. I don't want no bitterness coming between Jarvis and young Sara. The fact is they were both sweet on one another till Loman stuck his nose in. This way, maybe the two of them can patch things up between themselves."

"What if Hicks goes back to his old rounder's ways?" Sam asked.

"Aw," Tackett dismissed it, "he never was the rounder he professes to being. To tell you the truth, I believe he started getting bad about drinking and gambling after Gunderson came between the two of them. Jarvis loved that young woman. You could see it in his eyes .... Hers, too. I reckon that's what kept Gunderson so hostile all the time. He kept them apart, but he couldn't deny what he saw between them." Tackett shook his head slightly. "Such a shame it had to come to all this." He fell into a silent contemplation, studying the water glass in his hand.

"All right then, I'll send him," said Sam, "if he'll go."

"I'm sure he will," said Tackett. "It'd be the best thing for both him and her to talk about what happened here and get it out of the way."

"I suppose that does it for the peddler, too," said Sam. "Now that the bad blood between him and Jarvis Hicks is settled, he'll go on down the road."

"Yeah, it's all settled, for now anyway," said Tackett. "People go around for a while a-wanting to kill one another.

Then something comes along, takes their mind off it." He grinned. "Do you reckon it's all just part of our nature, Sam?"

"I hate to admit it if it is," the ranger said with a trace of a smile. "I'm not used to this kind of peacekeeping, settling disputes ... matchmaking. I don't see how you do it, Sheriff."

Tackett gave him a patient look. "It's part of sheriffing a town. Sometimes you have to look out for the innocent parties after the shooting stops. You might want to remember that, in case you ever sheriff a town someday."

"I don't look for that to happen," said the ranger, "but I'll remember your advice in case it does. The one thing I've learned about law work is that it can take some peculiar turns all of a sudden. It pays to keep an open mind I reckon."

"That it does, Ranger," said Sheriff Tackett, handing him the water glass and resting his head back down on the pillow. "That it does ...."

Victor Trumbough had ridden hard throughout the day, having left Halston early in the morning after visiting the ranger and Sheriff Tackett. The storm had left the ground sloppy and hard to travel at the opening of day; but by dark, the sun had done its job, drying the trails. Trumbough was not used to being this long in the saddle. He'd had to stop often throughout the day to rest both himself and the big buckskin he rode. When he'd come closer to the remote cattle ranch of Cochio Santavia, all he saw at first was the distant light shining in the darkness. After another half-an-hour ride, he came to the wide stone and wooden rail entrance to the ranch.

Trumbough slowed the big buckskin down to a halt. When he started to nudge it forward at a walk through the entrance, a voice spoke quietly from the darkness beneath the sound of a rifle hammer cocking. "Hold it right there, pilgrim. Keep your hands up where I can see them in the moonlight."

Trumbough stopped the buckskin again and sat with his hands chest high. "It's me, Victor Trumbough," he said to the shadowy figure walking cautiously toward him. "I was beginning to wonder if Cochio had posted a guard out here. Is that you, Link?"

"Yep, it's me," said Link Dawset. "We've got this whole place covered, Mister Trumbough," the man said, recognizing Victor Trumbough's voice. "There's three more men back there that ain't coming out where you can see them."

"Good work," said Trumbough, sitting still until the man came close enough to see his face in the pale moonlight.

Dawset looked at him warily, with the rifle cocked and loosely pointed at him. Once satisfied, the man lowered the rifle and motioned him forward. "If this Carlos the Snake comes showing his hide around here, we'll nail it to a board and tan it for him."

The man then turned and said to the darkness, "Randy, get on out here. Ride with Mister Trumbough to the house. Make sure nobody shoots him in the dark."

"Much obliged, Link," said Trumbough, seeing a rider step his horse forward and sidle up beside him.

"This is Randy Sparks," said Link Dawset, nodding toward the young man. "He'll escort you in."

Then he said to Randy Sparks, "See if you can get us a pot of hot coffee and bring it back. It's going to be a long night, and I better not catch any man with his chin on his chest."

"Right, Link," said Sparks. "I'll see what I can do." He pulled his horse back a step and jerked his head toward the light in the house, still a good ways off. "After you, Mister Trumbough. You've got nothing to worry about. Around here, there's nothing Link, Pecos, and the rest of us like better than to jerk a knot in somebody's back when they come looking for trouble."

Trumbough looked back at him. "Did you say, 'Pecos'? Is Pecos Bob here?"

"He sure is," said, Randy, "and Cochio says Wolf Avrial himself is going to show up. It'll look like a reunion here before long, all you guerrilla riders in one spot." Randy smiled.

But Victor Trumbough didn't return the smile. Instead, he murmured under his breath and heeled his horse forward.

When they rode into the front yard, Randy Sparks followed Trumbough around the side of the two-story, rough-lumber house to the rear, where the sound of voices resounded from a circling glow of firelight.

"Who's this?" said a young cowboy, standing with his hand on his pistol as he spoke. Another man rose beside him, a rifle swinging up from his lap and pointing in Victor Trumbough's direction.

"Easy, boys" said Randy Sparks, "it's Mister Trumbough. He was here the other day. Don't you recognize him?"

"Oh, yeah, sure, now that I got a better look," said the cowboy, both he and the others easing back down. "Sorry, Mister Trumbough," the young cowboy said.

Victor Trumbough only nodded and kept his horse walking until they reached a hitch rail near the back door. In the dark recess of the back porch, Trumbough saw a cigar flare up, then dim as a stream of smoke wafted out on a night breeze. "Cochio, it's Victor," Trumbough said, staying back and atop his horse for a moment.

"Yeah, Boss," said Randy Sparks, also staying atop his horse, "he rode in a few minutes ago .... Link had me bring him here."

A rocking chair squeaked to a halt on the dark porch. The cigar glow rose and fell again. Then a deep voice, full of barbed wire and gravel, said, "Come on up, Victor."

"Thanks," said Trumbough, stepping down and spinning his reins around the hitch rail.

Randy Sparks drew his horse back and took it around the fire toward where a chuck wagon sat, with its tailgate dropped. "How's it going out there, Randy?" a voice asked quietly from the circle of cowhands around the fire. "Catching any fireflies?"

"If I do, I'll save you some," said Randy, stepping down

from his saddle at the chuck wagon. He said to the cook, who sat washing dishes in a wooden bucket of water, "Link said see if we could take a pot of coffee out there for all of us." The cook only grunted and jerked his head toward an empty pot hanging just inside the open wagon bed.

On the dark porch, Trumbough saw Cochio Santavia raise a sawed-off shotgun from his lap and lean it against the house as he stood halfway up from his cushioned rocking chair. "I told you not to come here unless it is important," he said gruffly, looking closely at Trumbough with his one good eye. His other eye was covered by a black cloth patch. The long scar ran deep and jagged from under the patch, down across his cheekbone.

"I wouldn't be back here if it wasn't important," said Trumbough. "The cowhand told me Pecos Bob is here? Said Avrial is on his way?"

"That's right," said Cochio. He hooked his big thumb back toward the dark house. "Pecos is inside, asleep."

"I thought we agreed to keep apart from one another," said Trumbough.

"So did I," said Cochio, "but this is how it is. It was Wolf's idea. He sent word to Pecos, told him to come here."

"You still call him Wolf," said Trumbough. "He's not going to like that. It's strictly Jamison Avrial now. It has been for years."

"Sí." Cochio shrugged. "I have earned that right, if it suits me." He motioned for Trumbough to take a chair beside him. "Now seat yourself and tell me what is so important that you ride all this way to tell me."

"Gracias," said Trumbough, slumping down into the chair and taking a deep breath. On a small wooden table between the chairs stood a bottle of rye whiskey. Cochio took an upside-down whiskey glass, righted it, then filled it for his old war partner.

When Trumbough had finished the glass of whiskey and the

215

telling of what had happened to Dan Bristoe, Sheriff Boyd Tackett, and the rest of the recent grisly events involving Carlos the Snake, Cochio refilled his glass, corked the whiskey bottle and set it aside. "I see," Cochio said. A silence passed as he considered all Trumbough had just told him. Then he said with a dark ironic chuckle, "So, at last someone has sent Calvin Galt to hell, where he belongs. The way he kept gigging you for money, I should think you would be glad of it."

"Whether Dan Bristoe— I mean *Calvin Galt,*" said Trumbough, catching himself, "is dead or alive doesn't mean much to me one way or the other. He was on his last legs anyway. But all these other people, dying for something we caused so many years ago, Cochio! That's what has me troubled. No matter how I try to look at it, we're responsible for their deaths."

"You think too deep and too hard, *mi amigo,*" said Cochio, dismissing it with a wave of his thick hand. "I, too, am sorry for the terrible thing we did, but my sorrow is all the retribution I will pay. I cannot bring back the dead and change the turn of the past. Do you think you can?" he asked. "If so, be my guest. Make up for all of our sins .... Do for us what we cannot do for ourselves. Be*jesus,* if that suits you."

"Don't treat it this way, Cochio," said Trumbough. "All I'm saying is there has been too much bloodshed already. There must be a way to stop this before it gets worse."

"No, there is no way to stop it, except to kill this man. But you already knew this, so why do you even think any more about it? He finds us .... We kill him. Life does not have to be so complicated and thought about so much. You will drive yourself to madness if you are not careful."

He leaned in closer to Victor Trumbough. "Carlos the Snake knows this. He has known it since the day I stood looking for him across the desert of *Mejico*. He knew then as a child what he knows now as a man, that we must kill one another until this matter is over. These are things that few men realize when they first spill blood. Death gives no second chance, no reprieve. Death, and only death, is carved in stone."

"I didn't come here for a sermon on death," said Trumbough.

"Oh ... and why are you here?" said Cochio. "If you are as truly sorry as you say you are, why don't you wait in one spot, let this man catch up to you and kill you? That is all that would absolve you."

"I suppose I want to think there is some other way," said Trumbough. "I've tried to be a good man, tried to live right, deal fairly and—"

"Poor Victor." Cochio cut him off. Chuckling low under his breath and again shaking his head, he said with finality, "If this Carlos the Snake kills you before we kill him, we will see to it that those words are carved on your tombstone. 'Here lies Victor Trumbough, a good man who lived right and dealt fairly with people. The only bad thing he did was to kill a small child's mother and father.' "

"Shut up, Cochio! That's enough!" Victor Trumbough uncorked the bottle of rye, poured a glassful with a shaky hand and raised it to his lips. When he lowered the glass, he avoided Cochio's eyes and looked across the flickering flames of the glowing fire. "May God have mercy on our souls," he whispered.

CHAPTER 19

Before daylight, Sam was up from the cot in an empty cell and putting on his boots when he heard hard knocking on the door of the sheriff's office. In the cell next to him, Dutch Cull had just lit an oil lamp. At the sound of the knocking, Dutch raised the lamp's wick to a bright glow, and walked toward the front door. "All right, I'm coming!" said Dutch as the hard knocking resumed in urgency. He looked through the open cell door at the ranger, giving him a questioning glance in passing. "You'd think they could wait until after breakfast," he said.

As soon as Dutch opened the door, young Willie Burns burst inside, looking all around until he saw the ranger stepping out of the cell, shoving his shirttail into his trousers, behind his holster belt. "Ranger! You got to come quick! It's the Godawfulest thing you ever saw in your life! I showed it to the piano player, Ed Noble! He lost his breakfast right there on the spot!"

"Easy, lad," said the ranger, stepping close, putting a hand down on the boy's shoulder to keep him from bouncing up and down. "Settle down and tell us what you're talking about."

As he spoke, Sam reached down and picked his sombrero up from atop the sheriff's desk and placed it on his head. Dutch Cull had already set the lamp on the desk, turned the light out, and reached for his hat on a wall peg.

Willie Burns got a grip on himself, took a hard dry swallow, and said, "Over at the dump, Ranger. I found a man with his head eaten by rats!"

"Eaten by rats?" Sam asked, leaning down slightly in order to see the boy's eyes as he spoke.

Seeing the dubious look on the ranger's face, Willie Burns said quickly, "I swear it's the truth, Ranger! They ate his head plumb down to nothing but a pulp! Piano Ed told me to run over and get you. He couldn't come himself—puking and all! It's terrible, Ranger! Plumb awful!"

"Let's go look," said the ranger, giving Dutch Cull a glance. He picked up his rifle from the desk and swung it under his arm. On their way out the door, Sam asked Willie Burns, "What were you and Piano Ed doing at the dump before daylight anyway?"

"We go there early sometimes and smack sand rats!" said Willie, still excited. "I smack 'em with a shovel handle. Piano Ed's got a baseball bat somebody sent him all the way from Louisville, Kentucky! Boy, Ed can make 'em pop if he gets a good swing on one!"

"I bet he can," Sam said, giving Dutch Cull another glance as they closed the door behind themselves. They headed down off the boardwalk toward the dump just outside the town limits.

Ed Noble stood with one arm across his thin stomach, leaning against the remnants of an abandoned road wagon, with his head bowed as if in prayer. He wiped his mouth with a wrinkled white handkerchief and pointed at the bloody bundle a few feet away when Sam, Dutch Cull, and Willie Burns came walking up to him. "It's right there, Ranger," Ed said without looking up, or toward the sound of buzzing flies.

As soon as Sam looked at the partially rolled-up tent lying at the edge of the dump, he knew what to expect. "It's Dan Bristoe," he said quietly, sidelong to Dutch Cull standing beside him.

"How do you know for sure?" Dutch asked, equally as quiet.

"I don't for sure," said the ranger, picking up a short stick

219

Ralph Cotton

from the ground. "But that's the same canvas tent I found him wrapped in out on the desert. I brought him here wrapped in it." He swatted at flies, stepped closer, and reached out with the stick and uncovered what was left of the dead man's face. Then he let out a breath as he stepped back. "Yes, it's him all right," he said, tossing the stick aside.

Dutch Cull stepped forward now, looking down at the swarm of flies and mass of gore. "Good God! What did all that damage? Don't tell me rats." He looked all around the dump as if he might catch sight of such a hideous creature.

"Yes, it was so rats!" said Willie Burns, looking wide-eyed at the two men. "I saw one run off when I first found him."

"Willie," said the ranger, "a rat might have been there. But he was in this shape when I first found him and brought him to the undertaker. Gunshots did that to him." He looked at Dutch Cull as he continued. "A lot of gunshots, and one crazy human being doing the shooting."

"If you dropped him off at the funeral parlor, Ranger," asked Cull, "then how'd he end up here?"

"That's a good question, Dutch," said Sam, looking back toward the Halston rooftops in the thin early morning light. "I was wondering that myself." He lowered his eyes to the ground and looked all around until he caught sight of the set of deep wagon tracks in the now dry earth. He followed the tracks a few feet, seeing where someone had swung the rig off the trail closer to the piles of debris, as if they had barely slowed down in order to heave the body out onto the dump.

"What are you thinking, Ranger?" asked Cull, looking down and around with him, seeing the tracks himself and running a boot toe along one. "Is this what a funeral parlor does when they get too busy?"

"Lord, that ain't even funny," said Piano Ed behind them, his voice sounding weak. He bowed at the waist with one hand on his knee, ready to get sick again. Willie Burns picked up the stick the ranger had discarded and inspected the end of it.

Dutch and the ranger looked at both the man and boy, then stepped farther away from them. "Let's get over to the funeral parlor and see if Miss Darcy's there," said Sam.

"You don't think *she* would do something like this, do you?" asked Cull.

"No, but neither would Earl Blume or his boy Herman," said the ranger. "It's my hunch Miss Darcy is gone, hearse and all." His eyes followed the tracks until they passed out of sight on the trail leading northeast.

"If she is, do you figure she's been forced to leave against her will?" asked Dutch.

"That's a good question, too," said the ranger. "I can't wait to find out the answer. Ed," he said, turning to the thin piano player, "I'd like you to stay here for a few minutes, till I can send somebody for the body."

"I might as well," said Ed Noble, shooting a glance of disgust toward the swirl of flies above Dan Bristoe's remains. "My day's shot to hell now anyway."

The ranger and Dutch Cull walked to the rear door of Tennison's Funeral Parlor and knocked. After a moment of silence, the ranger knocked again, this time giving Dutch a curious look. In a second, when he'd started to knock a third time, the voice of Earl Blume called out behind him, "Can I help you, Ranger?"

Dutch and Sam looked around, seeing Earl Blume and Little Herman walking toward them. "You sure can, Earl," said Sam. "Willie Burns and Piano Ed found Dan Bristoe's body in the town dump. I need it picked up and brought back here." He gave Earl a stern look. "I also wonder if you've got any idea how it got there. It was in the hearse when I left it back here."

Earl's eyes widened. "No, I have no idea how it got there ... or who would do such a thing in the first place!"

The ranger waved his hand toward the door. "I can't raise anybody. Is Miss Darcy here?"

"Well, yes, she should be, as early as it is." Earl Blume stepped up with the key to the door and poked it into the lock. He opened the door and stepped inside the dark room. Little Herman, Dutch, and the ranger followed.

In the gloom, Stanley Baggs's body lay stretched out on the preparation table with a thin sheet covering it. As Earl Blume lit a lamp sitting near the table, Dutch Cull and the ranger saw the sheet over Stanley Baggs tremble and jerk. The sight of it caused Dutch Cull to gasp and throw his hand to his pistol butt.

"Don't worry," said Earl, seeing the look of terror on Cull's face. "It's just nerves. The change in the temperature overnight often causes—"

His words stopped short beneath Dutch Cull's shriek. Dutch's pistol came out of his holster cocked and pointed as Stanley Baggs's body jerked upward almost all the way into a sitting position and the sheet slid down off his pale ivory-blue face.

"Oh, dear Lord God!" Dutch shouted, almost firing before he could stop himself.

"Easy, Deputy," said Earl, "that happens sometimes, too."

Little Herman walked over giggling, climbed onto a chair sitting beside the table, reached out and pressed on Stanley Baggs's chest, forcing the body back flat on the table. Herman looked around at the ranger and Dutch with a broad grin, then flipped the sheet over Stanley's stonelike face.

"Whew," said Dutch, his hand trembling as he uncocked the pistol and slipped it down into his holster, "I came very near shooting a dead man by accident."

"That beats shooting a live one by accident I suppose," the ranger said, not wanting to embarrass Dutch any further.

"I'll just go see if Miss Darcy is in her quarters," said Earl Blume, holding the glowing lamp up to light his way along the dark hallway. Little Herman stood watching the two lawmen with a grim smile.

When Earl returned, the ranger saw the puzzled look on his face as he reentered the room. "She's not here," Earl said. "The big travel bag is even gone."

"That's what I was afraid of," said the ranger. He pointed with his rifle barrel at a bloodstained preparation table that had been folded and leaned in a corner. In a wastebasket on the floor, were wads of bloody gauze. "Did you use this table, Earl? Or all those gauze bandages?"

"Why, no, I didn't," said Earl, looking surprised, having not taken notice of these things before the ranger pointed them out to him. "Herman, did you use these?"

Little Herman only shook his head.

"Looks like you were right, Ranger," said Dutch Cull. "The wagon tracks belong to the hearse."

"But she told me she was taking the hearse to the livery barn," said Earl.

"Then let's go see if she did," Sam said, stepping over and opening the door.

They walked quickly to the livery barn, Little Herman almost having to run to keep up with them. Once inside the livery barn, it only took a quick glance to see that the hearse was not in the spot where it was always kept. Seeing the three men and Little Herman enter the barn, Willie Burns ran as fast as he could along the empty street and came in the door behind them. "What can I do for you, Ranger?" Willie asked, rubbing the palm of his hand up and down his trouser leg, anticipating a tip.

"Saddle Black-Pot for me, Willie," said the ranger, "and bring me a good strong spare horse from the corral." Fishing a silver dollar from his vest pocket, Sam flipped it to Willie for his stall bill and grain.

"Keep the change." He watched Willie Burns hook the coin out of the air with his small hand. "How's Piano Ed making out looking after Dan Bristoe's body?" the ranger asked.

"He got sick again, right after you left." Willie looked the coin

223

over and put it away. "I'll have your horse ready in no time." He hurried off toward one of the stalls at the end of the barn.

"Want me to ride with you, Ranger?" Dutch asked.

"No, I think Tackett needs you here looking after the town," Sam replied.

"We're both thinking the same thing," said Dutch. "That Carlos the Snake has come here wounded, and somehow forced the funeral parlor lady to leave with him, right?"

"That's an easy first conclusion, Dutch," said Sam. He considered it for a second, then said, "But I believe I'll do some more thinking on it along the trail."

He looked down at Little Herman and said, "Suppose you run over to the mercantile and get me a few days' supplies: coffee, jerked beef, some traveling grain for my stallion. Tell the clerk I'll pay him when I get there." He fished a nickel from his pocket and flipped it to the boy. "Here's a nickel for your trouble. I'll pick the supplies up in a few minutes."

"Sure thing!" Little Herman caught the nickel, turned and left the barn at a quick trot.

Seeing Willie Burns lead the saddled Appaloosa from its stall and down the center of the large barn toward him, the ranger raised his pistol from his holster, checked it, and put it away. "Tell Sheriff Tackett what we think's going on," said Sam. "Then tell him not to worry. I'll be back as soon as I can."

Dutch Cull nodded. "Will do. Be careful, Ranger. If this is Carlos the Snake, you saw what he did to Tackett ... not to mention what you just saw at the dump. Do you have any idea where they might be headed?"

"Yes, I do," said Sam. "Carlos ain't finished killing yet, not by a long shot." He reached out and shoved his rifle down into his saddle boot as Willie led the big stallion up to him. Then he and Dutch stood in silence until Willie Burns ran out to the corral and came out leading a big brown-and-white paint horse on a length of lead rope.

"Guess what?" said Willie Burns, handing the ranger the

lead rope as Sam looked the paint horse up and down. "I've got two saddles missing."

"Are you sure, Willie?" The ranger gave him a questioning gaze.

"I'm positive," said Willie. "I thought you might want to know."

"Much obliged," said Sam. He stepped up into the stirrup and swung into his saddle. "Let's go, Black-Pot," he said to the Appaloosa stallion, nudging it toward the barn door, leading the paint horse, "before they get too far ahead of us."

The hearse had only slowed them down, traveling over the soft ground. At dawn, from atop a cliff overlooking the flatlands, Darcy and Carlos stood beside the horses and looked on the abandoned hearse. It was now no more than a black dot on a sparkling bed of sand. There was a certain peace in her seeing the hearse grow smaller behind her. She wanted to get farther and farther away from it until at some point she would look back and find it had disappeared. That time would come, she reminded herself.

Beside her, Carlos said, "Are you ready? We need to keep moving. We lost time last night."

"Yes, I'm ready," Darcy said serenely. Then her eyes went to the fresh blood on his shirt, and she said, just as serenely, "You're bleeding again."

"I'll be all right," Carlos said. He adjusted the big rifle up under his arm.

"I brought some gauze," she said. "I can dress it for you. It will only take a minute!"

"I said I'm all right," said Carlos, looking away from her, toward the northeast.

Darcy glanced at the rifle, but only for an instant, not wanting him to see that she had made any connection between it and the long-range rifle that had killed her husband and had tried to kill her. No sooner than they had left Halston the night

Ralph Cotton

before, he had gotten her to stop the wagon near a short rise of rock. He'd gotten out of the hearse and walked away into the darkness for a moment. When he'd returned, she saw the rifle in his hands. But she never mentioned it, nor did he. Perhaps they each knew that the rifle spoke for itself and left nothing more to be said.

"Who is it you're searching for out there?" she asked quietly, seeing his distant gaze. "It's as if you're looking for ghosts."

Her words came soft and sudden. He felt them stab his conscience like sharp blades. "No," he said, "they're not ghosts, not yet anyway."

They mounted the horses and rode farther along the high ridge surrounding the basin. By midmorning, when the sun began to boil in the sky and draw what little moisture was left from the ground, they stopped the horses side by side again and looked down on the flatlands. The barren sand turned upward for aways, then spilled into a stretch of sparse grassland and black rock. A thin trail snaked across the grassland toward a rough-lumber house, whose weather-bleached walls glistened silver in the harsh sunlight.

"There," Carlos said dryly, "that's where we're going." The blood on his shirt had blackened and dried.

"And what are you going to do there, kill someone?" she asked matter-of-factly. "How will you know who to kill and who not to kill?"

For Carlos, the answer was simple. He'd already decided, when he got to the CS spread he'd kill them all. He looked at her, no longer wondering what she knew or what she thought she knew. She had done her part, she'd helped him. And in helping to keep him alive, she had aided his pursuit. Now there was no more pretense between them. Yet, there were things unsaid that he felt needed saying.

"I lied to you, Darcy," he told her, still not facing her. He heard her sigh, and he heard her horse scrape a hoof on the rocky ground.

226

Vengeance

When Darcy made no comment on the matter one way or the other, he said, "I lied about who I am and what I'm doing out here. I am Carlos the Snake. I am the man who killed your husband ... and tried to kill you." He waited, staring out across the endless land below them. He didn't know what he expected her to say. "You're free to go," he added, after a moment of silence. But when he heard no response, he turned to face her and saw that she had backed the horse quietly and was now looking back at him from twenty yards away.

"Are you coming or not?" she called back to him.

Carlos sat staring at her for a moment, not knowing what if anything she had heard—not knowing what if anything she had chosen not to hear. He heeled the horse firmly and set it into a gallop, saying as he sidled up to her on the narrow trail, "Yes, I'm coming. From here on, you stay behind me."

CHAPTER 20

In the early afternoon, before the sun had reached its hottest point of the day, the supply rig from Cochio's ranch to Little Dog Mesa moved along at a steady clip in front of its own rise of dust The run took less time than it ordinarily would have, owing partly to the fact the three cowboys had been ordered not to stop at the makeshift tent saloon for a few rounds of whiskey. Driving the buckboard was Duck Phillips, a young red-haired Texas cowhand who'd hired on with Cochio Santavia on his way back from a big drive to Wyoming.

Sitting next to Duck Phillips, with a shotgun across his lap, was an old wrangler known only as Greerson. Riding a rawboned cattle pony next to the buckboard, an experienced old Irish gunman named Pat Grimes kept a wary eye on the surrounding ridgelines above the sand basin. "Boys, it don't seem right leaving the mesa stone sober," said Greerson, wiping a bandanna across his face, then across the back of his neck. "I feel plumb guilty of something." He shook the bandanna out, looped it around his neck and tied it.

"Aye," said Pat Grimes, from his saddle, riding close beside the loaded buckboard, "and if we were to scratch deep enough, we'd no doubt find that you *are* guilty of something."

"Then don't go scratching." Greerson grinned. His voice rose above the squeak of the buckboard and the horses' hooves. "You know it might not be wise getting back this soon," he said. "The boss might start expecting us back this quick all the time." He gazed forward at a turn in the trail. Around the long turn stood the ranch house, less than two miles away.

"If it was any boss but Cochio, I might think so myself," said Pat Grimes. "But Cochio Santavia knows that a man needs his whiskey now and then ... just to keep the devils out of his dreams. Long as a man does a full day's work, Cochio ain't going worry about a couple sips of whiskey."

"What gets me about all this," said Duck Phillips, who'd been riding quietly for the past couple of miles, "is, why don't this Carlos the Snake come face Cochio and the rest of them, one at a time, if he had vengeance to settle? That's what I'd do, if I was him."

"Oh, would you indeed now?" said Pat Grimes, almost mockingly.

"Damn right," said Duck. "I'd want it known that I'd been wronged, and that I was there to settle it straight-up, face-to-face. Let the sun shine in the winner's face, and let the dirt fall in the face of the loser's. That's how we handle this kind of stuff in Texas."

"So it is, I'm sure," said Pat Grimes. "But men handle these situations in different ways. It's best not to speculate what you would do, or how you would do it, until this kind of thing happens to you. But pray to merciful God it never does," he pointed out, raising a gloved finger.

"That's the truth, Duck," said Greerson. "If you think about it, what worse way is there to torment a man, than for him to know that you might strike from out of nowhere at any second, when he least expects it. It's enough to drive a man crazy."

"It would me," said Grimes, "and it might others. I don't think it worries Cochio though."

"This is no easy thing for me to even side with, knowing the circumstances of it," said Greerson. "I think the world of Cochio, but damn ... it's hard to reconcile what him and the others did. As far as how Carlos goes about getting his revenge, I reckon he figures that's his call and nobody else's. Which I got to admit is how I would look at it, were it me."

"I didn't mean nothing by it one way or the other," said Duck, "but I'll be honest. I didn't hire on here as a gunman. I don't like being caught up in this."

"Neither do the rest of us, Duck," said Greerson. "But when you ride for a brand, you ride for it. You can't cut and run first time the lightning strikes. I sure as hell didn't figure I'd ever be ready to side with a man and fight for him over something he did years ago—especially something like this."

"I'd never say it to Cochio," Pat Grimes said, "but it's hard not to side with Carlos the Snake on this." He shrugged. "Sure, we cut across the border now and then, rustle us back some horses or cattle—just enough to keep our hands in. But that's to be expected, eh?" He grinned.

"That's right," said Greerson. "I wouldn't want to ride for a cattleman who had that much sand in his craw. But this other thing… killing a kid's family. Damned if that ain't cold as ice."

Duck slapped the reins to the team horses' backs, keeping them at a steady clip. "Well, one thing's for sure, as soon as this thing is—" His words stopped short with a deep grunt, as if someone had reached out with a hard fist and hit him in the chest. Beside him, Greerson saw the young man bolt back in the seat, then begin falling forward. As Greerson reached to stop Duck Phillips from tumbling headlong out of the buckboard, the shot that had just blown his heart out resounded across the floor of the sand basin.

"Glory be!" Pat Grimes shouted, his hand making a quick sign of the cross on his chest as he saw the gout of blood rise up from the exit wound on Duck Phillips's back.

Six hundred yards away, atop a flat cliff overhang, Carlos the Snake flipped the spent cartridge from his rifle and replaced it with a fresh load. Darcy stood thirty feet behind with her back to him, looking in the opposite direction as she held the horses' reins and tried to shut the sound of the big rifle out of her mind.

Carlos kept a firm grip on the cross sticks in his left hand and took aim again.

In the buckboard, Greerson had pulled Duck Phillips's body back up into the seat, just long enough to confirm what he and Pat Grimes already knew. "Lord have mercy!" Greerson said, seeing the large hole in the center of the young cowboy's chest. "He never knew what hit him!" Then he let the body slump down on its side in the seat.

"Neither will we if we don't get moving!" Pat Grimes shouted from atop his horse, jerking a rifle from his saddle boot, his eyes frantically scanning the ridgeline. Seeing Greerson take the reins to the buckboard, Grimes slapped the barrel of his rifle on the rump of the team horse nearest him. As the buckboard lunged forward, Grimes nailed his spurs to the sides of his horse and raced alongside it.

Pat Grimes heard the second shot and turned in his saddle, taking a quick look along the ridgeline again, seeing nothing. He didn't realize that Greerson had been hit until he noticed the buckboard swerve off the trail. As he continued racing forward, he saw the buckboard hit a rocky bump, and caught a glimpse of Greerson's body bounce out of the seat in one direction and Duck Phillips's in the other.

"Merciful savior!" Grimes shouted to himself. He jammed his spurs harder to his horse's sides, but the horse had no more to give. It raced along the trail in a high rising dust.

From atop the ridgeline, Carlos watched the toylike figure of the buckboard sail upward and back down, leaving a long stream of white powder in its wake. He watched the two billowing rows of dust split off from one another as the rider stuck to the trail and the buckboard raced wildly across rock and sand. As he watched the scene below, he flipped out the spent round and replaced it.

In the cattle pen behind the ranch house, the sound of the first shot made two of the men stand up slowly from branding

231

a calf and look off toward the ridges. On the porch, where Cochio sat peeling an apple, he stopped rocking and looked away from Pecos Bob and Victor Trumbough toward the distant sound.

When the second shot came, Cochio and the other two men stood up and walked down into the yard, where cowhands working the pens close by began to draw together, their eyes on the ridgelines. "What do you think it is, Link?" Randy Sparks asked Link Dawset.

"Sssh, hush, boy," Link said, his eyes still fixed toward the shots. All the men seemed to hold their breaths until finally a shot echoed in.

Link Dawset shook his head and walked over closer beside Cochio Santavia. "Boss, this ain't a good sign ... hearing three shots when we've got three men out there."

"Keep quiet, I know that," said Cochio, still staring off, a half-peeled apple in his right hand, a paring knife in his left.

Beside Victor Trumbough, Pecos Bob Denton said to him in a guarded tone, "Just how tough are these CS cowhands, if one man can do all this to them?"

Victor Trumbough gave his old saddle partner a grave look, seeing that Pecos Bob wasn't taking this as seriously as he should. "Bob, this man means to let nothing stop him until we are all dead. Do you understand that?"

Pecos Bob offered a thin smile. "Yeah, I understand that, Victor. Don't get your drawers in a knot. I was just saying, maybe he ain't caught up to the right ones of us yet. You might have spent the years behind a desk, but I've kept a shine on my saddle. Maybe I ought to ride and have a look-see."

Cochio, hearing part of the conversation, looked at Pecos Bob and said, "Neither of you leaves here until I send some riders and see what the shooting was about, *comprende?*"

"Comprende," said Trumbough. "You don't have to worry about me riding out there. I'm not trying to be a hero."

Pecos Bob looked all around at the cowhands, then at

Cochio Santavia. "With all respect, Cochio ... never yet had to have somebody else do my fighting for me. I ain't starting now. Besides, we don't know what that shooting was about. It might be somebody shooting at sand lizards." He grinned.

"Sí, it might be," said Cochio, "but I have three men out there on a supply run. I don't like what I feel about this." He looked at Link Dawset and Randy Sparks. "Link, the two of you get saddled, go take a look. If something looks bad, draw back and do some pistol shooting. We'll all come running."

"Right away, Boss," said Link, but the look on his face said his heart wasn't really in it.

"I'm riding with them," said Pecos Bob.

"I forbid it," said Cochio.

"Look, Cochio, *mi amigo,* " said Pecos, "let's don't start our reunion off with an argument. I ride where it suits me, when it suits me. Always have, always will."

Cochio let out a breath, then said in resolve, "All right, be bullheaded then ... I won't try to stop you."

"What say, boys?" Pecos asked Link Dawset and Randy Sparks. "Are we ready to ride?"

"I'll get the horses," said Link, he and Randy turning toward the corral.

"What about you, Victor?" said Pecos Bob, goading him. "Feel like going out there and seeing if we can flush us out an ambusher?"

"Stay here, Bob, for God sakes!" said Victor Trumbough. "This is no game!"

"Now that's where you're wrong, Victor," said Pecos Bob, pulling on his leather riding gloves as he spoke. "It's all a game. From the first breath you take, till the last breath seeps out of you." He looked around at the others with a slight smile. "Boys, it's all just one big ole game of life or death."

"He sounds like a crazy sonuvabitch," whispered an old cowboy at the rear of the gathering.

The ranger had pushed hard throughout the day, swapping the big Appaloosa for the paint horse every few miles, keeping both horses as rested as possible in the scorching heat. When he'd heard the rifle shots, he was surprised at how close they sounded, perhaps less than a mile away. He'd made good time, pushing the animals, but not overpushing them. "Good work, boys," he said to the sweaty horses, patting the paint horse's withers with his gloved hand.

No sooner than he'd left Halston, Sam had seen where the hearse had pulled over and stopped for a moment. He'd followed the boot prints out to where he saw scraping in the sand under a broad flat rock. He put two and two together and decided this was where Carlos the Snake had hidden his long-range rifle rather than carry it into town with him. "That's the way, Carlos," he said to himself, "get in a hurry... start making it easier for me."

Back in the saddle, pushing hard, the ranger had come upon the abandoned hearse before noon. He'd only stopped there long enough to look the funeral rig over while both horses stood resting. Then the ranger sipped some tepid water from his canteen, swapped the saddle back to the Appaloosa from the paint horse he'd been riding for the past hour, and rode on. He'd followed the hoofprints up from the sand flats into the surrounding ridges, knowing all along they would lead him to the CS spread.

Twenty minutes later, Sam eased down from his saddle and tied the horses to a sprig of juniper growing out of a rock crevice. His eyes followed the hoofprints left by Carlos and Darcy Tennison. Leaving the horses in the thin shade of the rock wall alongside the trail, Sam worked the rest of the way along the wall on foot, with caution until he reached a cliff overlooking the flatlands. Seeing no one around, he moved forward with his Colt drawn and cocked. Near the edge he saw the empty brass cartridge shells. He saw where the shooter had lain prone, taking all the time he needed to hone in on his targets a good seven hundred yards below.

Looking down, Sam saw the bodies on the sandy soil. A hundred yards away he saw the buckboard.

The team of horses stood with their muzzles down, picking at sparse clumps of wild grass, a line of spilled supplies reaching back toward the trail behind them. As he looked down, Sam felt a crawling sensation on the back of his neck. He turned to his left and looked around. Seeing a higher rise of ridgelines above him three hundred yards away, he immediately sprang back from the edge of the cliff.

Even as he dove to the ground and into a roll toward the cover of the rock wall, he heard the sound of a bullet strike the cliff and ricochet off with a loud whine. He scrambled on hands and knees, his Colt still in hand.

At the rock wall, he scooted into cover, uncocked the Colt and holstered it. The pistol was useless to him now. This was going to be a long-range rifle battle—just what Carlos the Snake seemed to like, he thought—until he could find a way to change it. Sam dusted his hands together, then began crawling along the wall back to the horses.

On the flatlands, Link Dawset, Randy Sparks, and Pecos Bob had begun rounding the turn in the trail that would soon flatten down and leave them exposed to the long ridgelines. At the sound of the rifle shot, Link sat back quickly on his reins, bringing his horse to sliding halt. "Unh-uh, boys! We're fools if we ride into that! Let's pull wide and slip in around the ridges on the other side of the basin."

But Pecos Bob would have none of it. "Are you out of your mind? That's seven miles at least!"

"Yep, it is," said Link Dawset, "and it's seven miles more than we'll get if we ride in this way. Every time I hear that rifle bark, I get the feeling somebody else just bit the dust."

"You two do what suits your nature," said Pecos Bob in a haughty tone. "I'm riding in, checking things out."

"Damn, Pecos Bob!" said Link Dawset "You heard Cochio ... if things look bad, we just fire some pistol shots, let him know to bring the whole crew out here, ready for bear!"

"Well, that's just fine, boys," said Pecos Bob. "When they get here, you tell Cochio I went on in .... Say I felt like hunting some snake." He grinned and kicked his horse forward.

"Damn it to hell, there he goes," said Link Dawset.

"Let the fool go," said Randy Sparks, "if he's got no better sense."

"But damn it, Cochio ain't going to like it, us letting his ole buddy get shot all to hell," said Link Dawset. He hesitated for a second, then said, "I best go with him."

"Wait, Link!" Randy Sparks shouted. But Link didn't even look back. "I hate it when people do me this way," Randy said, spinning his horse in a quick circle. He jerked his hat from his head and slapped it against his leg. "Dang it then! Wait up, Link, I ain't cutting out on ya."

CHAPTER 21

With the big Swiss rifle assembled, loaded, and in hand, Sam left the horses in the shade of the rock wall. He climbed upward along a jagged crevice until he estimated himself to be about at the same level as where the shot had come from. From behind rock cover, he looked out from the edge of his higher perch and saw the three riders strung out in a line along the flatlands' trail.

"No, go back," Sam said to himself. Quickly, he raised the Swiss rifle to his shoulder, aimed down through the tall ladder sight and hoped he could make his shot before Carlos the Snake made his.

On the flatland, Pecos Bob didn't hear the bullet thump into the ground and kick stinging sand up against the horse's foreleg. But he realized what had happened as the horse reared high with him and the sound of shot finally reached down to him from the ridgeline.

"Whoa!" he shouted, wrestling with the reins. The horse came down in a quick turn and started to race back along the trail with him. Farther back on the trail, Link and Randy heard the shot and veered toward cover along the lower level of rocks and ridges. As Pecos Bob took control of his horse, he guided it toward them.

The ranger breathed a sigh of relief. But then as he lowered his rifle, watching the three riders cut for cover eighty yards away, he heard the rifle explode on his left and saw Pecos Bob bolt upright in his saddle, then seem to melt backward off his horse.

Sam winced at the sight. Then he leaned forward quickly and looked around to his left, catching a quick glint of Carlos's rifle barrel before Carlos pulled it back out of sight.

On the flatlands, Link Dawset and Randy Sparks ducked into rock cover at the same time. Sliding their horses down and spinning them around for a look at Pecos Bob, they saw him crawling hand over hand across the rocky ground, a wide red patch of blood covering the back of his shirt.

"Lord, he's hit bad!" said Link Dawset, backing his horse a few steps deeper into the rock shade for safety's sake. Farther past Pecos Bob, they saw the bodies of the other cowboys who'd been with the buckboard.

"That poor sonuvabitch," said Randy Sparks, seeing Pecos Bob raise up on an elbow and reach a bloody hand out toward them, clawing the air fifty yards away. "There ain't a thing we can do for him either."

As if having heard Randy Sparks's words, Pecos Bob pleaded in a sobbing voice, "Boys ... you got to help me! I'm back shot" His words sounded hoarse and broken.

"Bob, lay still," Link called out to him. "We can't get to you right now. Just lay still ... it'll be dark before long!"

"Dark?" Pecos Bob said, pleading. "I'll be dead long before dark!"

"Hell, it's the truth, and he knows it," Link Dawset said to Randy Sparks. "If he ain't bled to death by then, the sun will have fried him like bacon."

"I know it," said Randy Sparks, getting a sick feeling low in his belly. "You cocky sonuvabitch!" he shouted at Pecos Bob. "You just had to go and do it, didn't you? Now look at you! Look at all of us!"

"Ain't no need cussing about it, Randy, it's already done now," said Link Dawset. He raised his pistol from his holster and emptied all six shots into the air. Then he sat, staring out at Pecos Bob as he punched out his empty shells and replaced them. "I always wondered where shots go when you fire them straight up that way," he said idly. "Always wondered why they don't fall straight back down and nail you in the top of the head."

"Please don't tell me we're going out there and try to drag him back here," said Randy.

"No, *we're* not ... but I am," said Link with determination, not facing him.

"Aw hell, Link! Look at him! He's dead either way! It's crazy getting yourself killed over a dead man," Sparks tried to reason.

"That's a good way of looking at it, Randy," said Link Dawset. "I ain't faulting you for it at all. I often wished I looked at things that way. But I never could. I druther die on slim odds of saving a person, than live knowing I didn't even try."

Staring out, the two cowhands saw Pecos Bob's horse walk up to him and prod him with its muzzle. Pecos reached up and took the stirrup. But suddenly, before he could even get a firm grip, the horse faltered sideways with a pitiful whinny and toppled to the ground as the sound of the shot echoed down.

"My God, now he's shot Bob's horse," said Link Dawset.

"See? Damn it, Link, don't go out there! He's just baiting us, trying to get us out there. You know that man will kill you. I can't even cover you from here! It won't be long before Cochio and the rest get here."

"Cochio and the rest will have better sense than to ride in here along the trail. They'll do like we should've done. They'll come wide around the bottom of the ridgelines over there. But that won't help Pecos Bob any."

"Neither will getting yourself killed help him," said Randy Sparks.

"Hush up," Link said, with a slight grin. "Just think what a big dog I'll be if I make it out there and back without so much as a scratch—you'll never hear the end of it, will you?"

"Damn it, Link." Randy Sparks shook his head. "Now stay

back here, Randy boy," said Link Dawset, "and don't go doing something foolish."

Atop the ridge, Sam ventured another glance around the edge of the rock, but there was still no sign of Carlos's rifle barrel. Yet, as soon as he looked down and saw the lone rider dart out of cover, lying down at his horse's side, Comanche style, Sam raised his rifle quickly to his shoulder and steadied it on the edge of the rock, pointed toward Carlos's position. The second Sam saw the big Remington's barrel reach out to take aim, he locked his sights onto the jagged edge of the cliff and squeezed the trigger.

Carlos felt the particles of sharp rock and sand sting his face as he pulled the trigger on the Remington, causing his shot to jerk to the left of his target.

Looking down quickly, Sam saw the rider stop his horse and leap down to the wounded man on the ground.

Keeping one rein in his hand as he scooped Pecos Bob up in his arm, Link Dawset said, "Come on, Pecos, help me all you can! He missed once, but he ain't apt to miss again!"

Even as he spoke and pulled Pecos Bob to his feet, Link Dawset scanned the ridges and saw the ranger perched to the left of where the shot had come front. But he had no time to even wonder about it right now. He shoved Pecos Bob up onto the saddle and flung himself up behind him. "Hang on, Pecos! This is going to be a rough one!" Dawset nailed his spurs to his horse's sides, sending the animal into a race for their lives.

"Hurry, man, hurry," Sam murmured, watching the horse race toward the cover of rock. At the same time, Sam counted the seconds in his mind as he kept an eye to the ridgeline, prepared for Carlos's next shot. The time he expected it to take Carlos to reload and fire moved by swiftly. The horse seemed too slow, the distance to the rock cover seemed too far. Yet, in a moment the horse and its two riders had disappeared behind the rocks without another shot being fired. Letting out a breath of relief, Sam looked down and saw the riders rounding the turn on the trail below.

On the flatlands, Randy Sparks also saw the riders, Cochio at the lead, come charging around the trail and spread out across the flatlands. Sparks reached up, caught Pecos Bob, and laid him down flat on the ground, propping his head against the rock wall protecting them. "Thought you said they would take the long way around," Randy Sparks said to Link Dawset. Randy then stooped and looked closely at the wound in Pecos Bob's chest.

"Looks like I was wrong." Dawset stepped down from his saddle with a canteen in his hands and hurried over, jerking his bandanna from around his neck. "It's a damn good thing. Pecos needs to be gotten out of here and taken care of."

"Who was that other shooter up there?" Randy Sparks asked, taking the canteen from Link, uncapping it and lowering it to Pecos Bob's lips.

"I don't know," said Dawset, "but I got a feeling I wouldn't be standing here if he hadn't been looking out for me. I'd like to buy him a drink sometime... provided, of course, that he buys me one in return." He squatted down, looked at the gaping wound in Pecos Bob's chest and shook his head, giving Randy a glance, both men knowing the Pecos Bob's back would look even worse. Blood rose in a puddle with each beat of Pecos's heart.

Pecos Bob coughed and blood spilled from his lips. "I'm done for, ain't I, boys?" His voice quivered as he spoke. "You can tell me straight.... I never liked being led around the bush."

"Then I'll give it to you straight, Bob," Link Dawset said, his voice turning gentle, "it looks pretty bad. Anything you want us to tell anybody?"

"No, I expect not," said Pecos Bob, blood pouring too thick and fast to stop it. "Much obliged for coming to get me .... I reckon I really shouldn't have asked."

"Don't mention it, Bob," said Link Dawset.

Pecos Bob motioned for another sip of water, but as Randy lowered the canteen to his lips, Bob went limp. His eyes turned flat and lifeless, staring straight ahead.

"See?" Randy Sparks said quietly to Link. "I told you he was done for."

"So what? At least I done him as right as I could. That's all a man has to do to live with himself." The two stood up waving the riders toward them, wondering what had happened to cause the rifle fire to stop.

"Is he dead?" asked Cochio, riding in first, the others closing in and forming around him, their eyes scanning in every direction.

"Yep, Boss, I'm afraid so," said Dawset. He stepped to one side to give Cochio a better look at Pecos Bob's body. "You got here awful quick," Dawset said.

"We didn't wait for the pistol shots," said Cochio. "As soon as we heard the rifle shot, we left Victor to watch about the place, and we headed out here. Was that shot we heard the one that killed Bob?"

"No, boss. There's another man up there. I believe he saved our lives."

"Too bad he didn't save Bob's," said Cochio. He looked around at the men, and said, "All of you with rifles spread out, work your way up there and kill the bastard who did this."

"What about the man who tipped us off, Boss?" Link Dawset asked.

"He'll see us coming ... he'll clear out. The only one left up there will be the one who wants to do some killing."

When the ranger saw that the rider and the wounded man had made it to safety, and that Carlos had stopped shooting, he climbed back down the crevice to where he'd left the horses, Atop the Appaloosa, leading the paint horse, he made his way along a snaking trail until he came close to the spot where Carlos had been firing. Once again, all he found of Carlos the Snake were his empty shells. The horses' hoofprints led off around the ridgeline.

Sam followed the hoofprints, but he did so warily at first, not wanting to leave himself exposed for too long to the higher ridges above. But the farther he followed the prints, the more he realized that Carlos wasn't waiting around to ambush him. It became plain to him that Carlos would let nothing stop him from reaching the ranch house beyond the turn in the long flatland trail.

Farther along the trail, headed down from the ridges, Darcy Tennison rode close beside Carlos, seeing the fresh blood on his shirt and the trickle of blood running down from the cut on his cheek left by one of the chips of rock Sam's rifle shot had kicked up. "We have to stop long enough to attend to your wounds," she said. "Surely your killing can wait that long."

"Keep moving," he said with determination.

"At least wipe the blood from your face," Darcy said.

Carlos rubbed his hand back and forth across his cheek, then said again, "Keep moving. I know who's behind us. It's the ranger. But he won't stop me, not until I've done what I set out to do."

"And after that?" Darcy asked, looking him up and down.

"After that, it doesn't matter much one way or the other," Carlos said.

When they stopped at the bottom of the ridgeline, they had half circled the house, bypassing the front entrance altogether and coming in from the side. They both stepped down from their horses. Carlos studied the house for a moment from the cover of dark shade and rock. He saw two older cowhands carrying rifles in the backyard. He saw another rifleman in the front. This one leaned against an ancient oak tree and kept a close eye on the main trail. "We tie the horses here," he said.

"Should I stay here and watch them?" Darcy asked.

"No, you stick close to me," said Carlos, shoving his rifle up under his arm, taking the reins from her hands and tying both horses' reins to a waist-high stand of juniper. "They'll be all right here for now. We go on foot from here. Keep down. If they see us, they'll shoot us."

Darcy started to object, but Carlos had already moved forward in a crouch, as if it made little difference to him whether she came with him or not. She cut a quick glance to the saddlebags herself, then crouched down and followed close behind him. They moved quietly and quickly and didn't stop until they reached a thirty-foot clearing between the house and a sandy field of brush.

"You wait right here," Carlos said. "Don't try to leave."

Although his words didn't reveal it, there was a threat in his voice. "I'll wait right here," said Darcy, looking into his dark eyes. "You don't have to worry about me. I'll stay here until it's over."

Inside the house, Victor Trumbough had found a coiled-up rope hanging on a wall peg just inside the back door. He'd carried the rope and a sawed-off shotgun to an upstairs bedroom, dropped them both on the bed, and slumped down in a rocking chair that matched the one on the back porch. He'd sat rocking for a good long while, with his face in his hands, listening to the chair creak beneath him. But then, when he'd heard a scuffling sound through the open front window, he got up, went to the window and looked down into the front yard.

"Is everything all right down there, Chancey?" Victor asked the rifleman.

Still leaning against the tree without turning toward him, Victor heard him say quietly, "Yep, everything's fine down here."

Victor looked out across the land in the direction the gunfire had come from earlier. "I hope Pecos Bob hasn't gone and done something foolish .... He was always good at that back when we rode guerrilla together." He paused, then added, "Well, I suppose we'll find out soon enough, eh?"

"I suppose so," said Chancey Kerns, still not looking up at him.

Victor studied him closely from the window, noting something different, but unsure about what it was. Then he turned from the window and walked back to the bed.

There were three things Victor Trumbough had not seen from his position in the window. He had not seen Chancey Kerns's dead eyes staring blankly across the land. He had not seen the circle of blood spilling down the front of Chancey's shirt, nor had he seen Carlos the Snake kneeling in front of the oak tree with the bloody knife in his hand.

Carlos had heard all he needed to hear. He knew the name Pecos Bob—he'd heard it from Dan Bristoe. Hearing that whoever it was at the window used to ride with Pecos Bob was good enough for Carlos. He wiped the knife blade back and forth on the ground, shoved it down into his boot well, and crept from the oak tree to the front porch without a sound, carrying his rifle across his chest.

Carlos slipped through the front door and flattened himself against the wall for a moment, looking up at the ceiling, at the sound of footsteps in the room above him. His eyes followed the footsteps across the floor, then back to the center of the room. There was silence for a moment, then a steady creaking sound back and forth.

Out back, through the open door, the sound of two voices drew closer to the back porch. Carlos could wait no longer. He hurried quietly to the stairs and went up them quickly, keeping his footsteps close to the wall to silence any sound from the wooden stair treads.

At the closed door to the bedroom, Carlos stopped long

enough to cock his rifle silently. He stood for a second longer, listening to the slow, steady creaking sound, noting that it had lessened since a while ago. Then he reached down, grabbed the doorknob, twisted it, and flung the door open. But he did not find the man sitting off-guard in a rocking chair as the sound had indicated. Instead, he looked straight into Victor Trumbough's face from less than ten feet away. Trumbough stood staring at him cold and wild-eyed, his arms poised at his sides as if ready to draw pistols and fire.

Instinctively, Carlos started to pull the trigger. But something stopped him. His eyes went to the bed, seeing the sawed-off shotgun there, then back to the face staring at him. Carlos let out a breath of defeat. Looking down, he saw that Trumbough's drooping boot toes swayed three inches off the floor with each steady creak of wood against rope on the rafter above him.

"You son of a bitch," Carlos hissed into Victor Trumbough's stunned purple expression, "this gets you nothing in my book." He spit in Victor's dead face.

CHAPTER 22

It had been quite a while since Carlos left Darcy Tennison waiting for him in the brush alongside the house. She'd waited as long as she was going to, At the sight of the CS riders coming along the path in the front yard, Darcy ducked farther down and slipped away quickly, back toward the horses. Whatever strange force, or spell, or slip of her own sanity, had held her bound to Carlos the Snake was now severed. She was free ... free of Carlos, free of Maximus, free of all encumbrances that life had placed upon her.

As she rushed through snagging thorns and clinging brush, it was as if a great fever had broken inside her, as if she'd suddenly been cured and rid of some terrible sickness. Tears streamed down Darcy's cheeks. Even if she'd had time to ask herself, she would not have been able to say if they were tears of sorrow or joy. Perhaps both. As she scrambled in a crouch, she heard the hoofbeats of the horses draw closer to the house. But that was no concern of hers. Whatever happened back there would happen in a time and place that was not a part of her world.

In the front yard, Cochio Santavia raised his hand as he slid his horse to a halt. Seeing the dark blood down Chancey Kerns's chest, he called out to the men following him, "Hold it, he's here! He's waiting for us!"

"What?" asked Link Dawset, sidling up close to him, his pistol coming up .out of his holster and cocking. The others followed suit. Pecos Bob's body lay in the buckboard the men had rounded up on their way back.

In the front window, Carlos the Snake cast an eye toward Darcy Tennison, seeing her flee through the brush as he cocked the big Remington rifle. At the other end of the stretch of brush and scrub juniper he saw the ranger step down from his saddle.

"You're running right into his arms," Carlos whispered, his finger slipping inside the trigger guard. A slight smile stirred across Carlos's lips. "I hope this clears things between us." He raised the rifle to his shoulder and sought his target.

Seeing sunlight glint off the rifle barrel, the riders opened fire on the front window. But it was too late. The explosion of the big rifle rocked the whole house. Victor Trumbough's body trembled on the end of its taut rope. Cochio Santavia shouted a curse as Carlos's shot lifted him from his saddle and twisted him sideways in the air, his eyes appearing to flash across the faces of his men before he slammed facedown on the ground.

"Boss!" one of the men cried out. Cochio raised the lower half of his body to his knees and tried crawling away, his cheek still pressed to the hot sand. The men scattered, taking cover from the big rifle while Carlos reloaded it. Out back, the two unsuspecting riflemen who had dove for cover when the shooting started, now rose up and raced across the backyard, up onto the back porch.

In the upper bedroom, seeing the men take cover out front and realizing the two men out back would be coming soon, Carlos leaned his loaded Remington beside the window, took out his Colt, checked it, and laid it on the window ledge, cocked and ready. He stepped over to the bed around Victor Trumbough's hanging body, picked up the sawed-off shotgun, checked it, snapped it shut, and let it rest over his forearm.

"Come and get it!" Carlos shouted through the open window. "I've got all day."

Vengeance

"Damn it," said Link Dawset to Randy Sparks, the two of them crouched behind a low stand of rock. They had shooed their horses away, fearing Carlos would shoot their animals the way he had shot Pecos Bob's. "You know he's killed Trumbough, otherwise, he wouldn't have made it into the house."

"Yeah, I reckon so," said Randy Sparks. He looked all around at the men scattered across the front yard, none of them finding much cover, each looking anxiously toward him and Link for some direction. "What are we going to do now?"

"Now, we're going to find out just who the hell else he's got to kill to end this." As he spoke, Link Dawset took his bandanna from around his neck and began tying it to the end of his pistol barrel.

In the far end of the stretch of brush, Darcy Tennison raced the last few yards toward the horses. Her breath heaved in her chest. Stiff sharp branches of low juniper and cactus had ripped her dress from one shoulder, causing her to cradle her partially bare breast in hand, protecting it against the biting slashing terrain.

Just as she rounded the far edge of the brush and saw the horses standing only a few feet away, Sam caught her arm, causing her to turn in her tracks, facing him. She almost screamed before recognizing him.

"Easy, Miss Darcy," Sam said, keeping his voice lowered to almost a whisper, "you're all right now. I've got you."

She trembled and collapsed against him, sobbing, "No, Ranger, you don't understand. I— I had to—"

"Sssh, Miss Darcy," said Sam. "Don't you say nothing right now. You need time to collect yourself." He held her against his chest and stroked the back of her head. "Is Carlos inside the house?"

She nodded instead of speaking.

"He's going to hold them off till he's finished killing the ones he came for?"

"I think so," Darcy said, sniffling, trembling.

Ralph Cotton

"All right now." Sam held her back at arm's length and nodded at her hand covering her breast. "You go ahead and cover yourself while I get the horses."

In the front yard, Link Dawset waved his pistol with the bandanna tied to it back and forth above his head. From the window, Carlos the Snake took aim on Dawset's forearm, positioning his rifle barrel to one side at the very point where Dawset's arm would stop for a split second, before swinging back the other direction.

"You're *loco,* Link!" said Randy Sparks. "He'll blow your arm off if he gets a chance!"

"Then I reckon he's got a chance," said Link. "I can't let these boys lay out here and get picked off like varmints. I got to try to stop him."

Carlos held his rifle targeted on the spot where the arm was headed. He took a breath and held it. This was not a hard shot for him, nor was it an important one. At less than thirty yards, he could strike a match with the big Remington. The arm swung into his sights, then past it a fraction and back. There was his lead. His finger closed back on the trigger, squeezing, squeezing. But at the last second, knowing it was too late to stop his shot, Carlos tipped the rifle barrel up as the explosion rattled the window frame.

Link Dawset jerked his arm down, a paleness sweeping over his startled face. Then he let out a breath and wiggled his finger around his pistol butt. "See, everything's still here," he said with relief.

"You're damn lucky he missed then," said Randy Sparks.

"Link!" a cowboy called out, lying prone behind a thin clump of grass. "What say? Reckon we better rush him?"

"Hold on, Rusty," said Link. He ran a hand across his brow. "I got to give it one more try."

"You're pushing your luck today, Link," Randy warned him. "He don't miss often."

"He didn't miss that time, Randy. He just changed his

250

mind," said Link. He raised the pistol again and waved the bandanna back and forth, calling out to the window, "What's it going to hurt, talking about this thing?"

Carlos opened the rifle chamber as he replied, "Talk then. I'm not going anywhere, neither are you." He reloaded and took a step to one side of the window.

"I'm betting Victor Trumbough is dead in there, am I right?" asked Link.

"Don't know his name ... but yeah, he's dead. He rode with Pecos Bob and that Mexican, Cochio, laying dead out there. I didn't kill this one though," Carlos added. "He must've realized what a murdering animal he was, and couldn't stand it any longer. He's swinging on a rope here." Carlos stopped talking and listened.

"But you son of a bitch, you killed Cochio, and them boys back there on the flatland!" said a voice, as if only then becoming aware of the fact. "I say we kill him, boys!"

"Easy there, damn it," Link called out over his shoulder to the rest of the men. "Everybody try to keep their heads here."

He raised his voice to the window again. "Mister, if he realized what a terrible thing he did, and hung himself for it ... what the hell more can you want from him?"

"Nothing more! Not from him anyway!" Carlos felt the heat of the room close in around him. He didn't want to think anymore. He only wanted to act. He only wanted to spill his rage like a rabid dog, until something or someone reached out and stopped him.

"Then, mister, you've killed them all?" Link called out.

"What the hell?" said Randy Sparks, stunned by Link Dawset's words. "Are you saying we back away—let this man leave, after killing Cochio? And Bob?"

"Shut up, Randy!" Link barked at him. "You didn't even know Pecos Bob. Two hours ago you didn't want to try and save his life! Now you're wanting to avenge his death? And you called me crazy?"

251

"But damn it, Link! We all could rush him. He might get one or two of us, but the rest of us would get him!" Sparks said.

"Yeah?" Link gave him a look. "Then you turn around right now and pick the ones you want to see die while we get him. Damn it, we've got no stomach for this kind of killing! Let's try cutting our losses here."

"What about the leader, Wolf Avrial?" Carlos called down from the window. "He's still alive."

Sparks and Dawset stared at one another for a second until Sparks's expression gave in and he nodded his head. "All right, I'm with you."

Link Dawset called out to Carlos, "Mister, I reckon there's lots of killers running loose. But me and these boys ain't them. We work cattle, mind our own business. There's a bloodbath waiting here, if that's what it's got to be. But it's senseless! We never wronged you."

Carlos took a deep breath and calmed himself. He holstered his pistol, and touched the warm wet spot on his chest where his wound had bled once again. "Are you saying I can ride out of here?" he asked, thinking that if he died here before killing Wolf Avrial that his vengeance would not be complete.

There was a silence while Link looked around at the others, his stare forcing them to go along with him. "Yep, mister, that's what I'm saying. The fact is, nobody I talked to here has been able to abide what Cochio and those men done to your folks. It's just that it all was a long time ago, before we knew Cochio and had come to be his friends."

Another silence passed, then Carlos said, "I'm coming out. Nobody follows me, or I'll chop them down in their tracks."

"Fair enough, mister," said Link Dawset, letting go of a tense breath. "Get on out of there .... You've got my word."

Carlos rubbed his face with both hands and started toward the door, the big rifle in his left hand. But before he reached the door, the two riflemen from the backyard had crept up the stairs. They sprang into the room, one firing his rifle, the other having shed his rifle and drawn his Smith & Wesson pistol for more up-close gun fighting.

"Get him, Slappy" shouted the one with the rifle.

On the ground out front, Link Dawset yelled, "No!" at the sound of gunfire. Broken glass flew out of the window frame. "Let him go! For God sakes, I gave him my word!"

In the deathlike silence that followed, all eyes in the front remained fixed on the broken upstairs window. Finally, Link Dawset called out, "Slappy? Are you and Mort all right up there?"

He saw the bloody face of Slappy Perkins appear at the window, seeming to stagger in place.

"Here comes Slappy!" Carlos shouted, giving the dying man a shove. The man tumbled out, taking the remaining broken glass with him. His body bounced once on the tin roof beneath the gabled window, then fell to the ground, causing a short burst of dust to rise up around him.

"Aw, Jesus," said Link Dawset.

Before Slappy Perkins's body hit the ground, Carlos had already taken off, running down the hall to an open window. His chest wound had broken open more. He felt fresh warm blood ooze down behind his belt and creeping down his lower belly. There was a graze on his left arm, but nothing serious. He climbed quickly out the window and down onto the wide tin roof covering the back porch.

Holding his rifle out to one side, Carlos leaped down from the roof and landed on both feet, going down into a squat, feeling the pain rip through his wounded chest. He stood up slowly, and in doing so, saw the ranger step into view less than fifteen feet away, the big Swiss rifle cocked, the butt of it propped against his hip, his finger on the trigger. "Don't make me do it, Carlos," said the ranger. "Let me take you in."

Carlos caught his breath, dropping his rifle from his left hand and clutching the pain in his chest. "Take me in?" He let out a low dark laugh. "Ranger, it's straight-up murder .... I knew it would be starting out."

"Yes, it is," said Sam. "But maybe ... just maybe, a jury will listen and show some mercy, given the circumstances."

"Strange, ain't it, Ranger?" said Carlos, Sam already seeing his right hand grow poised and ready near his pistol butt. "How everybody sees this thing the way I do ... but still the law won't rest till I pay for doing it. The thing is, I been paying for killing these men all my life, Ranger. Soon as I collect Wolf Avrial, I'm free of it."

"You don't get Wolf Avrial, Carlos," said Sam. "Give yourself up, or you know what I've got to do."

"I don't get Avrial?" Carlos asked with a wizened look. "Do you think I'm stupid, Ranger?"

"What are you talking about, Carlos?" Sam asked, keeping a close watch on that right hand, knowing it was ready to make its move any second.

"I'm talking about you, Ranger! The way you've showed up, hounded me through all this. I know who you are! You are Wolf Avrial! I remember your face plain as day! Ever since I was a boy!"

"Easy, Carlos," said the ranger, hearing footsteps run around the side of the house, but not about to take his eyes off Carlos right now, "you're talking out of your head now. You need to ease down, give yourself up."

"Unh-uh!" said Carlos the Snake, shaking his head, having none of it. "You are him, Ranger, you *are* Wolf Avrial .... I see it now. I should have seen it all along!"

"Stop it, Carlos," the ranger cautioned.

But Carlos couldn't stop. "Don't you see it? Huh, Ranger? Don't you see it yourself?" As he spoke, his voice grew more and more urgent, his hand twitched a fraction of an inch, just enough to show the ranger where it was headed.

"Yes, Carlos, I see it now," said the ranger. As Carlos grabbed for the pistol, Sam's finger closed back on the trigger of the big Swiss rifle. Carlos's pistol barrel never cleared the top of his holster. The butt plate of the big rifle bucked against Sam's hip, the explosion seeming to run the distance of the land like bad news from hell. Then the barrel lowered beneath a curl of smoke. "I reckon you're right, I am him," the ranger whispered.

As the cowhands gathered closer to the ranger, some still with their hands on their holstered pistols, Darcy Tennison stepped out of the surrounding brush leading four horses—the pair she and Carlos had ridden, and the ranger's two.

Randy Sparks almost drew his pistol before seeing it was a woman. "If you're going to keep acting skittish with that sidearm," said one of the older cowhands, half-jokingly, "we'll have to take it away from you."

"Ranger," said Link Dawset, "I sure am glad to see you show up here. I know that was you out there, shooting at Carlos whilst I made a run for Pecos Bob."

Sam only nodded, then watched Darcy walk in closer, the torn shoulder of her dress tied up in place with. a strip of the gauze she'd brought for Carlos's wound. The men looked her up and down, seeing her step over and bend down beside Carlos's body.

"Was she with him?" asked Link Dawset, keeping his voice down, but not low enough to keep Darcy from hearing him. She looked around at Link Dawset, then at Sam, seeming anxious to hear Sam's reply.

"Yep, she was with him," Sam said, eyeing her closely, "but it was against her will." He stopped for a moment as if to hear how that sat with her.

Then he continued. "Carlos killed her husband. Tried to kill her. Later, when he was wounded, he drifted into town, took her hostage, forced her to tend his wounds, then made her leave with him." He saw the look on Darcy's face. "That's pretty much how it happened, isn't it, Miss Darcy?"

"I came with him .... I don't know why, except that—"

255

Ralph Cotton

"That's all right, Miss Darcy," said Sam, cutting her off, "you just take it easy now .... It's all over. That's all you want isn't it? For all this to be over, so you can get on with your life somewhere?" His eyes searched deep into hers until there was nothing more required of her than a nod of her head.

Sam turned to Link Dawset, saying just between them, "She's still in a little bit of shock—it's understandable."

"Yep, it is," said Link Dawset. "Randy, run over there and get this woman some cool water—where's your manners anyway?"

All the way back to Halston the next day, Darcy Tennison kept expecting the ranger to ask her more questions about what she was doing with Carlos the Snake. But, to her surprise and relief, he didn't mention Carlos. But he did ask her about the bulging saddlebags hanging across the back of the horse Carlos the Snake had ridden—the horse she now rode, and had kept near her side ever since she'd led the animals into the yard.

"I suppose when Carlos made you come with him, he forced you to bring along any money you had close by?" Sam asked, as if preparing her for when they got to Halston and someone asked her the same question.

Darcy stared at him in silence for a moment as they rode along side by side, leading the spare horses toward the abandoned hearse on the scorched flatlands.

"Ranger, I don't like lying to you," she said. "When I woke up and finally realized Max was dead, that it wasn't just some bad dream ... and that I was stuck in that terrible business, I would have done anything to get out." She looked away for a moment and touched her fingers to her eyes. "I think something might have snapped inside me."

"You mean you haven't been yourself ... in a state of shock, like I've been telling everybody you were?" Sam asked.

She gave him a curious look, seeming to catch onto

256

something for the first time. "That's what people do, when they're in shock?"

"I've seen it time and again," said the ranger, looking ahead along the trail.

He paused as if considering something, then said in a gentle tone, "Miss Darcy ... Carlos took everything from you, your new husband ... your future, any family the two of you might have created for yourselves." He cut a glance back at the saddlebags, but only for an instant. "I reckon if there was any way for him to make that right, he would. If not, how much different was he than the men he hunted?"

"You mean, you think he might have wanted to make up for what he took from me, but didn't know how?"

"Nobody ever knows how to make up for something like that, Miss Darcy. I don't know what how much of what a man does is meant to make things right, or to make things wrong." To change the subject, he asked, "When we get back to Halston, where are you headed to?"

"I didn't say I was leaving Halston," Darcy said.

"I know you didn't," Sam said, offering a slight smile.

She blushed a bit. "I think I'll travel back East for a while, perhaps even go to Europe. I have no strings, Ranger. It's time I realize I can go where I please ... anywhere where I don't have to see bodies in the streets."

"Now you're talking." The ranger grinned. "I'm looking for a place like that myself."

Author Ralph Cotton

Vengeance, written in 2003 and published as *Vengeance is a Bullet*, was the eighth in the original issue, and is fourth in the new *Ranger Sam Burrack* series of Western Classics, written by national best-selling author Ralph Cotton. These very popular novels are also known as the *Big Iron Series*. Ralph has achieved notable success with the publication and sales of over fifty novels; most have been or are on the *New York Times* Bestseller List.

Ralph lives on the Florida Gulf Coast with his wife Mary Lynn. He writes prodigiously and his books remain top sellers in the Western and Civil War/Western genres. Ralph enjoys painting, photography, sailing and playing guitar. His imagination is comfortable building characters and working with events in the past, but he reaches to the present and future to find the best way to present them.

The Western Classic series of novels introduces Ralph Cotton to a new generation of readers who will enjoy them for the first time, and find pleasure in re-reading them for years to come.

Made in the USA
Las Vegas, NV
15 December 2024

14322752R00155